THE

S L A V E :

OR

MEMOIRS OF ARCHY MOORE.

Richard Hildreth

ALL men are by nature equally free and independent, and have certain IN-
HERENT RIGHTS, of which, when they enter into society, they cannot by any
compact deprive or divest their posterity, viz: the enjoyment of life and liberty,
with the means of acquiring and possessing property, and pursuing happiness
and safety. *Virginia Bill of Rights, Art. I,*

VOLUME I.

THE GREGG PRESS
UPPER SADDLE RIVER, N.J.

First published in 1836 by John H. Eastburn
Republished in 1968 by
The Gregg Press
121 Pleasant Avenue
Upper Saddle River, New Jersey, U.S.A.

Library of Congress Catalog Card Number: 68 - 57530

Printed in United States of America

ADVERTISEMENT.

It is unnecessary to detain the reader, with a narrative of the somewhat singular manner in which the MS. of the following Memoirs came into my possession. It is sufficient for me to say, that I received it, with an injunction to make it public—an injunction which I have not felt myself at liberty to disobey.

I would not be understood, however, as implicitly adopting all the author's feelings and sentiments ; for it must be confessed that he sometimes expresses himself with a force and a freedom, which by many will be thought extravagant. Yet, if I am not greatly mistaken, he preserves throughout, a moderation, a calmness, and a magnanimity, which have never yet been displayed upon the other side of the question ; and laying entirely out of account the author's personal grievances, I do not know how it is possible to be over zealous in a cause so just as that in which he pleads.

As to the conduct of the author, as he has himself described it, there are several occasions on which it is impossible to approve it. But he has written Memoirs, not an apology nor a vindication. No man who writes his own life, will gain much credit, by painting himself as faultless ; and few have better claims to indulgence than Archy Moore.—The Editor.

AMERICAN NOVELS OF MUCKRAKING, PROPAGANDA, AND SOCIAL PROTEST

The United States has suffered quite a few spells of sickness, if one may judge by the long and varied procession of novels dealing with the ills of its society. As each generation has sought assurances for the social hope that springs eternal in a democracy, muckraking, propagandizing, and advocating reforms have been not only implicit in partisan politics but also germane to literary production. While it has been said that Americans are readier to believe in charlatans than in utopias, there remains a sneaking feeling that maybe Oscar Wilde was right when he remarked: "Progress is the realization of utopias." Some such moral—if indeed moral it be—may be derived from the Gregg series of "American Novels of Muckraking, Propaganda, and Social Protest."

One purpose underlying the selection of the titles in the series is to provide examples of socio-economic novels which are presently out of print but which are nevertheless important in showing the history of the genre, a topic so far treated by historians only sporadically. Most of these works can rarely be found in the original editions; and many were printed on paper which is beginning to shatter. The series should prove a boon to librarians and to scholars who work in the fields of literary history and the social sciences. Its usefulness as supplementary reading for college courses in American studies and social history speaks for itself.

In turning the pages of the novels we begin with the groping 1830's and the fabulous 40's—when, as Emerson put it, every man in New England was running around with a plan for reorganizing society in his vestpocket. And we end with the "Era of the Muckrakers"—when the long-existent fervor to remake the world nearer to the mind's desire became a contagious fever, and phrases were bandied about like "frenzied finance," "conspicuous consumption," "malefactors of great wealth," "how the other half lives" and "the shame of the cities." In this series we find artifacts from the days following the panic of 1837, when Horace Greeley devoted a regular column in his *Tribune* to the kind of "associationism" that overtook Brook Farm; and we come along to the period early in the present century when the "yellow" journalism of Hearst and Pulitzer reached full flower and young Sinclair

Lewis swept the floors of Helicon Hall, the socialist community supported by Upton Sinclair with the profits of *The Jungle.* That was the epoch when the young intellectuals stormed college halls to hear Jack London expound the principles of socialism. In between, we find specimens emanating from the Gilded Age, with the ensuing clamor against business combinations eventuating in the Sherman Anti-Trust Act of 1890, and the agricultural depression that aroused Midwestern farmers to "raise less corn and more hell" or to align themselves with the People's Party. Business panics in 1873 and 1893 stirred up the coals, young preachers discovered the social gospel, bewhiskered anarchists were the chief "reds," strikes became for the first time a matter of wide public concern, and the play based on *Uncle Tom's Cabin* was the best money-maker on the stage.

One of the features of the list is a careful selection of works concerned with the Negro. The earliest is *The Slave,* by the historian Richard Hildreth. It was not only the first fully developed antislavery novel, but a pattern-maker for the many subsequent tales presenting the chief character as a light-skinned mulatto. The Russians translated it in the 1950's. Another is Harriet Beecher Stowe's *Dred,* a sequel to *Uncle Tom's Cabin* and perhaps more cogent propaganda. The idea that the Negro is constitutionally unable to cope with American society is curiously set forth in *Liberia,* by Sarah J. Hale, a staunch Yankee best known for her verses about Mary and her little lamb. Mrs. Hale was propagandizing for solving the slavery problem by returning the Negroes to Africa. Presenting the Southern side, *Aunt Phillis's Cabin,* by Mary H. Eastman, has been chosen from the batch of novels which sought in vain to counter the effect of Mrs. Stowe's world-famed classic of protest. The blasting of Northern prejudice against the Negro after the Civil War is well illustrated in two works: Rebecca Harding Davis's *Waiting for the Verdict,* a title still apt a century after it first appeared, and Albion W. Tourgée's tract for the times *Pactolus Prime,* which vitriolically scores the essential prejudice of white against black and is, apparently, the first American novel dealing with the Negro problem with a setting in Washington, D. C.

Joaquin Miller's *Life Amongst the Modocs* deals with the mistreatment of Indians. Few in number but judiciously chosen for illustrative purposes are stories exposing the white slave traffic—

from the days when the Mann Act was legislated and city slums were being muckraked both in and out of fiction to a degree probably more thorough than is the case even today. Among the other problems considered in these stories are divorce, prisons, and the criminal code, political corruption, pacificism, states rights, the social responsibilities of the churches, the plight of the Jew and the Immigrant, and even medical frauds.

But the theme governing the largest single element in this collection is the business tycoon and the battle between the capitalist power elite and the working class. The range in the picturization of "the typical American figure," as Henry James declared the captain of industry to be, runs quite a gamut in the series, from the romantic treatment in *Sevenoaks,* by the first editor of *Scribner's Magazine,* to the excoriation of corporation machinations by avowed socialists not unacquainted with Karl Marx. The tycoons pilloried range from bankers, real estate promoters, mill owners, and railroad magnates to lumber barons. One might view the development of this theme in the amazing profusion of fictional examples as a symbol of the growing unrest precipitated in a traditionally agrarian society bewildered by its confrontation with huge industrial corporations and big cities. But possibly it proves no more than the homely wisdom distilled into the humorist's wisecrack: "We have met the enemy—and the enemy is us!"

PROFESSOR CLARENCE GOHDES
Duke University
Durham, North Carolina

September, 1968

RICHARD HILDRETH

Richard Hildreth, novelist, historian, and pamphleteer was born in Deerfield, Massachusetts, in 1807, a descendant of Richard Hildreth, a freeman of the Massachusetts Bay Colony. His father was Professor of Mathematics at Phillips Exeter Academy, and he graduated from that school in 1822, then from Harvard in 1826. He was admitted to the bar four years later. From 1830 to 1832 he practiced in Boston and Newburyport, but closed down his practice in order to become Editor of the Boston *Daily Atlas.* He contributed articles on social and economic problems to this paper, as well as to the *American Monthly Magazine,* the *Ladies' Magazine,* and the *New England Magazine.* In 1834 he purchased a part ownership in the *Atlas,* but sold out to Caleb Cushing in order to go to Florida for his health. It was here that he wrote *The Slave; or Memoirs of Archy Moore,* which appeared in 1836. Returning north, he became Washington correspondent for the *Atlas,* but resigned in 1839 because the owners refused to print his articles advocating prohibition. His health broke down again, and Hildreth was forced to live in Demerara, British Guiana, but he continued to fight for social reform, particularly the abolition of slavery, editing the anti-slavery papers *The Guiana Chronicle* and the *Royal Gazette.* In 1844 he returned to America and married Caroline Neagus.

This was the beginning of the period of his historical writings. His intention was to write a universal history from the point of view of inductive science, but he wisely abandoned this project in order to write a history of the United States, next to *The Slave* his most famous work. This six-volume work has been hailed as the first scientific history. It is sober, free from Hegelian abstractions, and has a strong Federalist bias. It is read today for its closely reasoned analyses of the relationships between economics and politics, a completely opposite approach from that of Hildreth's great rival, George Bancroft, writer of the nationalistic, rhetorical *History of the United States.*

After finishing his *History,* Hildreth went to New York, and worked for Horace Greeley's *Tribune* from 1855 to 1861. In 1861 Lincoln appointed him Consul at Trieste, a position which he resigned in 1864. He died in 1865 in Florence, and was buried in the Protestant Graveyard near Theodore Parker.

Active throughout his life in politics on the side of the Whigs, Hildreth supported Harrison in his campaign against Van Buren. He wrote *The History of Banks,* which advocated the system of open competition in banking, and his concern with the problems of the age was further exemplified by his articles on tariffs and the ownership of land. He entered the field of theological controversy by attacking Andrews Norton in "A Letter to Andrews Norton on Miracles as the Foundation of Religious Faith."

"He took a decisive part in several campaigns, and was always esteemed a powerful friend and a bitter and formidable foe. Very decided in the utterance of his opinions, vehement and caustic in controversy. . .he was not likely to receive full justice for the finer qualities of his mind and heart." (*New England Historical and Genealogical Register, Jan. 1866.*)

The Slave is the first fully developed anti-slavery novel; an abolitionist classic second only to *Uncle Tom's Cabin* in its inflammatory effects on Northern opinion, and an exciting, skillfully plotted adventure tale with considerable value as a literary work. Thanks to Hildreth's slow, careful, coldly objective approach to his subject matter, *The Slave* transcends the usual work of pro-Negro propaganda. The horrors of servitude are described with clinical detachment, with the eye of the historian-novelist who can sympathize with the agony of his literary creations, avoiding overinvolvement with the material, which spoils so many exposé novels. He allows the octoroon hero to tell of his adventures and sufferings as though he were being interviewed by a reporter. Fortunately for the modern reader, Hildreth refuses to use Negro "dialect," an annoying and all-too-common trick used by novelists who try to be "realistic," and succeed in being unreadable. It was, perhaps, this happy combination of the passionate denunciation of a cruel bygone social institution and the scientific, unemotional approach of the author which led the Russians to translate *The Slave* in the 1950's.

Hildreth, no respecter of "genteel" New England literary traditions, writes frankly about the sexual abuses incident to slavery, a tabooed theme that only began to be explored very recently. *The Slave* is an extraordinary novel which, according to Van Wyck Brooks, "thrilled the younger generation," and which, more than any textbook or abolitionist pamphlet, tells us what it was really like to be a slave on a Louisiana plantation.

Upper Saddle River, N. J.   F. C. S.
October, 1968

MEMOIRS.

CHAPTER I.

Ye who would know what evils man can inflict upon his fellow without reluctance, hesitation, or regret; ye who would learn the limit of human endurance, and with what bitter anguish and indignant hate, the heart may swell, and yet not burst, peruse these Memoirs!

Mine are no silken sorrows, nor sentimental sufferings; but that stern reality of actual woe, the story of which, may perhaps touch even some of those, who are every day themselves the authors of misery the same that I endured. For however the practice of tyranny may have deadened every better emotion, and the prejudices of interest and education may have hardened the heart, humanity will still extort an involuntary tribute; and men will grow uneasy at hearing of those deeds, of which the doing does not cost them a moment's inquietude.

Should I accomplish no more than this; should I be able, through the triple steel with which the love of money and the lust of domination has encircled it, to reach one bosom—let the story of my wrongs summon up, in the mind of a single oppressor, the dark and dreaded images of his own misdeeds, and teach his conscience how to torture him with the picture of himself, and I shall be content. Next to the tears and the exultations of the emancipated, the remorse of tyrants is the choicest offering upon the altar of liberty !

But perhaps something more may be possible ;—not likely—but to be imagined—and it may be, even faintly to be hoped. Perhaps within some youthful breast, in which the evil spirits of avarice and tyranny have not yet gained unlimited control, I may be able to rekindle the smothered and expiring embers of humanity. Spite of habits and prejudices inculcated and fostered from his earliest childhood—spite of the allurements of wealth and political distinction, and the still stronger allurements of indolence and ease—spite of the pratings of hollow hearted priests—spite of the arguments of time-serving sophists—spite of the hesitation and terrors of the weak-spirited and wavering—in spite of evil precept and evil example, he dares—that generous and heroic youth !—to cherish and avow the feelings of a man.

Another Saul among the prophets, he prophecies terrible things in the ear of insolent and luxurious tyranny ; in the midst of tyrants he dares to preach the good tidings of liberty ; in the very school of oppression, he stands boldly forth the advocate of human rights !

He breaks down the ramparts of prejudice ; he dissipates the illusions of avarice and pride ; he repeals the enactments, which though destitute of every feature of justice, have sacriligiously usurped the sacred form of law ! He snatches the whip from the hand of the master ; he breaks forever the fetter of the slave !

In the place of reluctant toil, delving for another, he brings in smiling industry to labor for herself ! All nature seems to exult in the change ! The earth, no longer made barren by the tears and the blood of her children, pours forth her treasures with redoubled liberality. Existence ceases to be torture ; and to live is no longer, to millions, the certainty of being miserable.

Chosen Instrument of Mercy ! Illustrious Deliverer ! Come ! come quickly !

Come !—lest if thy coming be delayed, there come in thy place, he who will be at once, DELIVERER and AVENGER !

CHAPTER II.

THE county in which I was born, was then, and for aught I know, may still be one of the richest and most populous in eastern Virginia. My father, colonel Charles Moore, was the head of one of the most considerable and influential families in that part of the

country ;—and family, however little weight it may
have in other parts of America, at the time I was born,
was a thing of no slight consequence in lower Virginia. Nature and education had conspired to qualify
colonel Moore to fill with credit, the station in which
his birth had placed him. He was a finished aristocrat ; and such he showed himself in every word, look
and action. There was in his bearing, a conscious
superiority, which few could resist, softened and rendered even agreeable by a gentleness and suavity,
which flattered, pleased and captivated. In fact, he
was familiarly spoken of among his friends and neighbors, as the faultless pattern of a true *Virginian* gentleman—an encomium, by which they supposed themselves to convey, in the most emphatic manner, the
highest possible praise.

When the war of the American Revolution broke out,
colonel Moore was a very young man. By birth and
education, he belonged, as I have said, to the aristocratic party, which being aristocratic, was of course,
conservative. But the impulses of youth and patriotism
were too strong to be resisted. He espoused with zeal,
the cause of liberty, and by his political activity and
influence, contributed not a little to promote it.

Of liberty indeed, he was always a warm and energetic admirer. Among my earliest recollections of
him, is the earnestness with which, among his friends
and guests, he used to vindicate the cause of the
French revolution, which was then going on. Of this
revolution, throughout its whole progress, he was a most
eloquent advocate and apologist ; and though I under-

stood little or nothing of what he said, the spirit and eloquence with which he spoke could not fail to affect me. *The rights of man*, and the *rights of human nature* were phrases, which, although at that time, I was quite unconscious of their meaning I heard so often repeated, that they made an indelible impression upon my memory, and in after years, frequently recurred to my recollection.

But colonel Moore was not a mere talker ; he had the credit of acting up to his principles, and was universally regarded as a man of the greatest good nature, honor and uprightness. Several promising young men, who afterwards rose to eminence, were indebted for their first start in life, to his patronage and assistance. He settled half the differences of the county, and never seemed so well pleased as when, by preventing a lawsuit or a duel, he hindered an accidental and perhaps trifling dispute from degenerating into a bitter, if not a fatal quarrel. The tenderness of his heart, his ready active benevolence, and his sympathy with misfortune, were traits of his character which were spoken of by every body.

Had I been allowed to choose my own paternity, could I possibly have selected a more desirable father? But by the laws and customs of Virginia, it is not the father but the mother, whose rank and condition determine that of the child ;—and alas ! my mother was a concubine and a slave !

Yet those who beheld her for the first time, would hardly have imagined, or would willingly have forgotten, that she was connected with an ignoble and de-

1*

graded race. Humble as her origin might be, she
could at least boast the possession of the most brilliant
beauty. The trace of African blood, by which her
veins were contaminated, was distinctly visible ;—but
the tint which it imparted to her complexion only served to give a peculiar richness to the blush that mantled
over her check. Her long black hair, which she understood how to arrange with an artful simplicity, and
the flashing of her dark eyes, which changed their expression with every change of feeling, corresponded
exactly to her complexion, and completed a picture
which might perhaps be matched in Spain or Italy, but
for which, it would be in vain to seek a rival among the
pale-faced, languid beauties of eastern Virginia.

I describe her more like a lover than a son. But in
truth, her beauty was so uncommon, as to draw my
attention while I was yet a child ;—and many an hour
have I watched her, almost with a lover's earnestness,
while she fondled me on her lap, and tears and smiles
chased each other alternately over a face, the expression of which was ever changing, yet always beautiful.
She was the most affectionate of mothers ; the mixture
of tenderness, grief and pleasure, with which she always
seemed to regard me, gave a new vivacity to her beauty, and it was probably this, which so early and so
strongly fixed my attention.

But I was very far from being her only admirer.
Her beauty was notorious through all that part of the
country ; and colonel Moore had been frequently
tempted to sell her by the offer of very high prices.
All such offers however, he had steadily rejected ;

for he especially prided himself upon owning the swift-
est horse, the handsomest wench, and the finest pack
of hounds in all Virginia.

Now it may seem odd, to some people, in some
parts of the world, that colonel Moore being such a
man as I have described him, should keep a mistress
and be the father of illegitimate children. Such persons however, must be totally ignorant of the state of
things in the slave-holding states of America.

Colonel Moore was married to an amiable woman,
whom, I dare say, he loved and respected ; and in the
course of time, she made him the happy father of two
sons and as many daughters. This circumstance however, did not hinder him, any more than it does any other
American planter—from giving, in the mean time, a
very free indulgence to his amorous temperament among
his numerous slaves at Spring-Meadow,—for so his
estate was called. Many of the young women occasionally boasted of his attentions—though generally, at
any one time, he did not have more than one or two
acknowledged favorites.

My mother was for several years, distinguished by
colonel Moore's very particular regard ; and she
brought him no less than six children,—all of whom,
except myself, who was the eldest, were lucky enough
to die in infancy.

From my mother I inherited some imperceptible
portion of African blood, and with it, the base and
cursed condition of a slave. But though born a slave,
I inherited all my father's proud spirit, sensitive feelings and ardent temperament ; and as regards natural

endowments, whether of mind or body, I am bold to assert, that he had more reason to be proud of me than of either of his legitimate and acknowledged sons.

CHAPTER III.

THAT education is the most effectual, which commences earliest—a maxim well understood in that part of the world in which it was my misfortune to be born. As it sometimes happens there, that one half of a man's children are born masters and the other half slaves, it has become sufficiently obvious how necessary it is, to begin, by times, the course of discipline proper to train them up for these very different situations. It is, accordingly, the general custom, that young master, almost from the hour of his birth, has allotted to him, some little slave near his own age, upon whom he begins, from the time that he can go alone, to practice his apprenticeship of tyranny   It so happened that within less than a year after my birth, colonel Moore's wife presented him with her second son, James ; and while we both slept unconscious in our cradles, I was duly assigned over and appointed to be the body-servant of my younger brother.   It is in this capacity, of master James's boy, that following back the traces of memory, I first discover myself.

The natural and usual consequences of giving one child absolute authority over another, may be easily imagined. The love of domination is perhaps the strongest of our passions ; and it is surprising how soon the veriest child will become perfect in the practice of tyranny. Of this, colonel Moore's eldest son, William, or master William, as he was called at Spring-Meadow, was a striking instance. He was the terror and bug-bear, not only of Joe, his own boy, but of all the children on the place. That unthinking and irrational delight in the exercise of cruelty, which is sometimes displayed by a wayward child, seemed in him, almost a passion ; and this passion by perpetual indulgence, was soon fostered into a habit. When any delinquent slave was to be punished, he contrived if possible to find it out, and to be present at the infliction ;—so that he soon became an adept in all the disgusting slang of an overseer. He always went armed with a whip, twice as long as himself ; and upon the least opposition to his whims and caprices, was ready to show his skill in the use of it. All this he took some little pains to conceal from his father ; who however, was pretty careful not to see what he could, by no means, approve, but what, at the same time—indulgent father as he was—he would have found it very difficult to prevent or to cure.

Master James, to whose service, I was particularly appointed, was a very different boy. Sickly and weak from his birth, his temper was gentle and his mind effeminate. He had an affectionate disposition, and soon conceived a fondness for me, which I very thankfully returned. He protected me from the tyranny of master William by his entreaties, his tears, and what had much more weight with that amiable youth by threats of complaining to his father, and making a complete exposure of his brutal and cruel behaviour.

I soon learned to pardon and put up with an occasional pettishness and ill humor, for which master James' bad health furnished a ready excuse ; and by flattery and apparent obsequiousness—for a child learns and practices such arts as readily as a man—I presently came to have a great influence over him. He was the master, and I the slave ; but while we were both children, this artificial distinction had less potency, and I found little difficulty in maintaining that actual superiority, to which my superior vigor both of body and mind, so justly entitled me.

When master James had reached the age of five years, it was judged expedient by his father, that he should be initiated into the rudiments of learning. To learn the letters was a laborious undertaking enough,— but for putting them into words, my young master seemed to have no genius whatever. He was not destitute of ambition ; he was indeed very desirous to learn ; it was the ability, not the inclination that was wanting. In this difficulty, he had recourse to me, who was on all occasions, his chief counsellor. By putting our heads together, we soon hit upon a plan. My memory was remarkably good, while that of my poor little master was very miserable. We arranged therefore, that the family tutor should first learn me the letters and the abs, which my strong memory, we thought, would enable me easily to retain, and which I was gradually, and between plays, as opportunity served, to instil into the mind of master James. This plan we found to answer admirably. Neither the tutor nor colonel Moore made any objection to it ;—for all that colonel Moore desired was, that his son should learn to read, and the tutor was very willing to shift off the most laborious part of his task upon my shoulders.

As yet, no one had dreamed of those barbarous and abominable laws—unparalleled in any other codes and destined to be the everlasting disgrace of America—by which it has been made a *crime*, punishable with fine and imprisonment, to teach a slave to read.

It is not enough that custom and the proud scorn of unfeeling tyranny unite to keep the slave in hopeless and helpless ignorance, but the laws too have openly become a party to this accursed conspiracy ! Yes—I believe they would tear out our very eyes,— and that too by virtue of a regularly enacted statute— had they ingenuity enough to invent a way of enabling us to delve and drudge without them !

I soon learned to read, and before long, I made master James almost as good a reader as myself. As he was subject to frequent fits of illness, which confined him to the house, and disabled him from indulging in those active sports to which boys are chiefly devoted, his father obtained for him a large collection of books adapted to his age, which he and I used to read over together, and in which we took great delight.

In the further progress of my young master's studies I was still his associate ; for though the plan of teaching me first, in order that I might afterwards teach him, was pursued no longer, yet as I had a desire to learn, as well as a quick apprehension, I found no difficulty in extracting every day from master James, the substance of his lessons.   Indeed, if there was any difficulty in them, he was in the constant habit of appealing to me for assistance.   In this way, I acquired some elementary knowledge of arithmetic and geography, and even a smattering of latin.

These acquisitions however, I took great pains to conceal, since even the fact that I had learned to read, though it increased my consequence among the servants, exposed me to a good deal of ridicule to which I was very sensitive.   I was not looked upon, as I suppose they now look upon a slave, who knows how to read and who exhibits some marks of sense and ability, as a dreadful monster breathing war and rebellion, and plotting to cut the throats of all the white people in America.   I was regarded rather as a sort of prodigy, —like a three legged hen, or a sheep with four eyes ; a thing to be produced and exhibited for the entertainment of strangers.   Frequently at a dinner party, after the Madeira had circulated pretty freely, I was set to read paragraphs in the newspapers, to amuse my master's tipsy guests, and was puzzled, perplexed and tormented, by all sorts of absurd, ridiculous, and impertinent questions, which I was obliged to answer under penalty of having a wine glass, a bottle, or a plate flung at my head.   Master William especially, as he was prevented from using his whip upon me, as freely as he wished, strove to indemnify himself by making me the butt of his wit. He took great pride in the nick-name of the "learned nigger," which he had invented and always applied to me ;—though God knows, that my cheek was little less fair than his, and I cannot help hoping that at least, my soul was whiter.

These, it may be thought, were trifling vexations. In truth they were so—but it cost me many a struggle before I could learn to endure them with any tolerable patience. I was compensated in some measure, by the pleasure I took in listening—as I stood behind my master's chair—to the conversation of the company,— I mean their conversation before they set regularly in to drinking ; for every dinner party was sure to wind up with a general frolic.

Colonel Moore kept an open house, and almost every day, he had some of his friends, relatives, or neighbors, at his table. He was himself an eloquent and most agreeable talker ;—his voice was soft and musical, and he always expressed himself with a great deal of point and vivacity. Many of his guests were well informed men ; and though politics was always the leading topic of conversation, a great variety of other subjects were occasionally discussed. Colonel Moore, as I have already observed, was himself a warm democrat—republican was then the phrase—for democrat, however fond the Americans have since become of the name, was at that time regarded as an epithet of reproach. The greater part of those who frequented colonel Moore's house, entertained the same liberal opinions

2

on political subjects. I listened to their conversation
with eagerness and pleasure ;—and when I heard them
talk of equal rights, and declaim against tyranny and
oppression, my heart would swell with emotions of
which I scarcely understood the meaning. All this
time, I made no personal application of what I heard
and felt. It was only the abstract beauty of liberty
and equality, of which I had learned to be enamoured.
It was the French republicans with whom I sympathiz-
ed ; it was the Austrian and English tyrants against
whom my indignation was roused ; it was John Adams
and his atrocious gag law. I had not yet learned to think
about myself. What I saw around me I had always
been accustomed to see, and it appeared as it were,
the fixed order of nature. Though born a slave, I had,
as yet, experienced scarcely any thing of the miseries
of that wretched condition. I was singularly fortunate
in my young master, to whom I was, in many respects,
as much a companion as a servant. By his favor, and
through means of my mother, who still continued a favorite with colonel Moore, I enjoyed more indulgen-
ces than any other servant on the place. Comparing
my situation with that of the field hands, I might pro-
nounce myself fortunate indeed ; and though exposed
to occasional mortifications, enough to give me already
a foretaste of the bitter cup, which every one who
lives a slave must swallow, my youth and the buoyant
vivacity of my temper as yet sustained me.

At this time, I did not know that colonel Moore
was my father. That gentleman was indebted for no
inconsiderable portion of his high reputation, to a very

strict attention to those conventional observances which so often usurp the place of morals. Some observances of this sort, which prevail in America, are sufficiently curious. It is considered for instance, no crime whatever, for a master to be, if he chooses, the father of every infant slave born upon his plantation. Yet it is esteemed a very grave breach of propriety, indeed almost an unpardonable crime, for such a father ever, in any way, to acknowledge or take any notice, of any of his unfortunate children. Imperious custom demands that he should treat them, in every respect, like his other slaves. If he drives them into the field to labor,—if he sells them at auction to the highest bidder, it is all very well. But if he audaciously undertakes to exhibit towards them, in any way, the slightest indications of paternal tenderness, he may be sure that his character will be assailed by the tongue of universal slander ; that his every weak point and unjustifiable action will be carefully sought out, malignantly magnified, and ostentatiously exposed ; that he will be compelled to run a sort of moral gauntlet, and will be represented among all the *better sort of people*, as every thing that is infamous, base and contemptible.

Colonel Moore was by far too wise a man, to entertain the slightest idea of exposing himself to any thing of this sort. He had always kept the best society,—and though he might be a democrat in politics, he was certainly very much of an aristocrat and an exclusive in his feelings. Of course, he had the same sort of indescribable horror, at the thought of violating any of the settled proprieties of the society in which he moved, that a modern belle has, of cotton lace, or a modern dandy of an iron fork. This being the case, nobody will wonder,—so far at least as colonel Moore had any control over the matter—that I was still ignorant who my father was.

But though a secret to me, it certainly was not so to colonel Moore's friends and visitors. If nothing else had betrayed it, the striking resemblance between us, would certainly have done so ;—and although that same *regard to propriety*, which prevented colonel Moore from ever noticing the relationship, tied up the tongues of his guests,—yet, after I had learned the secret, there immediately occurred to my mind the true explanation of certain sly jests and distant allusions, which had sometimes been dropped towards the end of a dinner, by some of those guests whom deep potations had inspired at once with wit and veracity. These brilliancies, of which I had never been able to understand the meaning, were always ill received by colonel Moore, and by all the soberer part of the company, and were frequently followed by a command to me and the other servants to quit the room ; but why or wherefore—till I became possessed of the key above mentioned—I was always at a great loss to determine.

The secret which my father did not choose, and which my mother did not dare to communicate to me, I might easily have obtained from my fellow servants. But at this time, like most of the lighter complexioned slaves, I felt a sort of contempt for my duskier brothers in misfortune. I kept myself as much as possible, at a distance from them, and scorned to associate with

men a little darker than myself. So ready are slaves
to imbibe all the ridiculous prejudices of their oppressors, and themselves to add new links to the chains,
which deprive them of their liberty !

But let me do my father justice,—for I do not believe that he was totally destitute of a father's feelings.
Though he never made the slightest acknowledgment
of the claims which I had upon him, yet I am sure, in
his own heart, he did not totally deny their validity.
There was a tone of good natured indulgence whenever he spoke to me,—an air of kindness, which—
though he always had it—seemed toward me, to have
in it something peculiar. At any rate, he succeeded
in captivating my affections, for though I regarded him
only as my master, I loved him very sincerely.

CHAPTER IV.

I was about seventeen years old, when my mother
was attacked by a fever, which proved fatal to her.
She early had a presentiment of her fate ; and before
the disorder had made any great progress, she sent me
word that she desired to see me. I found her in bed.
She begged the woman who nursed her, to leave us
together, and bade me sit down by her bed-side.

2*

Having told me that she feared she was going to die, she could not think it kind to me, she said, to leave the world, without first telling me a secret, which possibly, I might find hereafter of some consequence. I begged her to go on, and waited with impatience for the promised information. She began with a short account of her own life. Her mother was a slave; her father was a certain colonel Randolph—a scion of one of the great Virginian families. She had been raised as a lady's maid, and on the marriage of colonel Moore, had been purchased by him and presented to his wife. She was then quite a girl. As she grew older and her beauty became more noticeable, she found much favor in the eyes of her master. She had a neat little house, with a double set of rooms—an arrangement, as much for colonel Moore's convenience as her own;— and though some light tasks of needle-work were sometimes required of her, yet as nobody chose to quarrel with master's favorite, she lived, henceforward, a very careless, indolent, but as she told me, a very unhappy life.

For much of this unhappiness she was indebted to herself. The airs of superiority she assumed in her intercourse with the other servants, made them all hate her, and induced them to improve every opportunity of vexing and mortifying her;—and to all sorts of feminine mortifications she was as sensitive as any belle that ever existed. But though vain of her beauty and her master's favor, she was not ill-tempered; and the foolish pride from which she suffered, sprung in her, as a similar feeling did in me, from a silly, though common prejudice. Indeed our situation was so superior to that of most of the other slaves, that we naturally imagined ourselves, in some sort, a superior race. It was doubtless under the influence of this feeling, that my mother, having told me who my father was, observed with a smile and a self-complacent air, which even the tremors of her fever did not prevent from being visible,—that both on the father's and the mother's side, I had running in my veins, the best blood of Virginia—the blood, she added, of the Moores and the Randolphs !

Alas ! she did not seem to recollect that though I might count all the *nobility* of Virginia among my ancestors, one drop of blood imported from Africa—though that too, might be the blood of kings and chieftains,—would be enough to taint the whole pedigree, and to condemn me to perpetual slavery, even in the house of my own father !

The information which my mother communicated, made little impression on me at the moment. My principal anxiety was for her ;—for she had always been the tenderest and most affectionate of parents. The progress of her disorder was rapid, and on the third day she ceased to live. I lamented her with the sincerest grief. The sharpness of my sorrow was soon over ; but my spirits did not seem to regain their former tone. The thoughtless gaiety, which till now had shed a sort of sunshine over my life, seemed to have deserted me. My thoughts began to recur, very frequently, to the information which my mother had communicated. I hardly know how to describe the

effect which it seemed to have upon me. Nor is it easy
to tell what were its actual effects, or what ought to be
ascribed to other and more general causes. Perhaps
that revolution of feeling, which I now experienced, should be attributed, in a great measure, to the
change from boyhood to manhood, through which I
was passing. Hitherto things had seemed to happen
like the events of a dream, without touching me deeply
or affecting me permanently. I was sometimes vexed
and dissatisfied,—I had my occasional sorrows and
complaints. But these sorrows were soon over, and
as after summer showers the sun shines out the brighter, so my transient sadness was soon succeeded by a
more lively gaiety, which, as soon as immediate grievances were forgotten, burst forth, unsubdued either by
reflections on the past, or anxieties for the future. In
this gaiety there was indeed scarcely anything of substantial pleasure :—it originated rather in a careless insensibility. It was like the glare of the moon-beams,
bright but cold. Such as it was however, it was far
more comfortable, than the state of feeling by which it
now began to be succeeded. My mind seemed to be
filled with indefinite anxieties, of which I could de-
vine neither the causes nor the cure. There was, as
it were, a heavy weight upon my bosom, an unsatisfied craving for something, I knew not what, a longing
which I could do nothing to satisfy, because I could
not tell its object. I would be often lost in thought,—
but my mind did not seem to fix itself to any certain
aim, and after hours of apparently the deepest medita-

tion, I should have been very much at a loss, to tell about what I had been thinking.

But sometimes my reflections would take a more definite shape. I would begin to consider what I was and what I had to anticipate. The son of a freeman, yet born a slave! Endowed by nature with abilities, which I should never be permitted to exercise; possessed of knowledge, which already, I found it expedient to conceal! The slave of my own father, the servant of my own brother, a bounded, limited, confined, and captive creature, who did not dare to go out of sight of his master's house without a written permission to do so! Destined to be the sport, of I knew not whose caprices, forbidden in anything to act for myself, or to consult my own happiness,—compelled to labor all my life at another's bidding, and liable every hour and instant, to oppressions the most outrageous, and degradations the most humiliating!

These reflections soon grew so bitter that I struggled hard to suppress them. But this was not always in my power. Again and again, in spite of all my efforts, these hateful ideas would start up and sting me into anguish.

My young master still continued kind as ever. I was changing to a man, but he still remained a boy. His protracted ill health, which had checked his growth, appeared also to retard his mental maturity. He seemed every day to fall more and more under my influence; and every day my attachment to him grew stronger. He was in fact, my sole hope. While I remained with him, I might reasonably expect to es-

cape the utter bitterness of slavery. In his eyes, I
was not a mere servant. He regarded me rather as a
loved and trusted companion. Indeed, though he had
the name and prerogatives of master, I was much less
under his control than he was under mine. There was
between us, something of a brotherly affection—at
least of that kind, which may exist between foster
brothers,—though neither of us ever alluded to our
actual relationship, and he probably, was ignorant of it.

I loved master James as well as ever ; but towards
colonel Moore, my feelings underwent a rapid and a
radical change. While I considered myself merely as
his slave, his apparent kindness had gained my affection ; and there was nothing I would not have done or
suffered, for so good natured and condescending a master. But after I had learned to look upon myself as
his son, I soon began to feel that I might justly claim
as a right, what I had till now, regarded as a pure gra-
tuity. I began to feel that I might claim much more,
—even an equal birth-right with my brethren. Occasionally, I had read the bible ;—and I now turned with
new interest to the story of Hagar, the bond-woman,
and Ishmael her son ;—and as I read how an angel
came to their relief, when the hard-hearted Abraham
had driven them into the wilderness, there seemed to
spring up within me, a wild, strange, uncertain hope,
that in some accident, I knew not what, I too might
find succor and relief. At the same time, with this
irrational hope, a new spirit of bitterness was poured into my soul. Unconsciously I clenched my
hands, and set my teeth, and fancied myself, as it were,

another Ishmael, wandering in the wilderness, every man's hand against me, and my hand against every man. The injustice of my unnatural parent, stung me deeper and deeper,—and all my love for him was turned into hate. The atrocity of those laws which made me a slave—a slave in the house of my own father,—seemed to glare before my prophetic eyes in letters of blood. Young as I was, and as yet untouched, I trembled for the future, and cursed the country and the hour that gave me birth !

I endeavored, as much as possible, to conceal these new feelings with which I was tormented ; and as deceit is one of those defences against tyranny, of which a slave early learns to avail himself, I was not unsuccessful. My young master would sometimes find me in tears,; and sometimes when I would be lost in thought, he would complain of my inattention. But I put him off with plausible excuses ; and though he suspected there was something which I did not tell him, and would frequently say to me, " Come Archy, boy, let me know what it is that troubles you,"—I would make light of the matter and laugh off his suspicions.

I was now about to lose this kind master, in whose tenderness and affection I found the sole palliative that could make slavery tolerable. His health which had always been bad, grew rapidly worse, and confined him first to his chamber and then to his bed. I attended him during his whole illness with a mother's tenderness and assiduity. Never was master more faithfully served ;—but it was the friend, not the slave, who rendered these attentions. He was not insensible to my services ; he did not seem to like that any one but I should be about him, and it was only from my hand that he would take his physic or his food. But it was not in the power of physician or of nurse to save him. He wasted daily, and grew weaker every hour. The fatal crisis soon came. His weeping friends were collected about his bed,—but the tears they shed were not as bitter as mine. Almost with his last breath he recommended me to the good graces of his father,— but the man who had closed his heart to the promptings of paternal tenderness, was not likely to give much weight to the requests of a dying son. He bade his friends farewell,—he pressed my hand in his ;— and, with a gentle sigh, he expired in my arms.

Would to God, I had died with him !

CHAPTER V.

THE family of colonel Moore knew well how truly I had loved, and how faithfully I had served my young master. They respected the profound depth of my grief, and for a week or two, I was suffered to grieve on unmolested. My feelings were no longer of that acute and piercing kind which I have described in the preceding chapter. The temperament of the mind is forever changing. That state of preternatural sensibility, of which I have attempted to give an idea, had disappeared when my attention became wholly occupied in the care of my dying master, and was now succeeded by a dull and stupid sorrow. Apparently I now had increased cause for agitation and alarm. That which I then dreaded, had now happened. My young master, on whom all my hopes were suspended, lived no longer, and I knew not what was to become of me. But the fit of fear and anxious anticipation was over; and I now waited my fate with a sort of stupid and careless indifference.

Though not called upon to do it, I continued as usual to wait upon my master's table. For several days, I took my place instinctively near where master James' chair ought to have stood; till the sight of the vacant place drove me in tears to the opposite corner. In the mean time, nobody called upon me to do anything, or seemed to notice that I was present. Even master William made an effort to repress his habitual insolence.

But this could not last long. Indeed it was a stretch of indulgence, which no one but a favorite servant could have expected;—since slaves, in general, are thought to have no business to be sorry—if it makes them unable to work.

One morning after breakfast, master William having discussed his toast and coffee, began by telling his father, that in his opinion, the slaves at Spring-Meadow, were a great deal too indulgently treated. He

3

was by this time, a smart, dashing, elegant young man, having returned, upwards of a year before, from college, and quite lately, from Charleston, in South Carolina, whither he had been to spend a winter, and as his father expressed it, to wear off the rusticity of the school-room. It was there perhaps, that he had learned the new precepts of humanity, which he was now preaching. He declared that any tenderness towards a slave only tended to make him insolent and discontented, and was quite thrown away on the ungrateful rascals. Then, looking about, as if in search of some victim on whom to practice a doctrine so consonant to his own disposition, his eye lighted upon me. " There's that boy Archy—I'll bet a hundred to one I could make him one of the best servants in the world. He's a bright fellow enough naturally, and nothing has spoil'd him, but poor James' over indulgence. Come father, just be good enough to give him to me, I want another servant most devlishly."

Without stopping for an answer, he hastened out of the room, having, as he said, two jockey races to attend that morning ; and what was more, a cock-fight into the bargain. There was nobody else at the table. Colonel Moore turned towards me. He began with commending very highly, my faithful attachment to his poor son James. As he mentioned his son's name the tears stood in his eyes, and for a moment or two he was unable to speak. He recovered himself presently, and added—" I hope now you will transfer all this same zeal and affection to master William."

These words roused me in a moment. I knew mas-

ter William to be a 'tyrant, from whose soul custom
had long since obliterated what little humanity nature
had ever bestowed upon him ;—and to judge from
what he had let drop that morning—he had of late improved upon his natural inclination for cruelty, and had
proceeded to the final length of reducing tyranny into a
system and a science. I knew too that from childhood, he had entertained a particular spite against me ;
and I dreaded, lest he was already devising the means
of inflicting upon me, with interest, all those insults
and injuries from which the protection of his younger
brother had hitherto shielded me.

It was with horror and alarm, that I found myself in
danger of falling into such hands. I threw myself at
my master's feet, and besought him, with all the eloquence of grief and fear, not to give me to master William. The terms in which I spoke of his son—though
I chose the mildest I could think of—and the horror I
expressed at the thought of becoming his servant—
though I endeavored as much as possible, to save the
father's feelings—seemed to make him angry. The
smile left his lip, and his brow grew dark and contracted. I began to despair of escaping the wretched fate
that awaited me ; and my despair drove me to a very
rash and foolish action. For emboldened by the danger of becoming the slave of master William, I dared
to hint—though distantly and obscurely—at the information which my mother had communicated to me on
her death-bed ; and I even ventured something like a
half appeal to colonel Moore's *paternal* tenderness,
At first, he did not seem to understand me ; but the

moment he began to comprehend my meaning, his face
grew black as a thunder cloud, then became pale, and
immediately was suffused with a burning blush, in
which shame and rage were equally commingled. I
now gave myself up for lost, and expected an instant
out-break of fury ;—but after a momentary struggle,
colonel Moore seemed to regain his composure,—even
the habitual smile returned to his lips,—and without
taking any notice of my last appeal, or giving any further signs of having understood it, he merely remarked,
—that he did not know how to refuse master William's
request, nor could he comprehend the meaning of my
reluctance. It was mighty foolish ; still he was willing to indulge me so far, as to allow me the choice of
entering into master William's service, or going into
the field. This alternative was proposed with an air
and a manner, which was intended to stop my mouth,
and allow me nothing but the bare liberty of choosing.
It was indeed, no very agreeable alternative. But any
thing,—even the hard labor, scanty fare, and harsh treatment, to which I knew the field hands were subjected,
—seemed preferable to becoming the sport of master
William's tyranny. I was piqued too, at the cavalier
manner in which my request had been treated, and I
did not hesitate. I thanked colonel Moore for his great
goodness, and at once, made choice of the field. He
seemed rather surprised at my selection,—and with a
smile, which bordered close upon a sneer, bade me
report myself to Mr Stubbs.

An overseer, is regarded in all those parts of slave-
holding America, with which I ever became acquainted,

very much in the same light in which people, in countries uncursed with slavery, look upon a jailor or a hangman ; and as these latter employments, however useful and necessary, have never succeeded in becoming respectable, so the business of an overseer is likely from its nature, always to continue contemptible and degraded. The young lady who dines heartily on lamb, has a sentimental horror of the butcher who killed it ; and the slave owner who lives luxuriously on the forced labor of his slaves, has a like sentimental abhorrence of the man who holds the whip and compels the labor. He is like a receiver of stolen goods, who cannot bear the thoughts of stealing himself, but who has no objection to live upon the proceeds of stolen property. A thief is but a thief ; and an overseer but an overseer. The slave owner prides himself in the honorable appellation of a planter ; and the receiver of stolen goods assumes the character of a respectable shop-keeper. By such contemptible juggle do men deceive not themselves only, but oft-times the world also.

Mr Thomas Stubbs was overseer at Spring-Meadow,—a personage with whose name, appearance and character I was perfectly familiar, though hitherto I had been so fortunate as to have had very little communication with him.

He was a thick set, clumsy man, about fifty, with a little bullet head, covered with short tangled hair, and stuck close upon his shoulders. His face was curiously mottled and spotted,—for what with sunshine, what with whiskey, and what with ague and fever, brown, red and sallow seemed to have put in a joint claim to

3*

the possession of it, without having yet been able to arrive at an amicable partition. He was generally to be seen on horseback, leaning forward over his saddle, and brandishing a long thick whip of twisted cow-hide, which from time to time, he applied over the head and shoulders of some unfortunate slave. If you were within hearing, his conversation, or rather his commands and observations, would have appeared a string of oaths, from the midst of which it was not very easy to disentangle his meaning. "You damned black rascal" was pretty sure to begin every sentence, and "by God," to end it. It was however, only when Mr. Stubbs had sole possession of the field, that he sprinkled his orders with this strong spice of brutality;—for when colonel Moore or any other gentleman happened to be riding by, he could assume quite an air of gentleness and moderation, and what appears very surprising, was actually able to express himself, with not more than one oath to every other sentence.

Mr Stubbs, in his management of the plantation did not confine himself to hard words. He used his whip as freely as his tongue. Colonel Moore had received an European education ; and like every man educated any where—except on a slave holding estate—he had a great dislike to all *unnecessary* cruelty. He was usually made very angry, about once a week, by some brutal act on the part of his overseer. But having satisfied his outraged feelings by declaring himself very much offended, and Mr Stubbs' proceedings to be quite intolerable, he ended, with suffering things to go on just as before. The truth was, Mr Stubbs under-

stood making crops ; and such a man was too valuable
to be given up, for the mere sentimental satisfaction of
protecting the slaves from his tyranny.

It was a great change to me, after having been accustomed to the elegance and propriety of colonel Moore's
house, and the gentle rule and light service of master
James, to pass under the despotic control of a vulgar,
ignorant and brutal blackguard. Besides, I had never
been accustomed to regular and severe labor ; and it was
trying indeed to submit at once to the hard work of the
field. However, I resolved to make the best of it. I
was strong,—and use would soon make my tasks more
tolerable. I knew well enough, that Mr Stubbs was
totally destitute of all humane feelings, but I had no reason to suppose that he entertained towards me any of
that malignity which I had so much dreaded in master
William. From what I had known of him, I did not
judge him to be a very bad tempered man ; and I took it
for granted that he cursed and whipped, not so much
out of spite and ill feeling, but as a mere matter of business. He seemed to imagine,—like every other overseer,—that it was impossible to manage a plantation in
any other way. The lash, I hoped, my diligence might
enable me to escape ; and Mr Stubbs' vulgar abuse,
however provoking the other servants might esteem it,
I thought I might easily despise.

Mr Stubbs listened to my account of myself very
graciously,—all the time, rolling his tobacco from one
cheek to the other, and squinting at me with one of his
little twinkling grey eyes. Having cursed me to his
satisfaction for "a damned fool," he bade me fol-

low him to the field. A large clumsy hoe, with a handle six feet long, was put into my hands, and I was kept hard at work all day.

At dark, I was suffered to quit the field, and the overseer pointed out to me a miserable little hovel, about ten feet square, and half as many high, with a leaky roof, and without either floor or window. This was to be my house,—or rather I was to share it with Billy, a young slave, about my own age.

To this wretched hut, I removed a chest, containing my clothes and a few other things, such as a slave is permitted to possess. By way of bed and bedding, I received a single blanket, about as big as a large pocket handkerchief ; and a basket of corn and a pound or two of damaged bacon, were given me as my week's allowance of provisions. But as I was totally destitute of pot, kettle, knife, plate, or dish of any kind,—for these are conveniences which slaves must procure as they can,—I was in some danger of being obliged to make my supper on raw bacon. Billy saw my distress and took pity on me. He taught me how to beat my corn into hominy ; and lent me his own little kettle to cook it in ; so that about midnight I was able to break a fast of some sixteen or twenty hours. My chest being both broad and long, served tolerably well for bed, chair and table. I sold a part of my clothes, which were indeed much too fine for a field hand ; and having bought myself a knife, a spoon and a kettle, I was able to put my house-keeping into tolerable order.

My accommodations were as good as a field hand had a right to expect ; but they were not such as to

make me particularly happy ; especially as I had been
used to something better. My hands were blistered
with the hoe, and coming in at night, completely exhausted by a sort of labor to which I was not accustomed, it was no very agreeable recreation, to be
obliged to beat hominy, and to be up till after midnight
preparing food for the next day, with the recollection
too, that I was obliged to turn into the field with the
first dawn of the morning. But this labor, severe as it
was, had been in a manner, my own choice. In choosing it, I had escaped a worse tyranny and a more bitter servitude. I had avoided falling into the hands of
master William.

As I shall not have occasion to mention this amiable
youth again, I may as well finish his history here.
Some six or eight months after the death of his younger
brother, he became involved in a drunken quarrel, at
a cock-fight. This quarrel ended in a duel, and master
William fell dead at the first fire. His death was a great
stroke to colonel Moore, who seemed for a long time,
almost inconsolable. I did not lament him either for
his own sake or his father's. I knew well, that in his
death, I had escaped a cruel and vindictive master;
and I felt a stern and bitter pleasure in seeing the be-
reavements of a man who had dared to trample upon the sacred ties of nature.

CHAPTER VI.

I had the same task with those who had been field hands all their lives ; but I was too proud to flinch or complain. I exerted myself to the utmost, so that even Mr Stubbs had no fault to find, but on the contrary, pronounced me, more than once, a "right likely hand."

The cabin which I shared with Billy, had a very leaky roof ; and as the weather was rainy, we found it, by no means comfortable. At length, we determined one day, to repair it ; and to get time to do so, we exerted ourselves to finish our tasks at an early hour.

We had finished about four o'clock in the afternoon, and were returning together to the *town*,—for so we called the collection of cabins, in which the servants lived. Mr Stubbs met us, and having inquired if we had finished our tasks, he muttered something about our not having half enough to do, and ordered us to go and weed his garden. Billy submitted in silence,—for he had been too long under Mr Stubbs' jurisdiction, to think of questioning any of his commands. But I ventured to say, in as respectful a manner as I could, that as we had finished our regular tasks, it seemed very hard to give us this additional work. This put Mr Stubbs into a furious passion, and he swore twenty oaths, that I should both weed the garden and be whipped into the bargain. He sprang from his horse, and catching me by the collar of my shirt—the only dress I had on,—he began to lay upon me with his whip. It was the first time, since I had ceased to be a child, that I had been exposed to this degrading torture. The pain was great enough, the idea of being whipped was sufficiently bitter,—but these were nothing in comparison with the sharp and burning sense of the insolent injustice that was done me. It was with the utmost difficulty, that I restrained myself from springing upon my brutal tormentor, and dashing him to the ground. But alas !—I was a slave. What in a freeman, is a most justifiable act of self-defence, becomes in a slave, unpardonable insolence and rebellion. I griped my hands, set my teeth firmly together, and bore the injury the best I could. I was then turned into the garden, and the moon happening to be full, I was kept weeding till near midnight.

The next day was Sunday. The Sunday's rest is the sole and single boon for which the American slave is indebted to the religion of his master. That master, tramples under foot every other precept of the Gospel without the slightest hesitation, but so long as he does not compel his slaves to work on Sundays, he thinks himself well entitled to the name of a christian. Perhaps he is so,—but if he is, a title so easily purchased, can be worth but little.

I resolved to avail myself of the Sunday's leisure to complain to my master of the barbarous treatment I had experienced the day before, at the hands of Mr Stubbs. Colonel Moore received me with a coolness and distance, quite unusual in him,—for generally he had

a smile for everybody,—especially for his slaves.
However, he heard my story, and even condescended to
declare that nothing gave him so much pain as to have
his servants unnecessarily or unreasonably punished,
and that he never would suffer such things to take
place upon his plantation.   He then bade me go about
my business, having first assured me, that in the course
of the day, he would see Mr Stubbs and inquire into
the matter.   This was the last I heard from colonel
Moore.   That same evening, Mr Stubbs sent for me
to his house, and having tied me to a tree before his
door, gave me forty lashes, and bade me complain at
the house again, if I dared.   " It's a damned hard
case," he added, " if I can't lick a damned nigger's
insolence out of him, without being obliged to give an
account of it !"

Insolence !—the tyrant's ready plea !

If a poor slave has been whipped and miserably
abused, and no other apology for it can be thought of,
the rascal's " insolence" can be always pleaded,—and
when pleaded, is enough in every slave-holder's estimation, to excuse and justify any brutality.   The
slightest word, or look, or action, that seems to indicate the slave's sense of any injustice that is done him,
is denounced as *insolence*, and is punished with the
most unrelenting severity.

This was the second time I had experienced the discipline of the lash ;—but I did not find the second dose
any more agreeable than the first.   A blow is esteemed among freemen, the very highest of indignities ;
and low as their oppressors have sunk them, it is es-

teemed an indignity even among slaves. Besides—as strange as some people may think it—a twisted cow-hide, laid on by the hand of a strong man, does actually inflict a good deal of pain ; especially if every blow brings blood.

I will leave it to the reader's own feelings to imagine, what no words can sufficiently describe,—the bitterness of that man's misery, who is every hour in danger of experiencing this indignity and this torture. When he has wrought up his fancy,—and let him thank God, from the very bottom of his heart, that in his case, it is only fancy,—to a lively idea of that misery, he will have taken the first step, towards gaining some notion, however faint and inadequate, of what it is, to be a slave !

I had now learned a lesson, which every slave early learns,—I found that I did not enjoy even the privilege of complaining ; and that the only way to escape a reiteration of injustice was, to submit in silence to the first infliction. I did my best to digest this bitter lesson, and to acquire a portion of that hypocritical humility, so necessary to a person in my unhappy condition. Humility,—and whether it be real or pretended, they care but little,—is esteemed by masters, the great and crowning virtue of a slave ; for they understand by it, a disposition to submit, without resistance or complaint, to every possible wrong and indignity,—to reply to the most opprobrious and unjust accusations with a soft voice and a smiling face ; to take kicks, cuffs and blows as though they were a favor,—to kiss the foot that treads you in the dust !

4

This sort of humility was a virtue, with which, I must confess, nature had but scantily endowed me ; nor did I find it so easy, as I might have desired, to strip myself of all the feelings of a man. It was like quitting the erect carriage which I had received at God's hand, and learning to crawl on the earth like a base reptile. This was indeed a hard lesson ;—but an American overseer is a stern teacher, and if I learned but slowly, it was not the fault of Mr Stubbs.

CHAPTER VII.

IT would be irksome to myself, and tedious to the reader, to enter into a minute detail of all the miserable and monotonous incidents that made up my life at this time. The last chapter is a specimen, from which it may be judged, what sort of pleasures I enjoyed. They may be summed up in a few words ;—and the single sentence which embraces this part of my history, might suffice to describe the whole lives of many thousand Americans. I was hard worked, ill fed, and well whipped. Mr Stubbs having once began with me, did not suffer me to get over the effects of one whipping before he inflicted another ; and I have some

marks of his about me, which I expect to carry with me
to the grave.   All this time he assured me, that what
he did was only for my own good, and he swore that
he would never give over, till he had lashed my
damned insolence out of me.

The present began to grow intolerable ;—and what
hope for the future has the slave ?   I wished for death;
nor do I know to what desperate counsels I might have
been driven, when one of those changes, to which a
slave is ever exposed, but over which he can exercise
no control, afforded me some temporary relief from my
distresses.

Colonel Moore, by the sudden death of a relation,
had recently become heir to a large property in South
Carolina.   But the person deceased had left a will,
about which there was some dispute, which had every
appearance of ending in a lawsuit.   The matter required colonel Moore's personal attention ; and he had
lately set out for Charleston, and had taken with him
several of the servants.   One or two also had recently
died ; and Mrs Moore, soon after her husband's departure, sent for me to assist in filling up the gap which
had been made in her domestic establishment.

I was truly happy at the change.   I knew Mrs
Moore to be a lady, who would never insult or trample
on a servant, even though he were a slave—unless she
happened to be very much out of humor,—an unfortunate occurrence, which in her case, did not happen
oftener than once or twice a week—except indeed in
the very warm weather, when the fit sometimes lasted
for days together.

Besides, I hoped that the recollection of my fond
and faithful attachment to her younger son, who had
always been her favorite, would secure me some kindness at her hands. Nor was I mistaken. The contrast of my new situation, with the tyranny of Mr
Stubbs, gave it almost the color of happiness. I regained my cheerfulness, and my buoyant spirits. I was
too wise, or rather this new influx of cheerfulness
made me too thoughtless, to trouble myself about the
future ; and satisfied with the temporary relief I experienced, I ceased to brood over the miseries of my
condition.

About this time, Miss Caroline, colonel Moore's
eldest daughter returned from Baltimore, where she
had been living for several years with an aunt, who
superintended her education. She was but an ordinary girl, without much grace or beauty. But her maid
Cassy,* who had formerly been my play-fellow, and
who returned a woman, though she had left us a child,
was truly captivating.

I learned from one of my fellow servants, that she
was the daughter of colonel Moore, by a female slave,
who for a year or two had shared her master's favor
jointly with my mother, but who had died many years
since, leaving Cassy an infant. Her mother was said
to have been a great beauty, and a very dangerous rival
of mine.

So far as personal charms extended, Cassy was not
unworthy of her parentage, either on the father's or

* Cassandra.

the mother's side. She was not tall, but the grace
and elegance of her figure could not be surpassed ; and
the elastic vivacity of all her movements afforded a
model, which her languid and lazy mistress,—who did
nothing but loll all day, upon a sofa,—might have imitated with advantage. The clear soft olive of her complexion, brightening in either cheek to a rich red,
was certainly more pleasing than the sickly, sallow
hue, so common, or rather so universal, among the
patrician beauties of lower Virginia ;—and she could
boast a pair of eyes, which for brilliancy and expression, I have never seen surpassed.

At this time, I prided myself upon my color, as
much as any white Virginian of them all ; and although
I had found, by a bitter experience, that a slave,
whether white or black, is still a slave ; and that the
master, heedless of his victim's complexion, handles
the whip, with perfect impartiality ;—still, like my
poor mother, I thought myself of a superior caste, and
would have felt it as a degradation, to put myself on a
level with men a few shades darker than myself. This
silly pride had kept me from forming intimacies with
the other servants, either male or female ; for I was
decidedly whiter than any of them. It had too, justly
enough, exposed me to an ill will, of which I had
more than once felt the consequences, but which had
not yet wholly cured me of my folly.

Cassy had perhaps more African blood than I ; but
this was a point—however weighty and important, I
had at first esteemed it—which, as I became more acquainted with her, seemed continually of less conse-
4*

quence, and soon disappeared entirely from my thoughts.
We were much together ; and her beauty, vivacity, and
good humor, made, every day, a stronger impression
upon me.   I found myself in love before I had thought
of it ; and it was not long before I discovered that my
affection was not unrequited.

Cassy was one of nature's children, and she had
never learned those arts of coquetry,—often as skilfully
practised by the maid as the mistress,—by which courtships are protracted.   We loved ; and before long,
we talked of marriage.   Cassy consulted her mistress ;
and the answer was favorable.   Mrs Moore listened
with equal readiness to me.   Women are never happier, than when they have an opportunity to dabble a
little, in match-making ; nor does even the humble
condition of the parties quite deprive the business of
all its fascination.

It was determined that our marriage, should be a
little festival among the servants.   The coming Sunday was fixed on as the day ; and a Methodist clergyman, who happened to have wandered into the neighborhood, readily undertook to perform the ceremony.
This part of his office, I suppose, he would have performed for any body;—but he undertook it the more readily for us, because Cassy, while at Baltimore, had
become a member of the Methodist Society.

I was well pleased with all this ;—for it seemed to
give to our union something of that solemnity, which
properly belonged to it.   In general, marriage among
the American slaves, is treated as a matter of very little
moment.   It is a mere temporary union, contracted

without ceremony, unrecognized by the laws, little or not at all regarded by the masters, and of course, often but lightly esteemed by the parties. The recollection that the husband may be, any day, sold into Louisiana, and the wife into Georgia, holds out but a slight inducement to draw tight the bonds of connubial intercourse;—and the certainty that the fruits of their marriage—the children of their love—are to be born slaves, and reared to all the privations and calamities of hopeless servitude, is enough to strike a damp into the hearts of the fondest couple. Slaves yield to the impulses of nature, and propagate a race of slaves;—but save in a few rare instances, slavery is as fatal to domestic love as to all the other virtues. Some few choice spirits indeed, will still rise superior to their condition, and when cut off from every other support, will find within their own hearts, the means of resisting the deadly and demoralizing influences of servitude. In the same manner, the baleful poison of the plague or yellow fever—innocent indeed and powerless in comparison!—while it rages through an infected city, and sweeps its thousands and tens of thousands to the grave, finds, here and there, an iron constitution, which defies its total malignity, and sustains itself by the sole aid of nature's health-preserving power.

On the Friday before the Sunday which had been fixed upon for our marriage, colonel Moore returned to Spring-Meadow. His return was unexpected; and by me, at least, very much unwished for. To the other servants, who hastened to welcome him home, he spoke with his usual kindness and good nature;—but

though I had come forward with the rest of them, all
the notice he took of me, was a single stare of dissatis-
faction. He appeared to be surprised—and that too
not agreeably—to see me again in the house.

The next day, I was discharged from my duties of
house servant, and put again under the control of Mr
Stubbs. This touched me to the quick ;—but it was
nothing to what I felt, the day following, when I went
to the house to claim my bride. I was told that she
was gone in the carriage with colonel Moore and his
daughter, who had ridden out to call upon some of the
neighbors ;—and that I need not take the trouble of
coming again to see her, for Miss Caroline did not
choose that her maid should marry a field hand.

It is impossible for me to describe the paroxysm of
grief and passion, which I now experienced. Those
of the same ardent temperament with myself will easily conceive my feelings ; and to persons of a cooler
temper, no description can convey an adequate idea.
My promised wife snatched from me,—and myself
again exposed to the hateful tyranny of a brutal overseer !—and all so sudden too—and with such studied
marks of insult and oppression !

I now felt afresh the ill effects of my foolish pride in
keeping myself seperate and aloof from my fellow servants. Instead of sympathizing with my misfortune,
many of them openly rejoiced at it ; and as I had
never made a confidant or associate among them, I had
no friend whose advice to ask, or whose sympathy to
seek. At length, I bethought myself of the Methodist
minister, who was to come that evening to marry us,

and who had appeared to take a good deal of interest in the welfare of Cassy and myself. I was desirous not only of seeking such advice and consolation as he could afford me, but I wished to save the good man from a useless journey,—and possibly from insult at Spring-Meadow ; for colonel Moore looked on all sorts of preachers, and the Methodists especially, with an eye of very little favor.

I knew that the clergyman in question, held a meeting, about five miles off ; and I resolved, if I could get leave, to go and hear him. I applied to Mr Stubbs for a pass,—that is, a written permission, without which no slave can go off the plantation to which he belongs, except at the risk of being stopped by the first man he meets, horsewhipped, and sent home again. But Mr Stubbs swore that he was tired of such gadding, and he told me that he had made up his mind to grant no more passes for the next fortnight.

To some sentimental persons, it may seem hard after the poor slave has labored six days for his master, and the blessed seventh at length gladdens him with its beams, that he cannot be allowed a little change of scene, but must still be confined to the hated fields, the daily witnesses of his toils and his sufferings. Yet many thrifty managers and good disciplinarians are, like Mr Stubbs, very much opposed to all gadding, and they pen up their slaves, when not at work, as they pen up their cattle, to keep them, as they say, out of mischief.

At another time, this new piece of petty tyranny, might have provoked me ;—but now, I scarcely regarded it;—for my whole heart was absorbed by a greater passion. I was slowly returning towards the servants' quarter, when a little girl, one of the house servants, came running up to me, almost out of breath. I knew her to be one of Cassy's favorites, and I caught her in my arms. As soon as she had recovered her breath, she told me she had been looking for me, all the morning, for she had a message for me from Cassy;—that Cassy had been obliged, much against her inclination, to go out that morning with her mistress, but that I must not be alarmed or down-hearted, for she loved me as well as ever.

I kissed the little messenger, and thanked her a thousand times for her news. I then hastened to my house. This was quite a comfortable little cottage, which Mrs Moore had ordered to be built for Cassy and myself, but of which, I expected every moment to be deprived. The news I had heard, excited new commotions in my bosom. I had no sooner sat down, than I found it impossible to keep quiet. My heart beat violently,—the fever in my blood grew high. I left the house and I walked about, within the limits of my jail yard,—for so I might justly esteem the plantation; I used the most violent exercise, and tried every means I could think of to subdue the powerful emotions of mixed hope and fear, with which I was agitated, and which I found more oppressive than even the certainty of misery.

As evening drew on, I watched for the return of the carriage; and at length, its distant rumbling caught my ear. I hastened towards the house, in the hope of

seeing Cassy, and perhaps, of speaking with her.
The carriage stopped at the door, and I was fast approaching it ; but at the instant, it occurred to me, that
it would be better not to risk being seen by colonel
Moore, who, I was now well satisfied, entertained a
decided hostility towards me, and whom I believed to
be the author of the cruel repulse I had that morning
met with. This thought stopped me, and I drew back
and returned home, without catching a glimpse, or exchanging a word.

I threw myself upon my bed ;—but I turned contin-
tinually from side to side, and found it impossible to
compose myself to rest. Hour after hour dragged on ;
but I could not sleep. It was past midnight ; when I
heard a slight tap at the door, and a soft whisper,
which thrilled through every nerve. I sprung up—I
opened the door—I clasped her to my bosom. It was
Cassy—it was my betrothed wife.

She told me, that since colonel Moore's return,
every thing seemed changed at the House. Miss
Caroline had told her, that colonel Moore had a
very bad opinion of me, and was very much displeased
to find, that during his absence I had been again employed as one of the house servants. She added, that
when he was told of our intended marriage, he had declared that Cassy was too pretty a girl to be thrown
away upon such a scoundrel, and that he would undertake to provide her with a much better husband. So
her mistress had bidden her to think no more of me;—
but at the same time, had told her not to cry, for she
would never leave off teazing her father, till he had ful-

filled his promise ; and if you get a husband, the young lady added, that you know is all that any of us want. So thought the mistress ;—the maid, I have reason to suppose, was rather more refined in her notions of matrimony.

I was not quite certain how to interpret this conduct of colonel Moore's. I was strongly inclined to consider it, only as a new out-break of that spite and hostility, which I had been experiencing, ever since my useless and foolish appeal to his fatherly feelings. It occurred to me however, as possible, that his opposition to our marriage might spring from other motives. Whatever I might imagine, I kept my own counsel. One motive which occurred to me, I could not think of myself, with the slightest patience ; and still less could I bear to shock and distress poor Cassy, by the mention of it. Another motive, which I thought might possibly have influenced colonel Moore, was less discreditable to him, and would have been flattering to the pride of both Cassy and myself. But this, I could not mention, without leading to disclosures, which I did not see fit to make.

Cassy knew herself to be colonel Moore's daughter ; but early in our acquaintance, I had discovered that she had no idea, that I was his son. I have every reason to believe, that Mrs Moore was perfectly well informed as to both these particulars,—for they were of that sort, which seldom or never escape the eagerness of female curiosity, and more especially, the curiosity of a wife.

Whatever she might know, she discovered in it no

impediment to my marriage with Cassy. Nor did I;
—for how could that same regard for the *decencies of
life*—such is the soft phrase which justifies the most
unnatural cruelty—that refused to acknowledge our
paternity, or to recognize any relationship between us,
pretend at the same time, and on the sole ground of
relationship, to forbid our union ?

But I knew that Cassy felt, rather than reasoned ;—
and though born and bred a slave, she possessed great
delicacy of feeling. Besides, she was a Methodist,
and though as cheerful and gay hearted a girl as I ever
knew, she was very devout in all the observances of
her religion. I feared to put our mutual happiness in
jeopardy ;—I was unwilling to harrass Cassy, with
what I esteemed unnecessary scruples. I had never
told her the story of my parentage, and every day I
grew less inclined to tell it. Accordingly I made no
other answer to what she had told me, except to say,
that however little colonel Moore might like me, his
dislike was not my fault.

A momentary pause followed ;—I pressed Cassy's
hand between mine, and in a faultering voice, I asked,
what she intended to do :

" I am your wife ;—I will never be any body's but
yours," was the answer. I clasped the dear girl to
my heart ; we knelt together, and with upraised hands
invoked the Deity to witness and confirm our union.
It was the only sanction in our power ; and if twenty
priests had said a benediction over us, would that have
made our vows more binding, or our marriage more

5

complete ?   I hope at least, it would have rendered it
more fortunate.

CHAPTER VIII.

It was impossible for my wife to visit me except by
stealth.   She slept every night upon the carpet in her
mistress' room,—for a floor is esteemed in America, a
good enough bed for a slave, even for a favorite and a
woman.   She was liable to be called upon in the night,
at the caprice of a mistress, who was in fact, a mere
spoiled child ;—and she could only visit me at the risk
of a discovery, which might have been attended with
very unpleasant consequences ;—for if these clandes-
tine visits had been detected, I fear that not all Cassy's
charms—whatever poets have fabled of the power of
beauty—could have saved her from the lash.

Yet short and uncertain as these visits were, they
sufficed to create and to sustain a new and singular state
of feeling.   My wife was seldom with me, but her
image was ever before my eyes, and appeared to
make me regardless of all beside.   Things seemed to
pass as in a happy dream.   The labor of the field was
nothing ;—the lash of the overseer was scarcely felt.

My mind became so occupied, and as it were, filled up, with the pleasure which I found in our mutual affection, and the anticipated delights of each successive interview, that it seemed to have no room for disagreeable emotions. Strong as was my passion, there was nothing in it, uneasy or unsatisfied. When I clasped the dear girl to my bosom, I seemed to have reached the very height of human fruition. I was happy ;—and greater happiness I could not imagine, and did not desire.

The intoxication of passion is the same in the slave and in the master ;—it is exquisite ; and while it lasts, all-sufficient in itself. I found it so. With almost everything to make me miserable, still I was happy,— for the excess of my passion rendered me insensible to any thing save its own indulgence.

But such extacies are unsuited to the human constitution. They are soon over, and perhaps are ever purchased at too dear a price ;—for they are but too apt to be succeeded by all the anguish of disappointed hope, and all the bitterness of deep despair. Still I look back with pleasure to that time. It is one of the bright spots of my existence which eager memory discovers in her retrospections, scattered and scarcely visible,— tiny islets of delight, surrounded on all sides, by a gloomy and tempestuous ocean.

We had been married about a fortnight. It was near midnight, and I was sitting before my door, waiting for my wife to come. The moon was full and bright ; the sky was cloudless. I was still at the height and flood of my intoxication ; and as I

watched the planet, and admired her brightness, I gave
thanks to heaven that the base tendencies of a servile
condition, had not yet totally extinguished within me,
all the higher and nobler emotions of man's nature.

Presently I observed a figure approaching. I should
have known her at any distance, and I sprang forward
and caught my wife in my arms. But as I pressed her
to my heart, I felt her bosom to be strangely agitated;
and when I brought her face to mine, my cheek was
moistened with her tears.

Alarmed at these unusual indications, I hurried her
into the house, and hastily inquired the cause of her
agitation. My inquiries appeared to increase it. She
sunk her head upon my breast; burst into sobs;
and seemed wholly incapable of speaking. I knew not
what to think, or what to do. I exerted myself to
compose her; I kissed off the tears that trickled fast
down her cheeks; I pressed my hand against her beating heart, as if, in that way, I could have checked its
palpitations. At length she grew more calm;—but it
was by slow degrees, and in broken sentences, that I
learned the origin of her terror.

It seemed that colonel Moore, ever since his return,
had distinguished her by particular kindness. He had
made her several little presents; had sought frequent occasions to talk with her,—and was ever, half jocosely,
complimenting her beauty. He had even dropped
certain hints, which Cassy could not help understand-
standing, but of which, she thought it best to take no
notice. He was not to be repelled in that way; but
proceeded to words and actions, of which, it was not

possible for her to affect to misunderstand the meaning. Her native modesty—her love for me—her religious feelings, were all alarmed ; and the poor girl began to tremble at the fate that seemed to await her. But as yet, she kept her terrors to herself. She was reluctant to torture me with the story of insults, which however they might pierce my heart, I had no power to repel.

That day, Mrs Moore and her daughter had gone to visit one of the neighbors, and Cassy was left at home. She was employed on some needle-work in her mistress' room, when colonel Moore entered. She rose up hastily and would have gone away; but he bade her stop and listen to what he had to say to her. He did not seem to notice her agitation, and appeared perfectly self-possessed himself. He told her that he had promised her mistress to provide her with a husband, in place of that scoundrel Archy ; that he had looked about, but did not see any body that was worthy of her ; and, on the whole—he had concluded to take her himself.

This he said with a tone of tenderness, which no doubt, he meant to be irresistible. To many women, in Cassy's situation, it would have been so. They would have esteemed themselves highly honored by their master's notice, and would have felt not a little flattered, by the delicate terms under which he concealed the real character of his proposals. But she— poor child—heard him with shame and horror ; and was ready,—she told me,—to sink into the earth, with terror and dismay. In relating it, she blushed—she

5*

hesitated—she shuddered—her breathing became short and quick—she clung to me, as if some visible image of horror were present before her ;—and, bringing her lips close to my ear, she exclaimed in a trembling and scarcely audible whisper—" Oh Archy !—and he my father !"

Colonel Moore, she believed, could not have misunderstood the sort of feelings with which she listened to his proposals. But if so, he disregarded them ;—for he proceeded to enumerate all the advantages she would derive from this connexion, and strove to tempt her by promises of idleness and finery. She stood with her eyes upon the floor,—and only answered him by sobs and tears, which she strove in vain to suppress. Upon this colonel Moore, in a tone of pique and displeasure, told her not to be a fool ;—and catching one of her hands in his, he threw his arm about her waist, and bade her not provoke him by a useless resistance. She uttered a scream of surprise and terror, and sunk at his feet. At that moment, the sound of the carriage wheels fell—she said—like heavenly music on her ear. Her master heard it too ;—for he let go his grasp, and muttering something about another time, hastily left the room. She remained almost senseless, on the floor, till the sound of her mistress' footsteps in the passage, recalled her to herself. The rest of the afternoon and evening, she had passed, she hardly knew how. Her head, she told me, was dizzy,—a cloud swam before her eyes, and she had hardly been sensible of anything but a painful feeling of langour and oppression. She had not dared to leave her mistress' room ; and had waited with impatience for the hour that would permit her to throw herself into the arms of her husband, her natural protector.

Her natural protector !—alas, of what avail is the natural right of a husband to protect his wife against the assaults of a villain, who is at once her owner and his !

Such was Cassy's story ; and strange as it may seem, I heard it almost unmoved. Although I held the panting, trembling, weeping narrator in my arms, I listened to her story with far less emotion, than I have since experienced in recounting it. In truth, I was prepared for it ; I had anticipated it ; I expected it.

I knew well that Cassy's charms were too great not to excite a voluptuary in whom a long indulgence had extinguished all the better feelings, and rendered incapable of controlling himself ;—and to whom, neither the fear of punishment, nor the dread of public scorn and indignation, supplied the place of conscience. What else could be reasonably expected of a man, who knew well—let him proceed to what extremities he might— not only that the law would justify him, but that any body who might think of calling him to account, before the bar of public opinion, would be denounced by the public voice, as an impertinent intermeddler in the affairs of other people ?

Little of paternal tenderness as colonel Moore ever showed me—at least, from the moment that he found I knew him to be my father,—I have too much of filial respect to entertain the wish of misrepresenting him. Though he was of a warm and voluptuous temperament, he was naturally a good natured man ; and his honor was, as I have said, unquestioned. But honor is of a very diverse character. There is honor among gentlemen, and honor among thieves ;—and though both these codes contain several excellent enactments, neither can fairly claim to be considered a perfect system of morality. Of that code in which he had been educated, colonel Moore was a most strict observer. To have made an attempt on the chastity of a neighbor's wife or daughter, he would have esteemed—and so the honorary code of Virginia esteems it,—an offence of the blackest die ; an offence, he well knew, to be expiated only by the offender's life. But, beyond this, he did not dream of prohibition or restraint. Hardened and emboldened, by certain impunity, provided the sufferer were a slave,—he regarded the most atrocious outrage that could be perpetrated upon the person and feelings of a woman, rather as a matter of jest—a thing to be laughed at over the fourth bottle— than a subject of serious and sober reprehension.

Of all this, I was well aware. I had from the first foreseen, that Cassy would be devoted by her master to the same purposes which had been fulfilled by my mother and her own. It was from these intentions, as I had all along believed, that his opposition to our marriage had originated. In imagining that it might spring from another cause, I had done him an honor, to which —as was now too evident—he had not the slightest title. What I had just now heard, I had daily expected to hear. I had expected it ;—yet such had been my intoxication, that even anticipations terrible as this,

had not been able to alarm or to distress me ;—and now
that anticipation was changed into reality, still I remained unmoved. The ecstacy of passion still supported me ; and as I pressed my wretched, trembling
wife to my bosom, I still rose superior to the calamity
that assailed me ;—even yet, I was happy.

This seems incredible ?—

Love then as I did ;—or if that suits your temperament better, hate with the same intensity with which I
loved. Be absorbed in any passion, and while the fit
continues, you will find yourself endowed with a surprising and almost superhuman energy.

My mind was already made up. The unhappy slave
has but one way of escaping any threatening infliction ;
—a poor and wretched resource, to which he recurs
always at the imminent risk of redoubling his miseries.
That remedy is flight.

Our preparations were soon made. My wife returned to the house, and gathered up a little bundle of
clothing. In the mean time, I employed myself in
collecting such provisions as I could readiest lay my
hands on. A couple of blankets, a hatchet, a little
kettle, and a few other small articles, completed my
equipments ; and by the time my wife returned, I was
ready for a start. We set out, with no other companion, but a faithful dog. I did not wish to take him, for
fear that some how or other, he might lead to our detection ; but I could not drive him back, and I was
afraid to tie him, lest his howlings might give an alarm,
and lead to an immediate pursuit.

Lower Virginia had already began to feel the effects

of that curse, which has since lighted so heavily upon her, and which, in truth, she has so well deserved. Already her fields were beginning to be deserted ; already impenetrable thickets had commenced to cover plantations, which, had the soil been cultivated by free-men, might still have produced a rich and abundant harvest. There was a deserted plantation about ten miles from Spring-Meadow. I had formerly visited it several times, in company with my young master, James, who, when he was well enough to ride about, had a strange taste for wandering into out-of-the-way places. It was thither that, in the hurry of the moment, I resolved to go.

The by-road which had formerly led to it, as well as the fields on both sides, were grown over with small scrubby pines ; so close and tangled as to render the thicket almost impenetrable. I contrived however, to keep on in the right direction. But the difficulties of the way were so great, that the morning had dawned before we reached the plantation buildings. They were still standing ; but in a most dilapidated condition. The great House had been a structure of large size, and considerable pretentions. But the windows were gone, the doors had dropped from their hinges, and the roof was partly fallen in. The court yard was completely grown up with young trees. Wild vines were creeping over the house ;—and all was silent, desolate and deserted. The stables, and what had been the servants' quarter, were mere heaps of ruins, overgrown with weeds and grass.

At some distance behind the house, there was a

rapid descent, which formed one side of a deep ravine; and near the bottom of this hollow, a fine bubbling spring, burst from under the hill. It was now half choked with leaves and sand, but its waters were pure and cool as ever. Near the spring, was a little low building of brick, which perhaps had been intended for a dairy, or some such purpose. The door was gone, and half the roof had tumbled in. The other half still kept its position, and the vacancy occasioned by the part that had fallen, served well enough to admit the light and air, and to supply the place of windows, which had formed no part of the original construction. This ruinous little building was shaded by several large and ancient trees ; and was so completely hidden by a more recent growth, as to be invisible at the distance of a few paces. It was by mere accident that we stumbled upon it, as we were searching for the spring, of which I had drank upon my former visits, but the situation of which, I did not exactly recollect. It struck us at once, that this was the place for our temporary habitation ; and we resolved forthwith to clear it of the rubbish it contained, and to turn it into a dwelling.

CHAPTER IX.

I knew that the place where we now were, was very seldom visited by any body. The deserted house had the reputation of being haunted; and this, as well as its seclusion from the road, and the almost impenetrable thickets by which it was surrounded, would serve to protect us against intruders. There were several plantations about it;—for it occupied the highest ground between two rivers, which flowed at no great distance apart, and of which the low grounds were still in cultivation. But there were no cultivated fields nearer than four or five miles; and no houses nearer than Spring-Meadow, which, I have said, was some ten or twelve miles distance. I judged that for the present, we might remain secure in this retreat; and it seemed our best policy to suffer the search for us to be pretty well over, before we attempted to continue our flight.

In the mean time, we exerted ourselves to make things as comfortable as possible. It was the height of summer; and we anticipated but little inconvenience from the openness of our habitation. A heap of pine straw, in one corner of our ruinous hovel, formed our bed; and sweeter slumbers, not down itself could have ensured. Out of such materials as the wainscoting of the deserted house supplied, I made two rude stools, and something that served for a table. The spring furnished us with water;—our principal concern was to provide ourselves with food. The woods and thickets produced some wild fruits ; and the peach-orchard near the house, though choked and shaded by a more recent growth, still continued to bear. I was an adept in the art of snaring rabbits, and such other small game as the woods supplied. The spring which furnished us with water, was one of the heads of a little brook which discharged, at a short distance, into a larger stream. In that stream there were fish. But our chief resource was in the neighboring corn-fields, which already furnished roasting ears, and from which I did not scruple to draw a plentiful supply.

On the whole,—though we were both quite unaccustomed to so wild a livelihood,—we passed our time very agreeably. Those who are always idle can never know the true luxury of idleness—the real pleasure, with which he who has been pushed to work against his will, relaxes his strained muscles, and delivers himself up to the delight of doing nothing. I used to lie for hours, in a dreamy sort of indolence, outstretched upon the shady slope, enjoying the sweet consciousness of being my own master, and luxuriating in the idea that I need come or go at no one's bidding, but might work or be idle as suited my own good will. No wonder that emancipated slaves are inclined to indolence. It is to them a new pleasure. Labor, in their minds, is indissolubly associated with servitude and the whip ; and *not to work*, they have ever been taught to look upon as the badge and peculiar distinction of freedom.

The present was passing pleasantly enough ; but it was necessary to be thinking about the future. We

6

had always regarded our present place of refuge as
temporary only ; and it was now time to think of leaving it.   I should have thought it delightful indeed, to
pass a whole life of solitude and seclusion with Cassy ;
where, if we had lacked the pleasures of society, we
might have escaped its ten-fold greater ills.   But this
was not possible.   The American climate was never
meant for hermits.   Our present station would answer well enough for a summer retreat ; but the winter
would render it untenable ;—and before long, winter
would be approaching.   Our hope was to escape into
the free states,—for I knew that north of Virginia
there was a country where there were no slaves.   If we
could once get away from the neighborhood of Spring-
Meadow, where I was well known, we should enjoy
one great advantage during the rest of our flight.   Our
complexions would not betray our servile condition ;
and we should find no great difficulty, we thought,
in passing ourselves as white citizens of Virginia.
Colonel Moore had, no doubt, filled the country round,
with advertisements, in which our persons were accu-
rately described, and every peculiarity of each of us
carefully noted.   It was therefore necessary to use
great caution ; and I considered it essential to our
escape that Cassy should adopt some disguise.   What
this should be, or where we should get it was now the
question.

We finally determined to assume the character of
white people travelling to the north to seek our fortunes ; and we arranged that Cassy should adopt a man's
dress, and accompany me in the character of a younger

brother. The night, on which we had left Spring-
Meadow, I had brought away my best suit,—one of
the last gifts of my poor master James, and such as
would well enough enable me to play the part of a travelling Virginian. But I had neither hat nor shoes ; nor
any clothes whatever, in which to dress up Cassy.

Luckily I had a small sum, the accumulated savings
of master James' liberality, which I had always kept in
reserve, in the hope and expectation that I should
sometime have a use for it. This money, I had been
careful to take with me ; and it was now our sole reli-
ance not only for the expenses of the road, but for
procuring the means, without which we could not start
at all.

But though we had the money, how could we make
any use of it, without running a very serious risk of
detection ?

There lived, about five or six miles from Spring-
Meadow, and near the same distance from us, one Mr
James Gordon. He kept a little store ; and his principal customers were the slaves of the neighboring plantations. Mr James Gordon, or Jemmy Gordon, as he
was familiarly called, was one of those *poor white men,*
of whom the number in lower Virginia, is or was, very
considerable ; and who are spoken of, even by the
very slaves, with a sort of contempt. He had neither
lands nor servants ; for his father before him, had been a
poor white man. He had been educated to no trade ;
for where every planter has his own mechanics on his
own plantation, a white tradesman can expect no encouragement. The only resource of a man in Jemmy

Gordon's situation, is to find employment as an overseer for some of his richer neighbors. But in Virginia, there are more persons who desire to be overseers than there are plantations to oversee. Besides,
Mr Gordon was one of those careless, easy, good natured, indolent sort of men, who are generally pronounced good-for-nothing. He never could bring himself to that ever watchful scrutiny, and assiduous over-
sight, which is necessary among slaves, whose maxim
it is to work as little as possible, and to steal all they
can. He was apt enough to get into a passion, and
cut and slash, right and left, without discrimination ;
but he was incapable of that regular severity, and systematic cruelty, by which other overseers gained the
reputation of excellent disciplinarians. Moreover, on
a certain plantation, of which he had been the manager,
some large vacancies had appeared in the corn-crib,
which were never very clearly accounted for. How
far this was occasioned by negligence, or how far by
dishonesty, was never, so far as I know, satisfactorily
determined. All I can say is, that Mr Gordon was
dismissed from his employment, and found it so difficult to get a new situation, that he gave up the search
in despair, and resolved to turn trader. He had nothing to begin upon ; and of course, traded in a very
small way. He dealt principally in whiskey,—but in
addition, kept shoes, and such articles of clothing as
slaves are in the habit of purchasing to eke out the
miserable and insufficient supply, which they receive
from their masters. He took money in payment ;—but

likewise corn and other produce, without any strict inquiry how his customers came into possession of it.

It is this class of men against whom the legislators
of Virginia have exercised all their ingenuity in the
construction of penal statutes ; and against whom, they
have exerted all the severity which they have dared to
use towards men, who might still claim the title and
demand the rights of " free white citizens." But these
penal enactments, have failed, in a great measure, of
their object. Though the trade with slaves is dangerous and disgraceful, and the traders, in consequence,
are desperate and reckless, their number is still so
great as to furnish the planters with an inexhaustible
topic of declamation and complaint,—and to supply the
slaves with numerous little comforts and luxuries which
they might in vain have expected from the indulgence
or humanity of their masters.

These traders are, no doubt, the receivers of plunder ; and no small proportion of what they sell is paid
for in that way. It is in vain, that tyranny fences itself
about with the terrors of the law. It is in vain, that the
slave-holder flatters himself with the hope of appropri-
ating to his own sole use, the entire fruits of the forced
labors of his fellow men. The slave cannot resist the
compulsion, with which the law has armed the hand of
his master. The lash is an ensign of authority and of
torture, to which the stoutest heart, and the most stub-
born will, is soon compelled to yield. But fraud is the
natural counterpart to tyranny ; and cunning is ever the
defence of the weak against the oppressions of the
strong. Can the unhappy slave, who has been com-

6*

pelled to plant in the day time, for his master's benefit
be blamed, if he strives in the night, to gather some
gleaning of the crop, for his own use ?

Blame him you who can !   Join, if you will, in the
clamor of the master against the cursed knavery of his
slaves !   This same master, who thinks it no wrong to
rob these slaves of their labor,—their sole possession,
their only earthly property !   He to talk about theft !
—he—the slave-holder—who has carried the art of pillage to a perfection of which robbers and pirates never
dreamed !   They are content to snatch such casual
spoils as chance may offer ; but the slave-holder—whip
in hand—extorts from his victims, a large, a regular,
an annual plunder !   Nay more ; he sells for money,
he has inherited from his father, and he hopes to trans-
mit to his children, the privilege of continuing this
systematic pillage !

I had once saved Mr Gordon's life, and for this
piece of service he had always expressed the greatest
gratitude.   This had happened several years since.   He
was fishing on the river, not far from Spring-Meadow,
when a sudden squall upset his boat.   It was no great
distance from the shore,—but Mr Gordon was no
swimmer, and was in the greatest danger.   Master
James and myself happened to be walking along the
beach.   We saw a man struggling in the water, and
I plunged in after him, and caught him as he was
sinking the third time.   This service, Mr Gordon
was in the habit of acknowledging by occasional little
presents ;—and I flattered myself with the hope that he
would not refuse his aid in my present circumstances.

My plan was, to get from Mr Gordon, a hat and shoes for myself, a man's dress for Cassy, and such information as he could give us about the route we ought to follow. A great many difficulties presented themselves to my mind in the prosecution of the journey ;—I resolved however not to afflict myself with borrowed trouble, but to leave the future to take care of itself.

The first thing was, to see Mr Gordon, and find out how far he was disposed to assist me. His house and store—both under the same roof—were in a lonely part of the country, near the crossing of two roads, and out of sight of any other buildings. I did not think it safe to trust myself upon the high-way before midnight ; and it was considerably past that hour before I approached Mr Gordon's house. When I came within sight of it, I hesitated, and more than once, came to a halt. .I did not like to trust my liberty, and all my hopes of happiness, to the unsure guardianship of any man's gratitude, and least of all, such a man as Mr Gordon. The risk seemed too great ;—and my heart sunk within me, when I called to mind how frail was the prop on which depended, if not my life, every thing that made life desirable.

I was on the point of turning back ;—but I recollected that this was my only resource. Mr Gordon must help me to escape, or my chance was worth nothing. This thought pushed me on. I plucked up my courage and approached the door. Three or four dogs which kept watch about the house, immediately opened in full chorus ; but though they barked loud enough, they gave no signs of any intention to attack me. I knocked again ;—and pretty soon, Mr Gordon thrust his head from the window, bade his dogs be quiet, and inquired who I was, and what I wanted. I begged him to open the door and let me in, for I had business with him. Expecting perhaps, to drive a profitable trade with some midnight customer, he hastened to do as I had requested. He opened the door;—the moon-light, as I entered, fell upon my face, and he recognized me at once.

" My God ! Archy, is it you"—and he spoke it with an air of the greatest surprise—" where, in the devil's name, did you spring from ?—I hoped you were clear out of the neighborhood a month ago,"—and with these words he drew me into the house and shut the door.

I told him, that I had a place of concealment near by, and that I had come to get a little of his assistance in making my escape.

" Any thing in reason, Archy ; but if I were caught helping off a run-away, it would ruin me forever. There's colonel Moore, your master, and major Pringle, and captain Knight, and a half dozen more, were over here, it's only yesterday, and they swore if I did not leave off trading with the hands, they'd pull my house down about my ears, and ride me on a rail out of the county ;—and now if I were caught helping you, by God, Archy, 't would do my business for me with a witness. I'm not quite such a fool as all that."

I used tears, and flatteries, and entreaties. I reminded Mr Gordon how often he had wished for an opportunity to serve me ; I told him that all I wanted

was a few articles of dress, and some directions about
the road I ought to follow.

"True, Archy, by God;—You saved my life, boy;
—I can't deny it;—and one good turn deserves another. But this business of yours is a damned bad business, at the best. What, the devil, must you and that
wench be running away for? I never knew any mischief in my life, that a woman was'nt at the bottom of
it. It's that damned tattling widow Hinkley, that
brought colonel Moore and the rest of 'em over here
yesterday;—damn the envious old jade, she wants to
drive me out of the neighborhood, and get all the custom for herself."

I knew that Mr Gordon had no turn for sentiment,
and that it would be casting pearls before swines' feet
to waste any upon him. So I told him it was too late
to talk about our reasons for running away,—run away
we had—and the only thing now was, to avoid being
taken.

"Aye, aye, boy, I understand you. It's a damned
silly business, and you beg into be ashamed of it already. You had better make up your minds now to go in,
take your whippings, and make the best of it. It's the
loss of the wench that colonel Moore is most angry
about; and I dare say, if you were to go in, Archy,
and make a merit of telling where he could find her,
you might get off mighty easy, and shift all the blame
upon her shoulders."

I concealed the indignation which this base proposal
excited. Such treachery to one another is too common among slaves, and is promoted and rewarded by

the masters. I could not expect Mr Gordon to rise
very far above the level of current morals. So I passed by this proposal in silence ; I only said, that I had
made up my mind to undergo every thing rather than
return to Spring-Meadow. If he was resolved not
to assist me, I would be off, as soon as possible,—
trusting to his honor, to say nothing about this visit.
As a last resource, I hinted that I had the money to pay
for all I wanted, and that I should not dispute about
the price.

Whether it was this last hint, or some more generous motive, or the combined effect of both, I shall not
undertake to determine ; but certain it is, that Mr Gordon began to exhibit a more favorable disposition.

" As to money Archy, between friends like us,
there is no need of speaking about that. And if you
will have your own way, considering what has happened between us, 'twould be mighty unkind in me not
to let you have the things you 're wanting. But you 'll
never get off—mind now what I tell you—you 'll never
get off. Why, boy, the colonel swares he 'll spend
five thousand dollars but what he 'll catch you. He 's
got printed handbills stuck up all through the country,
with *Five Hundred Dollars Reward*, at the head of 'em.
Come into the store here, and I 'll show you one.
Five hundred dollars !—somebody is to pocket that
money, I reckon."

I did not like the tone in which this was spoken.
The emphasis with which Mr Gordon dwelt on the five
hundred dollars, was rather alarming. The idea of

this reward was evidently taking strong hold of his imagination.

Mr Gordon's establishment consisted of but two rooms, of which, one was his parlor, bed-room and kitchen, and the other his store. All this time we had been in the bed-room, with no light but that of the moon. I now followed him into the store. He struck a light, kindled a piece of light-wood, and holding it up to a large handbill posted opposite the door, I read, to the best of my recollection, pretty much as follows;

"FIVE HUNDRED DOLLARS REWARD.

Ran away from the subscriber, at Spring-Meadow, on Saturday evening last, two servants, Archy and Cassy, for whose apprehension the above reward will be paid.

They are both very light colored. Of the two, Cassy is a shade the darker. Archy is about twenty-one years of age, five feet eleven inches high, and a stout muscular frame. He has a firm erect walk, and is a very likely fellow. Smiles when spoken to. His hair is a light brown, and curls over his head ; he has blue eyes and a high forehead. Said boy was raised in my family, and has always been kindly treated. It is not known what clothes he wore away.

Cassy is about eighteen, five feet three inches, or thereabouts, and a handsome face and figure. She has a head of long dark hair, and a very bright black eye. When she smiles there is a dimple in her left cheek. She has a good voice, and can sing several songs. No other marks particularly recollected, except a mole on her right breast. She has been raised a lady's maid, and she took a variety of good clothing with her. Said slaves have gone off in company as is supposed.

Whoever will return them to me, or lodge them in any jail, so that I can get them, shall be paid the above reward ; or one half for either separately.

CHARLES MOORE.

N. B. I suspect they have taken the road to Baltimore, as Cassy formerly lived in that city. No doubt they will attempt to pass off for white people."

While I was reading this advertisement, Mr Gordon looked over my shoulder, and added his comments upon each sentence of it. Neither his remarks, nor the advertisement, itself, were calculated to make me feel very comfortably. Perhaps Mr Gordon observed it ; for he handed me a glass of whiskey, and bade me keep up my spirits. He swallowed one himself ; and drank to my escape. This re-assured me a little,—for to tell the truth—I was a good deal startled at Mr Gordon's very evident hankering after the five hundred dollars. The whiskey he drank,—and he was not content with a single glass,—seemed to rekindle his gratitude. He swore he would run any risk to serve me, and told me to pick out such articles as I wanted.

I fitted myself with hat and shoes, and selected the same for Cassy. But it was necessary to have a man's dress for her. Mr Gordon did not deal in ready made clothing,—but he had some cloth, which I thought, would answer our purpose ; and he undertook to get the suit made up for me. I gave him the measure by guess, and was to return in three days, by

which time he promised to have the clothes done. I
had much rather have finished the business at once,
and have started directly on our journey ; but this was
impossible. A disguise for Cassy was absolutely necessary ; it would have been foolish to have attempted to
escape without it. I pressed him to be sure and have
the clothes finished, at the time appointed ; for a reward
of five hundred dollars, and the chance of making
friends with colonel Moore, and rising in the world by
his assistance, was a temptation to which I wished to
keep Mr Gordon exposed, as short a time as possible.
I now inquired what I had to pay for my various purchases. Mr Gordon took his slate and began to figure
it up. He proceeded very diligently for a few minutes,
and then suddenly came to a full stop. He looked at
the goods I had selected, and then at the slate. For a
moment, he hesitated,—then looking at me. "Archy,"
he said, " you saved my life,—you 're welcome to
them 'ere things, by God."

I knew well how to value this instance of generosity.
Whatever money Mr Gordon got, was pretty sure to
go in gambling and dissipation. Of course he was not
only poor, but often distressed and tormented to get
the means of indulging his propensities ;—money was
to him, what whiskey is to the lips of the drunkard.
For such a person to be generous, is hard indeed ;
and I ceased at once, to distrust a man, who gave
so substantial a proof of his inclination to assist me. I
bade him good night, and set out on my return home,
with a heart much lightened.

Mr Gordon put me some questions about the place

7

of my retreat, to which I thought it best to return rather an equivocal answer. Though greatly reassured, I still could see no good purpose to be answered by too great confidence ; and at setting out from Mr Gordon's, I was careful to take a direction quite wide of the true one. Once or twice, I thought I was followed. The moon was now setting, and her light was scanty and uncertain. My path led through a scattered growth of stunted trees and bushes. A pursuer might easily have concealed himself,—but when I stopped to listen, all was silent ; and I soon dismissed my fanciful fears.

Taking a considerable circuit, I struck into the direction of the deserted plantation, and arrived there about day-break. Cassy came out to meet me. It was the first time we had been so long separated since our escape from Spring-Meadow. I felt as overjoyed to see her, as if I had returned after a year's absence ; and the eagerness with which she flew into my arms, and pressed me again and again to her bosom, satisfied me that I was not alone in the feeling. We spent the three days in making preparations, starting and answering difficulties, and sometimes in pleasing ourselves with anticipations of future happiness.

At the appointed time I set off for Mr Gordon's. I approached the house, not trembling and hesitating, as before, but with the confident step with which one hastens to the dwelling of a tried friend. I knocked. In a moment Mr Gordon opened the door ; he caught me by the arm, and would have drawn me into the

house ; but the door half opened enabled me to discover that there were others there, beside himself.

I snatched myself from his grasp, and starting back,
I said in a whisper, " Good God ! Mr Gordon, who
have you in the house ?"

He returned me no answer ; but almost while I
spoke, I heard Stubbs' grum voice growling " sieze
him, sieze him ;"—and that moment I knew I was
betrayed. I ran ;—but very soon I felt somebody
grasping at my shoulder. Luckily I had a thick stout
stick in my hand, and turning short round, with one
blow, I struck my pursuer to the ground. It was the
traitor Gordon. I was tempted to stop and renew the
blow,—but that moment, a pistol ball whizzed by my
head, and looking round, I saw Stubbs and another
man, with pistols in their hands, close upon me.
There was no time to loose. I sprang forward, and
ran for my life. Two or three shots were fired, in
quick succession, but without effect ; and presently I
reached a thicket, where I felt myself more safe. It
was soon evident that I was much the best runner of
the party ; for before long, I was out of sight and hearing of my pursuers. I kept on for near half an hour ;
when, almost exhausted, I sunk upon the ground, and
strove to recover my breath and to collect my thoughts.
There was no moon ; the starlight was obscured by a
thin mist ; and I did not well know where I was.
Having determined, as well as I was able, the probable direction of the deserted plantation, I again set forward. In the race, I had sprained one of my ancles.
This I had scarcely observed, at the moment ; but it

now became painful, and I moved with difficulty. However, I kept forward the best I could, and flattered myself with the hope of getting back before daylight. I passed, for a considerable distance, through fields and thickets, with which I was not acquainted ; but presently, I reached a brook which I knew. I quenched my thirst, and pushed forward with greater alacrity. I was still five or six miles from the deserted plantation, and was obliged to take a very circuitous route. I kept on as fast as I was able ; but the sun was up, some hours, before I arrived at the spring. Cassy was anxiously watching for me. She had become exceedingly alarmed at my delay ;—nor did the disorder of my dress, and my appearance of haste and fatigue tend to reassure her. I hastened towards the spring, and was stooping to drink, when Cassy suddenly gave a loud shriek. I looked up, and saw two or three men rushing down the side of the hollow. I sprang upon my feet ; but immediately, I felt myself seized from behind. Two other men had rushed down the hollow, upon the other side, and while I was preparing to give battle to those I had first seen, before I was aware of my danger, I found myself in the grasp of their confederates.

CHAPTER X.

I learned afterwards, that when Mr Stubbs and his companion, who were waiting for me at Gordon's, had failed to bring me down with their pistols, discovering that I ran too fast for them, they soon gave over the chase and returned to the store. They sent off immediately for assistance; and were presently joined by two men, and what was of more importance, by a dog, named Jowler, and celebrated through the county for his skill in tracking out runaway slaves.

Jowler had no sooner arrived, than they tied a string about his neck, the other end of which, one of the party held in his hand. The dog was then put upon my track, and he trotted slowly forward with his nose to the ground, followed by Mr Stubbs and the rest of the party. All the latter part of the way, I had walked quite slowly, and Jowler, and his company had gained so fast upon me, that they reached the spring almost as soon as I did. Having discovered my retreat, they resolved to make every thing certain; and dividing into two parties, they rushed down both sides of the hollow, at the same time, and secured me in the manner I have related.

Poor Cassy was seized at the same instant; and almost before we knew what had happened, we found our hands tied, and ourselves connected by a heavy chain, the ends of which were made fast by padlocks

7*

about our necks. This was sad business for Cassy ; and the poor girl, when she felt the iron about her neck, wept bitterly. I do not believe the chain was drawn much tighter than was necessary ;—yet when I saw the tears of my poor wife, I could not help feeling a choking sensation about my throat. What aggravated my distress, and my indignation, was the brutal jests of our captors. It was well my hands were fast, for had they been free, I verily believe I should have found the means to finish one or another of the scoundrels. Mr Gordon was one of the party. His head was bound up in a bloody handkerchief; but instead of joining in the jests of his companions, he tried to keep them from vexing and insulting us.

" I'll tell you what Stubbs—you damned infernal blackguard—let that gal Cassy be. Ain't it I who 've taken them ? Ain't it I who am to have the reward ? Let them be I say ; I tell you they are under my protection."

" A damned fine sort of protector they 've found in you," answered Stubbs, with a loud laugh, in which he was joined by his companions,—" No question, they 're mightily obliged to you. The devil take your nonsense and yourself into the bargain ; I'll say what I please to the gal, and do what I please too. Ain't I the overseer ?"—and here he broke out with a fresh string of ribaldry, addressed to poor Cassy.

It was only by a promise to treat his companions to a quart of whiskey, that Mr Gordon could prevail on them to let us alone. The word " whiskey" worked like a charm, and by the influence of it, he persuaded the others to drop a little behind, and to give him a chance, as he expressed it, to have some private conversation with me. He had no objection, he said, to their hearing what he said to me, but he did not want to be interrupted by their damned clatter.

I was a good deal surprised at all this. Mr Gordon had betrayed me ;—and after doing me so base and irreparable an injury, what could he mean by these little marks of good will ? Mr Gordon was, as I have described him, a good natured fellow. He had not been able to resist the temptation of five hundred dollars, and all the other advantages, which he expected to gain by betraying me ;—but for all that, he had not forgotten that I had saved his life. He walked up beside me, and stammering and hesitating, he attempted to enter into conversation.

" That was a damned hard blow you struck me, Archy," he began.

" I am sorry it was not harder," was my answer.

" Come, come now, don't be in such a devilish savage humor. Why, boy, I thought I might as well get the five hundred dollars, as to let it slip through my fingers, and all for nothing too. I knew right well, you were sure to be taken,—and for all you pout so about it, I 've made better terms for you, than any body else would have done. Come, boy, cheer up, and I 'll tell you how it all was. You see, when you left me 't other night, I could not sleep a wink for thinking. Says I to myself, that 's a damned foolish project of Archy's. He is sure to be caught ; and then it will be coming out as how I helped him, and then there will be the devil and all to pay. He 'll be whipped, and I 'll be fined and sent to jail, and for any thing I know, ridden on a rail out of the county, as colonel Moore and them others threatened me ;—and then,—to make a bad matter worse,—somebody else will get the reward. Now that boy Archy, said I to myself, saved my life—there's no denying that, any how,—and if I can save him a whipping, and at the same time, put five hundred dollars into my pocket, it will be a mighty pretty business for both of us.

" So the next morning, I got up early and started off for colonel Moore's ;—and a mighty fluster I found the colonel in, to be sure, for he could hear no news of you nowhere. So says I, colonel, says I, I hear as how you have offered five hundred dollars reward to any body that 'll catch them 'ere runaways of yours. Yes, says the colonel, cash down ;—and he looked me in the face, as though he thought I knew where to find you.

" Just so, colonel, says I ;—and perhaps I might,— if you 'll promise me something in the first place.

" Promise you something, said the colonel ;—have 'nt I promised five hundred dollars already,—what is it you mean ?

" Says I, colonel, it is 'nt the reward I was thinking of,—the reward is handsome—a very pretty reward surely. Pay me four hundred and fifty dollars colonel, and promise me not to whip Archy, when you get him, and I 'll not ask for the other fifty.

" Pshaw, nonsense, says the colonel. Pray Mr

Gordon, what is it to you how much I whip the scoundrel, provided you get your money ?

"Says I, colonel, Jemmy Gordon is not the chap to forget a favor. That boy Archy, saved my life, it 's three years ago, this very month ; and if you 'll promise me upon your honor, not to punish him for running away, I will undertake to hunt him up for you; —and not otherwise.

" The colonel higgled and haggled a good deal ;—but when he found he could not get round me no how,— he promised all I had asked him. So I told him how you had been at my house, and how you were coming again ; and he sent Stubbs and them other fellows to help me take you,—and that 's the long and the short of the whole matter. So don 't be sulky Archy, but cheer up and take it kindly. You see, I meant to do what was best for us both."

" I wish you much joy, Mr Gordon of your part of the bargain ; and may you loose your five hundred dollars, the next time you play cards, and that will be before you are twelve hours older."

" You 're in a passion, Archy, or you would not talk in that way. Well, boy, to tell the truth, I don 't much wonder at it. But by and by, you 'll think better of it. I should think you might be content with having broken my head ;—by God, Archy, but it aches as though it would split open." So saying, Mr Gordon broke off the conversation and joined his companions.

Little reason as I have to speak well of him, I am bold to say there are a great many men in the world,

not much better than Jemmy Gordon. Five hundred
dollars was a great temptation to him. Besides, he
hoped to secure the good graces of colonel Moore, and
expected by his assistance, to get into the way of getting a living respectably ;—at least, as respectably as
any poor man can, in that country. He not only qui-
eted his conscience with the idea that, if he did not
betray me, somebody else would,—but he had made
terms with colonel Moore, for my benefit ; and actually seemed to have flattered himself into the notion,
that he was doing me a favor by betraying me.

There is many a *gentleman* in slave-holding America,—for anti-republican as it may seem, in no part
of the world is the distinction between *gentlemen*
and the *common people*, more distinctly marked,—who
would consider it an insult to be compared with
Jemmy Gordon, but whose whole life is a continued
practice of the very principles on which that man act-
ted, when he made up his mind to play the traitor.
Many is the gentleman in slave-holding America, who
knows full well,—and in the secret recesses of his own
soul, most unequivocally acknowledges,—that to keep
his fellow men in bondage, is a gross, flagrant, and
high-handed violation of the very first and clearest
principles of justice and equity,—a practice, abstractly
considered, fully more criminal than piracy or high-
way robbery. Slavery, in the abstract, he acknowledges to himself and to others, to be totally indefensi-
ble. But then his slaves are his estate,—and he cannot live, *like a gentleman*, without them. Besides, he
treats his servants particularly well,—so very well,

that he does not hesitate to argue that they are much happier as slaves, than freedom, under any form, could possibly make them !

When men of sense and education, can satisfy themselves with such wretched sophistry as this, let us learn to have some charity for poor Jemmy Gordon.

CHAPTER XI.

It was past noon before we arrived at Spring-Meadow, where colonel Moore, had been, for some time, impatiently expecting us.   But as he happened to have a large party to dine with him, he was too busy in entertaining his company, to pay any immediate attention to us.   Yet, no sooner had he received notice of our arrival, than he sent out Mr Gordon's five hundred dollars.   It was a large roll of bank notes ;—the fellow's eye kindled up at the sight of it, and he snatched it eagerly. I was looking steadily at him,—and his eyes met mine. The change was sudden. He blushed and grew pale by turns,—and shame, remorse and self-contempt were painted in his face. He thrust the money hastily into his pocket, and walked away without speaking a word.

Cassy and myself were driven to the stables, and locked up in a close, narrow, dark room, which served sometimes as a corn-crib, and sometimes as a sort of dungeon for refractory slaves. We sat down upon the floor,—for there was nothing else to sit upon,—and poor Cassy sunk into my arms. Her grief and terror seemed to burst out afresh, and she wept bitterly. I kissed away her tears, and tried to console her. But she would not be comforted ;—and little indeed, was the comfort I had to offer. The more I said to her, the more she wept ; and she clung to me closer and closer, till her embrace became almost convulsive. " He will kill us—He will separate us forever ;" she murmured, in a low, inarticulate voice,—and it was the only reply she made to all I could say to her.

Our situation was indeed pitiable. Had we fallen into the hands of an ordinary pirate or robber, there might have been some room for hope. The consciousness of his own violence, might perhaps alarm him ; the fear of avenging justice might stay his hand. At the worst, death, and that too a speedy and an easy one, would be the farthest limit of his malice. But we,—unhappy creatures,—could flatter ourselves with no such prospect. We were runaway slaves, who had fallen again into the hands of their master ;—a master, whom the very recollection that he *owned* us, inspired with rage at our insolence, in daring to run away from him ; and who knew well, that both the law and public opinion would amply justify him in the infliction of any tortures not likely to result in immediate death.

It is true that we had fled from the greatest outrage

that can be inflicted upon a wife and a husband. But this was no excuse,—not even the slightest palliation. Slaves are not permitted to fly at all. It is their duty —alas! that such a word should be so prostituted!— to submit without a murmur, to all the insults, outrages and oppressions of their masters.

I clasped my wife to my bosom, with almost the same trembling earnestness, with which she clung to me. I felt, as she did, that it was the last time ;— and this idea sunk into my heart with a bitterness, which all my late ecstacies served only to aggravate. I almost stiffled her with eager kisses ;—but the fever that glowed in her cheek was not the flush of pleasure ; and those deep sighs she heaved,—they could not be mistaken for the pantings of delight. The speedy separation that threatened us, was not only terrible in anticipation, but it seemed to destroy all our capacity for present enjoyment. But for this, with Cassy in my arms, what should I have cared for chains and a dungeon !—Dreading this, her lips lost all their sweetness, her bosom was an uneasy pillow, and though I could not leave her, every embrace seemed to increase both my distress and hers.

We passed several hours in this way, without any interruption. We had not tasted food that day,—and nobody brought us even a cup of cold water. The heat and closeness of the room, into which the air had no admission, aggravated the fever in our blood, and made our thirst almost intolerable. How I longed for the cool spring, the balmy air, the freedom, we had lost !

8

Toward evening, we heard somebody approaching ; and I soon recognized the voices of colonel Moore and his overseer. They opened the door, and bade us come out. At first, the light dazzled my eyes so that I could scarcely distinguish one object from another ; but in a little while I was enabled to see that our visitors were accompanied by Peter, a tall fellow, with a very suspicious smile, the spy and tell-tale of the place, the detestation of all the servants, but the especial favorite of Mr Stubbs, and his regular assistant on all occasions.

Colonel Moore's face was a good deal flushed, and I judged that he had been drinking. This was a practice very unusual with him. For though every dinner at his house, was pretty sure to end by putting the greater part of the guests upon the floor, colonel Moore generally passed the bottle, under the plea that his physician had forbidden it, and commonly rose up, the only sober man from his own table. It was too plain, that on the present occasion, he had forgotten his accustomed sobriety. He spoke not a word to me, and I found it impossible to catch his eye ;—but turning to his overseer, he said, in an under tone, and with the air of being a good deal irritated—" It was a damned blunder, Mr Stubbs, to shut them up together. I thought you understood my orders better."

The overseer mumbled out some unintelligible apology, of which colonel Moore took no notice ; and without further preface or explanation, he ordered Mr Stubbs to tie me up.

The padlock by which the chain was fastened about

my neck was undone. They stripped me almost naked. Mr Stubbs produced a piece of rope with one end of which he bound my hands, and the other end, he made fast, with Peter's assistance, to a beam over my head ;—not however, till he had drawn it so tight as almost to lift me from the floor.

Colonel Moore then ordered them to free Cassy from the chain. He put a heavy whip into her hand, and pointing to me, " Take care my girl," he said, " that you lay it on to some purpose."

Poor Cassy looked about in utter amazement. She did not understand him,—she had no idea of such re-fined cruelty, such ferocious revenge.

He repeated his commands, with a tone and a look that were frightful. " If you wish to save your own carcass, see that you bring blood at every blow. I 'll teach you,—both of you,—to trifle with me."

She now comprehended his brutal purpose ;—and giving one look of mingled horror and despair, sunk senseless to the ground. Peter was sent for water. He dashed it in her face, and she soon revived. They placed her on her feet, and colonel Moore again put the whip into her hand and repeated his orders.

She threw it down, as if the touch had stung her ; and looking him full in the face, the tears, all the while, streaming from her eyes, she said in a tone firm, but full of entreaty, " Master, he is my husband !"

That word *husband*, seemed to kindle colonel Moore into a new fury, which totally destroyed his self-com-mand. He struck Cassy to the ground with his fists, trampled on her with his feet, and snatching up the whip which she had thrown down, he laid it upon me with such violence, that the lash penetrated my flesh at every blow, and the blood ran trickling down my legs and stood in little puddles at my feet. The torture was too great for human endurance ; I screamed with agony. " Pshaw," said my executioner, " his noise will disturb the House ;"—and drawing a handkerchief from his pocket, he thrust it into my mouth, and rammed it down my throat with the butt-end of his whip-handle. Having thus effectually gagged me, he renewed his lashes. How long they were continued I know not ; a cloud began to swim before my eyes ; my head grew dizzy and confused ; and a fortunate fainting-fit soon put me beyond the reach of torture.

––––––––––

CHAPTER XII.

WHEN I recovered my senses, I found myself stretched upon a wretched pallet, which lay on the floor, in one corner of a little, old, and ruinous hovel. I was very weak and hardly able to move ; and I after-terwards learned that I had just passed through the paroxysm of a fever. A deaf old woman, too much superanuated to be fit for any thing but a nurse, was my only companion. I recognized the old lady, and forgetting that she could not hear me, I put her a thousand questions in a breath. I dreaded,—yet I wished to learn the fate of poor Cassy ; and it was to her that most of my questions related. But to all my inquiries the old woman returned no answer. I might scream myself deaf, she said, and she could not hear a word. Besides, she told me, I was too sick and weak to talk.

I was not to be silenced in this way, and only bawled the louder, and added signs and gestures, to enable the old woman to understand me. But it was plain that aunt Judy had no intention to gratify my curiosity; for when she found she could not quiet me, she went out and locking the door after her, left me to my own meditations. These were not very agreeable. As yet however, my thoughts were so confused, and my head so dizzy, that I could scarcely be said to reflect at all.

I learned afterwards, that it was more than a week, that I had remained delirious, the effect of the violent fever into which I had been thrown, and which threatened a speedy termination to my miserable existence. But the crisis was now past. My youth and the vigor of my constitution had carried me through it, and had preserved me for new sufferings.

I recovered rapidly, and was soon able to walk about. Lest I should make an undue use of my returning strength, and attempt another escape, I was presently accommodated with fetters and handcuffs. My fetters were taken off once a day, for about an hour, and under Peter's supervision, I was allowed to

8*

breathe the fresh air, and to take a short walk about
the plantation.   It was in vain that I attempted to get
from Peter any information concerning my wife.   He
could not, or he would not tell me anything about her.

I thought that perhaps he might sell the information
which he refused to give ; and I promised to make
him a present of some clothes, if he would allow me to
visit my former house.   We went together.   This
house, I had been enabled, in anticipation of my marriage, and through the bounty of Mrs Moore and her
daughter, to fit up quite comfortably.   It was furnished
with a variety of things, seldom seen in a slave's cabin.
But I found it stripped and plundered ; every article
of furniture was gone, and my chest was broken open
and all my clothes taken away.   For this I was no
doubt indebted to my fellow servants.   The strongest,
or almost the strongest passion of the human mind, is
the desire of acquisition.   This passion, the slave can
only gratify by plunder.   Besides, such is the baneful
effect of slavery, that it almost destroys the very germ
of virtue.   If oppression makes the wise man mad, it
too often makes the honest man a villain.   It embitters
the feelings, and hardens and brutifies the heart.   He,
who finds himself plundered from his birth, of his liberty and his labors—his only inheritance, becomes selfish, reckless, and regardless of everything save the immediate gratification of the present moment.   Plundered of every thing himself, he is ready to plunder in his
turn, even his brothers in misfortune.

Finding my house stripped, and my clothes stolen,
it put me in mind to feel in my pockets, for my

money. That was gone too. Indeed I soon recollected, that when surprised and seized by Mr Gordon and his assistants, Mr Stubbs had searched my pockets, and transferred their contents to his own. This, of course, was the last that I expected to see of my money. According to the Virginia code of morals, Mr Stubbs was a very respectable man, who did what was perfectly proper. Certainly, it was highly dangerous to trust a rogue and a runaway with the possession of a considerable sum of money. But according to the same code, the servants who had stolen my clothes, were a set of outrageous thieves, who richly deserved a whipping. So Mr Stubbs declared, whom we happened to meet, as we were returning, and to whom I complained that my house had been plundered. That honest gentleman worked himself quite into a passion, and swore roundly that if he could catch the thieves he would make them smart for it. Notwithstanding this outburst of virtuous indignation, Mr Stubbs said nothing about returning my money, and I judged it safest not to introduce the subject myself.

In two or three weeks I had nearly recovered my strength, and the gashes with which my back had been scored were quite healed over. I was beginning to wonder what colonel Moore intended to do with me ; when, one evening, I received a message from Mr Stubbs, to be up by sunrise, the next morning, and ready for a journey. Where we were going, or what was to be the object of our travels, he did not condescend to inform me ;—nor did I feel much curiosity to know. I had now one great consolation. Do what

they pleased, it was impossible to render me any
more miserable. It was this idea which sustained me,
and enabled me to regard the future with a sort of careless and stupid indifference, at which, when I reflect
upon it, I am myself surprised.

In the morning, Mr Stubbs came for me. He was
on horseback, whip in hand, as usual. He undid my
fetters, but allowed me to retain my handcuffs. He
tied a piece of rope about my neck, and fastened the
other end of it to his own waist. Thus guarded against
escapes, he mounted his horse, and bade me walk beside him. I was still rather weak, and sometimes my
pace flagged a little ;—but a stroke from Mr Stubbs'
whip soon quickened me into vigor. I inquired where
we were going. "You 'll know when you get there,"
was the answer.

That night we lodged at a sort of tavern. We both
occupied one room,—he the bed, and I the floor. He
took the cord from my neck and bound my legs with
it. It was so tight, and caused me so much pain, that
I could not sleep. Several times I complained to Mr
Stubbs ; but he bade me hold my damned tongue, and
not be troubling him with foolish complaints. The
next morning when he came to untie me, he found my
ancles a good deal swollen. He seemed sorry that he
had paid no more attention to my appeals, but excused
himself by saying, that we were all such a devilish
pack of liars there was no telling when to believe us ;
and he did not want to be at the trouble of getting up
for nothing.

The next day we continued our journey ;—but I

was so broken down by the fatigues of the day previous, and by the want of sleep, that nothing but the frequent application of Mr Stubbs' whip could stimulate me into the necessary exertion. My spirits and that stubbornness of soul, which hitherto had sustained me, seemed to fail at the same time with my strength, and I wept like a child. At last, we reached our journey's end. Late that evening, we entered the city of Richmond. I am not able to describe the town ; for I was hurried off to the jail, and there locked up for safe keeping.

I was now told why we had come. Colonel Moore, according to Mr Stubbs' account, was sick of such an unruly fellow, and had determined to sell me. I had not seen him since the day I had fainted under the energy of his paternal discipline. Nor did I ever see him afterwards. A strange parting that, between a son and a father !

CHAPTER XIII.

THE next day I was to be sold.   There was to be
a public sale of slaves ; and several besides myself,
were to be disposed of.   I was fettered and handcuffed, and taken to market.   The rest of the merchan-
dize was already collected ; but it was sometime before
the sale began, and I occupied the interval in looking
about me.   Several of the groups particularly attracted
my attention.

The first that caught my eye, was an old man,
whose head was completely white, and a pretty little
girl,—his grand-daughter, as he told me,—about ten or
twelve years old.   Both the old man and the little girl
had iron collars about their necks, which were connected by a heavy chain.   One would have imagined,
that the old age of the man, and the youth of the girl,
would have made such savage precautions unnecessary.
But their master, so far as I could learn, had resolved
to sell them in a fit of passion, and the chains perhaps
were intended more for punishment than security.

A man and his wife with an infant in her arms, stood
next to the old man and his daughter.   The man and
wife were quit young, and apparently fond of each
other ;—at least, they seemed very much distressed at
the idea of falling into the hands of different purchasers.   The woman now and then would address some
one or other of the company, who seemed to indicate

an intention of buying. She would beg them to purchase both herself and her husband ; and she ran over,
with great volubility, the good qualities of both. The
man looked on the ground, and preserved a moody and
sullen silence.

There was another group of eight or ten men and
women, who seemed to regard the sale with as much
unconcern, as if they were merely spectators. They
laughed, and talked, and jested with one another with
as much gaiety as any of the company. An apologist
for tyranny, would no doubt, rejoice in such a specta-
cle, and would be emboldened to argue, that after all
being sold at public auction is not so terrible a thing,
as some weak people are apt to imagine. The argument would be quite as sound as any that the slave-
holder ever uses ; and for ingenuity and conclusive-
ness, deserves to be compared with that of the philoso-
pher who, having seen through the grates of a prison,
a parcel of condemned criminals laughing and jesting
together, concluded that the expectation of being hung,
must have something in it very exhilirating.

The truth is, that the human mind, in its eager,
though too often unavailing struggle after happiness,
will still make the most of its means ;—and even in
the valley of despair, or under the ribs of death itself,
still strives to create some matter of enjoyment. Even
the poor slave will sing at his task ; he can laugh too,
though he finds himself sold like an ox in the market.
The tyrant discovers that all his wrongs and oppressions have not been able to extinguish in the soul of
his victim, the capability of enjoyment ; and he points

you to these outbursts of a nature not yet totally subdued, and dares to boast of the happiness he causes !

But to be sold, is not always a laughing matter.
The first bargain which the auctioneer offered to the
company, was a man apparently about thirty, with a
fine, open, prepossessing countenance. He had no
expectation of being sold, till the moment he was placed upon the table ; for it appeared that his master who
lived near the city, had lured him to town under the
delusive pretext of an intention to hire him out to some
of the citizens. When the poor fellow found that he
was actually to be sold, he was seized with such a
trembling that he could scarcely support himself. He
shook from head to foot ; and his face indicated the
greatest terror and distress. The two principal bidders,—and they seemed to enter into a pretty warm
competition,—were a gentleman of the neighborhood,
who appeared to know the poor fellow on sale, and
a dashing, buckish young man, who, it was said, was
a slave-trader from South Carolina, who had come to
purchase slaves for that market.

As the sale proceeded, it was curious, but at the
same time most distressing, to observe the anxiety
of the poor slave. When the slave-trader took the
lead, his jaw fell, his eyes rolled wildly, and he seemed
the very picture of despair ; but when the Virginian
bid higher, a sudden gleam of pleasure shot across his
face, the tears ran down his cheeks, and his earnest
" God bless you, master !" was enough to touch the
hardest heart. He interrupted the sale by his cries
and vociferations, and not even the whip could keep

him still. He called upon his favorite bidder by name, and entreated him to persevere, by every motive he could think of. He promised to serve him faithfully to the last minute of his life, and work himself to death in his service, if he would only buy him, only save him from being wholly separated from his wife and children, and sent away—he knew not whither—from the place where he was born and raised, and where, as he said, he had always behaved well, and borne a good character. Not that he had any particular objections to the other gentleman either,—for the poor fellow began to see the danger of offending a man. who was likely to become his master ;—no doubt he was a very fine gentleman too ; but he was a stranger, and would take him out of the country, and carry him far away from his wife and children ;—and as he mentioned them, his voice sunk, choked and interrupted, by an inarticulate sobbing.

The bidders kept up the contest with much spirit. The man was evidently a first-rate hand. Aside from this, the Virginian seemed touched by the poor fellow's entreaties, and dropped some hints about slave-traders, which put his opponent into a violent passion, and came near ending in a quarrel. The interposition of the by-standers, kept the competitors apart ;—but the slave-trader, whose passions were roused, swore that he would have the " boy," cost what he might,—if it was only to teach him a little good manners. One or two of the company cried shame, and called upon the slave-trader to leave off bidding, and suffer the poor fellow to remain in the country. He replied

9

with an oath, and a sneer, that he was not fool enough to
be bamboozled by any such nonsense ; and immediately
rose fifty dollars on the last bid.   This was more than
the Virginian could afford to sacrifice to a fit of good
nature, and piqued and chagrined, he yielded up the
contest.   The auctioneer knocked off the purchase,
and the man, more dead than alive, was delivered into
the hands of the slave-traders' attendants, who received
orders to give him twenty lashes on the spot, for his
" damned ill-manneredly Virginia insolence."

The sneering emphasis, with which this was spoken,
created no little sensation among the by-standers ; but
as the slave-trader strutted about with his hand on his
dirk handle, and as two pistols might plainly be seen
sticking out of his pockets, nobody saw fit to question
this provoking exercise of " his sacred right of property," and the sale proceeded as before.

At length my turn came.   I was stripped half
naked, the better to show my joints and muscles, and
placed upon the table or platform, on which the subject
of the sale was exposed to the examination of the purchasers.   I was whirled about, my limbs were felt, and
my capabilities discussed, in a slang much like that of
a company of horse-jockeys.   Various were the remarks that were made upon me.   One fellow declared
that I had a damned sullen look ; another swore that
my eye was devilish malicious ; a third remarked that
these light colored fellows were all rascals ;—to which
the auctioneer replied, that he never knew a slave of
any smartness, who was not a rogue.

Abundance of questions were put me, as to where I

was raised, why I was sold, and what I was fit for.
To all these inquiries I made the shortest and most indefinite answers. I was not in a humor to gratify this
curiosity ; and I had none of that ambition to bring a
high price, so common among slaves, the last and
lowest form in which is displayed that love of superiority, which is the main-spring of human action, the
source of all social improvement, and the origin of so
much crime and misery.

Mr Stubbs kept in the back ground, and said nothing. He had his own reasons, I suppose, for this reserve. The auctioneer did his best. According to
his account, there was not a stronger, more laborious,
docile and obedient servant to be bought in all the States.
Notwithstanding all these praises, a suspicion seemed
to spread itself that my master had some reasons for
selling me, which he did not think fit to avow. One
suggested that I must be consumptive ; another thought
it likely I was subject to fits ; while a third seemed to
think that I was an unruly fellow and mighty hard to
manage. The scars on my back tended to increase
their suspicions ;—and I was knocked off, at last, at a
very low price, to a portly, smiling old gentleman, by
name, major Thornton.

No sooner had the auctioneer's hammer struck upon
the table, than my new master spoke kindly to me, and
ordered my irons to be knocked off. Against this, Mr
Stubbs and the auctioneer remonstrated very earnestly;
and assured the purchaser that if he unchained me, he
did it at his own risk. "I know it," replied my new

master, "the risk is mine,—but I will never own a servant who wants to run away from me."

CHAPTER XIV.

WHEN my new master had learned that I had but just recovered from a fever, and that my strength was not yet entirely restored, he procured a horse for me, and we set out together. He lived a considerable distance west of Richmond, in that part of the State, known as Middle Virginia. During the ride, he entered into conversation with me, and I found him a very different person from any I had met with before.

He told me that I might consider myself lucky in falling into his hands ; for he made it a point to treat his servants better than anybody in the neighborhood. " If they are discontented, or unruly, or apt to run away," he added, " I sell them at once, and so get rid of them. I don't want any such fellows about me. But as my servants know very well, that they stand no chance to better themselves, by changing their master, they are very cautious how they offend me. Be obedient, my boy, and do your task, and I will ensure you plenty to eat, enough clothes, and more indulgence

than you will be likely to get from any other master."
Such was the amount of major Thornton's lecture,
which, it took him however, some five or six hours to
get through with.

It was late in the evening before we arrived at Oakland,—for that was the name of major Thornton's
property. The house was of brick, with wooden por-
ticos. It was not large, but neat and very handsome,
and presented many more appearances of substantial
comfort than are to be found about most of the houses
of Virginia. The grounds around it, were prettily
laid out, and ornamented with flowers and shrubbery,
—a thing quite uncommon, and which I had seldom
seen before. At a distance, on a fine swell, were the
servants' cabins, built of brick, neat and substantial ;
not placed in a straight line, but clustered together in
a manner that had something picturesque about it.
They were shaded by fine large oaks ; no underbrush
nor weeds were suffered to grow about them, and altogether, they presented an appearance of neatness and
comfort, as new and singular as it was pleasing. The
servants' cabins, on all the plantations I had ever seen
before, were a set of miserable ruinous hovels, with
leaky roofs and clay floors, almost buried in a rank
growth of weeds, and as dirty and ill-kept as they were
uncomfortable.

The children, who were playing about the cabins,
furnished a new occasion of surprise. I had been accustomed to see the children of a plantation, running
about stark naked, or dressed—if dressed at all—in a
shirt of dirty osnaburgs, hanging in tatters about their

9*

legs, and never washed after it was once put on. But the children at Oakland were neatly and comfortably clothed, and presented nothing of that squalid, pinched, neglected and half-starved appearance, to which my eye was so well accustomed. Their merry faces, and boisterous sports, called up no idea of juvenile wretchedness. I observed too, that the hands, who were just coming in from their work, were all well clothed. I saw none of those patched, tattered, ragged and filthy garments so common on other plantations.

Major Thornton was not a planter ;—that is to say, he did not make tobacco, and he chose to call himself a farmer. His principal crop was wheat ; and he was a great advocate for the clover system of cultivation, which he had adopted and pursued with much success. He owned some thirty or forty working hands ; the children and superanuated, made his entire stock of slaves upwards of eighty. He kept no overseer, but managed for himself. Indeed it was a maxim with him, that an overseer was enough to ruin any man. He was naturally stirring and industrious, and agriculture was his hobby,—a hobby which he rode to some purpose.

In all these things, and many others, he was the perfect contrast of all his neighbors ; and for that reason, very little liked by any of them. He carefully avoided horse-racing, cock-fights, political meetings, drinking, gambling, and frolicing of every sort. His money, he used to say, cost him too much to make it, to be thrown away upon a bet ; and as to frolics, he had neither time nor taste for any such nonsense. His neighbors revenged themselves for this contempt of their favorite sports, by pronouncing him a mean-spirited money-making fellow. They went further, and accused him of being a bad citizen and a dangerous neighbor. They complained most bitterly, that his excessive indulgence to his servants made all the slaves in the neighborhood, uneasy and discontented ; and at one time, some of them went so far as to talk about giving him warning to move out of the county.

But major Thornton was a man of spirit. He understood his own rights ;—he knew well the people among whom he lived, and what sort of reasoning would influence them most. He contrived to get hold of an offensive remark of one of the busiest of his ill-disposed neighbors, and sent him a challenge. It was accepted ; and his antagonist was shot through the heart at the first fire. Henceforward,—though his neighbors liked him no better than before,—they took very good care how they talked about him, and allowed him to go on in his own way, without any interference.

Major Thornton had not been bred a planter, and this perhaps was the reason, why he departed so much from the ordinary routine, and managed things so very differently from all his neighbors. He was born of a good family, as they say in Virginia, but his father died when he was a mere boy, and left but a very scanty property. He began life, in a small way, in a country store. His shrewdness, economy, and attention to his business, enabled him, in the course of a few years, to lay up a considerable sum of money. In

Virginia, trade is hardly looked upon as respectable,—
at least, such was the case at the time of which I am
speaking,—and any body who desires to be any thing,
aims at becoming a landed proprietor.   About the time
that major Thornton had made enough to think of
changing his store for a plantation, the proprietor of
Oakland, having already wasted two good estates on
dogs, horses, and wild debauchery, became so pressed
for money, as to be obliged to bring his remaining
property under the hammer.   Major Thornton became
the purchaser ;—but the place he bought, was very different from Oakland as I saw it.   The buildings which
were old and ugly, were all out of repair and just tumbling to the ground ; and the land was nearly ruined by
that miserable, thriftless system of cultivation, so universal throughout the slave-holding states of America.

In a few years after the property had passed into the
hands of major Thornton, every thing was changed.
The old houses were torn down and new ones built.
The grounds about the house were enclosed and ornamented ; and the land, under skilful management, was
fast regaining its original fertility.   Those who had
been born and bred planters, and whose estates were
very much in the same way in which Oakland had
been before it fell into the hands of major Thornton,
looked at what was going on there, with astonishment
and envy, and wondered how it could possibly happen.   Major Thornton was always ready to tell them ;
for he was extremely fond of talking,—particularly
about himself and his system of farming.   But though
he had explained the whole matter at least ten times,

to every one of his neighbors, he never could make a single convert. He had three favorite topics ; but he was equally unsuccessful upon all of them. He never could pursuade any one of his neighbors that clover was the true cure for sterile fields ; that the only way to have a plantation well managed, was to manage it one's self ; or that to give servants enough to eat was a sure method to prevent them from plundering the corn-fields and stealing sheep.

But though major Thornton could gain no imitators, he still persevered in farming according to his own notions. In no respect was he more an innovator than in the management of his slaves. A merciful man, he used to say, was merciful to his beast ; and not having been raised on a plantation, he could not bear the idea of treating his servants worse than his horses. " It may do very well for you, colonel," he said one day, to one of his neighbors, " to tie a fellow up and give him forty lashes with your own hand ; you were born and bred to it, and I dare say you find it very easy. But as odd as you may think it, I had much rather be whipped myself than to whip one of my servants ; and though sometimes I am obliged to do it, it is a great point with me to get along with as little whipping at possible. That 's a principal reason why I keep no overseer,—for a cow-hide and a pair of irons, are the only two things those fellows have any notion of. They have no wish, and if they had, they have not the sense, to get along in any other way ;—the devil take the whole generation of them. Every body, you know, has their oddities. For my part, I hate to hear the crack of a whip on my plantation, even though it be nothing more than a cart whip.''

The above speech of major Thornton's, is a brief summary of his system. He was, what every other slave-holder is, and from the very necessity of his condition must be,—a tyrant. He felt no scruple in compelling his fellow man to labor, in order that he might appropriate the fruits of that labor to his own benefit, —and in this certainly, if in any thing, the very essence of tyranny consists. But though a tyrant, as every slave-holder is and must be, he was a reasonable and, as far as possible, a humane one,—which very few slave-holders either are or can be. He had no more thought of relinquishing what he and the laws, called his property in his slaves, than he had of leaving his land to be occupied by the first comer. He would have been as ready as any of his neighbors, to have denounced the idea of emancipation, or the notion of limiting his power over his servants, as a ridiculous absurdity, and an impertinent interference with his '' most sacred rights.'' But though in theory, he claimed all the authority and prerogatives of the most unlimited despotism, he displayed in his practice, a certain share of common sense and common humanity, —two things, which so far as re lates to the management of his slaves, it is extremely uncommon for a slave-holder to have,—or if he has them, very difficult for him to exercise.

These unusual gifts led him to a discovery, which at the time was entirely new in his neighborhood ;— though I hope before now, it has become general. He discovered that men cannot work without eating ; and that so far as the capability of labor is concerned, there is the same policy in attending to the food, shelter and comfort of one's slaves, as in spending a little money on corn and stabling for one's horses. Feed well and work hard, was major Thornton's motto and practice, —a motto, and a practice, which in any other country than America, would never have subjected him to the charge of unreasonable and superfluous humanity.

As to whipping, major Thornton, to use his own phrase, could not bear it. Whether he felt some qualms of conscience at the barefaced, open tyranny of the lash,—which I do not think very probable, for I once heard him tell a Methodist parson, who ventured to say something to him on that delicate subject, that he had as much right to flog his slaves as to eat his dinner ;—or whether it was the influence of that instinctive humanity which is wanting only in brutal tempers, and which, till evil custom has worn it out, will not permit us to inflict pain, without feeling ourselves a sympathetic suffering ; or whatever might be the reason ; unless major Thornton was put into a passion,—to which he was but seldom liable,—he certainly had a great horror of using the whip.

But this was not all. Another man might have detested it as much as he did ; but the practice of a year or two in planting, and the apparent impossibility of dispensing with its use, would have taught him to get rid of so inconvenient a squeamishness. There are very few men indeed,—and of all men in the world, very few planters,—whose good sense and knowledge

of human nature, would enable them to manage their
slaves by any other means. Major Thornton, however, contrived to get on wonderfully well ; and in all
the time I lived with him,—which was nearly two
years,—there were not more than a half a dozen whippings on the place. If one of his servants was guilty
of any thing, which in a slave, is esteemed especially
enormous ; such as running away, repeated theft, idleness or insubordination, major Thornton sent him off
to be sold. By a strange, but common inconsistency,
this man of feeling, who could not bear to whip a
slave, or to see him whipped, or even to have him
whipped on his own plantation, felt no scruples at all,
at tearing him from the arms of his wife and children,
and setting him up at public sale, to fall into the hands
of any ferocious master, who might chance to purchase
him !

This dread of being sold, was ever before our eyes ;
and was as efficacious as the lash is on other plantations, in forcing us to labor and submission. We
knew very well, that there were few masters like major
Thornton ;—and the thought of exchanging our nice,
neat cottages, our plentiful allowance, our regular supply of clothing, and the general comfort and indulgence
of Oakland, for the fare and the treatment to be expected from the common run of masters, was more
terrible than a dozen whippings. Major Thornton understood this well ; and he took care to keep up the
terrors of it, by making an example of some delinquent, once in a year or two.

Then he had the art of exciting our emulation by

little prizes and presents ; he was very scrupulous never to exact any thing beyond the appointed task ; and he kept us in good humor, by allowing us, when not at work, to be very much our own masters, and to go where, and do what we pleased. We were rather cautious though, how we visited the neighboring plantations,—for with a magnanimity worthy of slave-holders, some of major Thornton's neighbors were in the habit of gratifying their spite against him, by improving every opportunity that offered, to abuse his servants. And here I may as well relate an incident that happened to myself, which will serve, at once, as a curious illustration of Virginia manners, and a proof of what I believe, will be found to be true all the world over,—that where the laws are designed for the oppression of one half the people of a country, they are seldom treated with much respect by the other half.

Captain Robinson was one of major Thornton's nearest neighbors, and a person with whom he had frequent altercations. I was passing along on the public road one Sunday, at a little distance from Oakland, when I met captain Robinson on horseback, followed by a servant. He bade me stop, and inquired if I was the fellow whom that damned scoundrel Thornton sent to his house yesterday with an insolent message about his lower-field fences. I answered, that I had been sent yesterday with a message about the fence, which I had delivered to his overseer.

" A mighty pretty message it was, by God. I 'll tell you what my boy, if my overseer had known his

10

business, he would have tucked you up on the spot and given you forty lashes."

I told him that I had only delivered the message which my master had sent me with, and it seemed hard to blame me for that.

" Don 't talk to me, don 't talk to me, you infernal scoundrel—I 'll teach both you and your master what it is to insult a gentleman. Lay hold of him Tom, while I dust that new jacket of his a little."

Having received these orders from his master, captain Robinson's man Tom, jumped off his horse and laid hold of me ; but as I struggled hard and was the stronger of the two, I should soon have got away, if the master had not dismounted and come to the aid of his servant. Both together, they were too strong for me ; and having succeeded in getting me down, they stripped off my coat and bound my hands. Captain Robinson then mounted his horse, and beat me with his whip, till it was quite worn out. Having thus satisfied his rage, he rode off followed by Tom, without taking the trouble to loose my hands. They had no sooner left me, than I began to look about for my hat and coat. Both were missing ;—and whether it was the captain or his servant that carried them off, I never could discover. I suppose though, it was the servant,—for I recollect very well seeing Tom, a few Sundays after, strutting about at a Methodist meeting, with a blue coat on, which I could almost have sworn to be mine.

When I got home, and told my master what had happened, he was in a towering passion. At first, he was for riding at once to captain Robinson's and calling for an explanation. But he happened to recollect that the county court was to meet the next day, at which he had business. This would give him an opportunity to consult his lawyer ; and after a little reflection, he thought it best not to move in the affair till he had a legal opinion upon it.

The next day he took me with him. We called upon the lawyer ; I told what had happened to me, and major Thornton inquired what satisfaction the law would afford him.

The lawyer answered, that the law in this case was very clear, and the remedy it provided, all-sufficient. " Some people," he said, " who know nothing about the matter, have asserted that the law in the slave-holding States, does not protect the person of the slave against the violence of the whites, and that any white man may flog any slave, at his own good pleasure. This is a very great mistake, if not a wilful falsehood. The law permits no such thing. It extends the mantle of its protection impartially over bond and free. In this respect, the law knows no distinction. If a freeman is assaulted, he has his action for damages against the assailant ; and if a slave is assaulted, the master of that slave, who is his legal guardian and protector, can bring his action for damages. Now in this case, major Thornton, it is quite plain that you have good ground of action against captain Robinson ; and the jury, I dare say, will give you a swinging verdict. I suppose you are able to prove all these facts ?"

"Prove them—to be sure" answered my master, "here is Archy himself who has told you the whole story."

"Yes, my good sir, but you do not seem to remember that a slave cannot be admitted to testify against a white man."

"And pray tell me then," said major Thornton, "what good the law you speak of is going to do me? Did not Robinson catch Archy alone, and abuse him as he has told you? You don't suppose he was fool enough to call in a white man on purpose to be a witness against him. Why, sir, notwithstanding the protection of the law, which you commend so highly, every servant I have, may be beaten by this Robinson every day in the week, and I not be able to get the slightest satisfaction. The devil take such law I say."

"But my dear sir," answered the lawyer, "you must consider the great danger and inconvenience of allowing slaves to be witnesses."

"Why yes," said my master with a half smile, "I fancy it would be rather dangerous for some of my acquaintances;—quite inconvenient no doubt. Well sir, since you say the law can't help me in this matter, I must take care of myself. I cannot allow my servants to be abused in this way. I'll horsewhip that scoundrel Robinson at sight."

With these words, my master left the office, and I followed behind him. We had gone but a little way down the street, when he had an unexpected opportunity of carrying his threat into execution,—for as it chanced, we met captain Robinson, who had business, it seemed, at the county court, as well as major Thornton. My master did not waste many words upon him, but began striking him over the shoulders with his riding whip. Captain Robinson drew a pistol ;—my master dropped his whip and drew a pistol also. The captain fired, but without effect ; major Thornton then levelled his weapon,—but Robinson called out that he was unarmed and begged him not to fire. Major Thornton hesitated a moment, and then dropped his hand. By this time, quite a crowd had collected about us, and some friend of captain Robinson's handed him a loaded pistol. The combatants renewed their aim, and fired together ; and captain Robinson fell desperately wounded. His ball missed my master, but passed through the body of a free colored man, who was the only person, of all the company, who made any attempt to separate the parties. The poor fellow fell dead ; and the people about declared that it was good enough for him,—for what right had a damned free fellow like him to be interfering between gentlemen ?

Captain Robinson's friends took him up and carried him home. Major Thornton and myself walked off the field in triumph,—and so the affair ended. Such affrays are much talked about ; but the grand jury very seldom hears any thing of them ; and the conqueror is pretty sure to rise in the public estimation.

10*

CHAPTER XV.

SOME persons perhaps may think that having fallen into the hands of such a master as major Thornton, I had now nothing to do, but to eat, to work and to be happy.

Had I been a horse or an ox, there would be good ground for this idea ; but unfortunately, I was a man ; and the animal appetites are by no means, the only motive of human action, nor the sole source of human happiness or misery.

It is certainly true that several of major Thornton's servants, born perhaps with but little sensibility, and brutalized by a life of servitude, seemed very well content. This was the sort of servant, which major Thornton especially admired. In this particular, he did not differ much from his neighbors. The more stupid a field hand is, the more he is esteemed ; and a slave who shows any signs of capacity, is generally set down as certain to be a rogue and a rascal.

I soon discovered my master's fondness for stupid fellows ; and I took care to play the fool to his entire satisfaction. In a short time, I made myself quite a favorite ; and my master having taken a fancy to me, I was more indulged perhaps, than any servant on the place. But this could not make me happy.

Human happiness—with some very limited exceptions—is never in fruition, but always in prospect and pursuit. It is not this, that, or the other situation that can give happiness. Riches, power or glory, are nothing when possessed. It is the pleasure of the pursuit and the struggle, it is the very labor of their attainment, in which consists the happiness they bring.

Those moralists who have declaimed so copiously on the duty of contentment, betray an extreme ignorance of human nature. No situation, however splendid, in which one is compelled to remain fixed and stationary, can long afford pleasure, and on the other hand, no condition, however destitute or degraded, out of which one has a fair prospect, or any thing like a rational hope of rising, can justly be considered as utterly miserable. This is the constitution of the human mind ; and in this, we find the explanation of a thousand things, which without this key to their meaning, seem full of mystery and contradiction.

Though all men have not the same objects of pursuit, all are impelled by the same love of pursuing. Nothing can satisfy the vast desires of one man, but immense wealth, great political power, the myrtle wreath or the laurel crown ;—another aims no higher than to rise from abject poverty to a little competency, or,—if his ambition is of another sort,—to be the chief personage in his native village, or the oracle of a country neighborhood. How different are these aims !—and yet, the impulse that prompts them, is the same. He whom circumstances permit to yield to this impulse of his nature, and to pursue—successfully or not, it matters little—but to pursue with some tolerable prospect of success, the objects which have captivated his fancy, may be regarded as having all the chance for happiness, which the lot of humanity allows ; while he, whom fate or fortune or whatever malignant cause, compels to suppress and forego the instinctive impulses and wishes of his heart,—whatever in other respects may be his situation,—is a wretch entitled to the greatest pity. To the one, toil is itself a pleasure. He is a hunter whom the sight of his game fills with delight, and makes insensible to fatigue. Desire sustains him, and hope cheers him on. These are pleasures the other never knows ; for him, life has lost its relish ; rest is irksome to him, and labor is intolerable.

This is no digression. He who has taken the pains to read the preceding paragraph, will be able to understand, how it happened, that even with such a master as major Thornton, I was neither happy nor content.

It is true I was well fed, well clothed, and not severely worked ; and in these particulars,—as my master was fond of boasting, and as I have since found to be the case,—my situation was far superior to that of very many freemen. But I lacked one thing which every freeman has ; and that one want was enough to make me miserable. I wanted liberty ; the liberty of laboring for myself, not for a master ; of pursuing my own happiness, instead of toiling at his pleasure and for his gain. This liberty can lighten the hardest lot. He knows but little of human nature, who has not discovered that, to all who rise one step above the brutes, it is far pleasanter to starve and freeze after their own fashion, than to be fed and clothed and worked upon compulsion.

I was wretched,—for I had no object of hope or rational desire. I was a slave ; and the laws held out no prospect of emancipation. All the efforts in the world, could not better my condition ;—all the efforts in the world could not prevent me from falling—perhaps tomorrow—into the hands of another master, as cruel and unreasonable as evil passions and hard-heartedness could make him. The future offered only the chance of evils. I might starve with cold and hunger as well as another ; I might perish by gun-shot wounds, or the torture of the lash ; or be hung up, perhaps, without judge or jury. But of bettering my condition, I had neither chance, nor hopes. I was a prisoner for life ; at the present moment, not suffering for food or clothing, but without the slightest prospect of liberation ; and likely enough at any moment, to change my keeper, and under the discipline of a new jailor, to feel the pains of cold and hunger, and to tremble daily beneath the whip. I was cut off and excluded from all those hopes and wishes, which are the chief impulses of human action. I could not aim to become the master of a little cottage, which, however humble, I might call my own,—to be the lord of one poor acre, which however small or barren, might still be mine. I could not marry—alas, poor Cassy !—and become the father of a family, with the fond hope, that when age should overtake me, I might still find pleasure and support, in the kindness of children and the sympathy of a wife. My children might be snatched from the arms of their mother, and sold to the slave-trader ; the mother might be sent to keep them company,—and I be left old, desolate, uncomforted. Motives such as these,—motives which strengthen the freeman's arm and cheer his heart, were unfelt by me. I labored ;—but it was only because I feared the lash. The want of willingness unnerved me, and every stroke cost a new effort.

It is even true, that major Thornton's humanity,— or to speak more correctly—his sense of his own interest, while it preserved his servants from the miseries of hunger and nakedness, at the same time, exposed those among them, whom slavery and ignorance had not completely brutalized, to other and more excruciating miseries. Had we been but half fed and half clothed, like the servants on several of the neighboring plantations, we should, like them, have enjoyed the excitement of plunder. We should have found some exercise for our ingenuity, and some object about which to interest ourselves, in plans and stratagems for eking out our short allowance by the aid of theft.

As it was, stealing was but little practiced at Oakland. The inducement was too small, and the risk too great,—for detection was certain to result in being sold. Money was no object to us ; we could only spend it on food and clothes, and of these we had enough already. Whiskey was the only luxury we wanted ; and we could make enough to purchase that, without the necessity of theft. Mr Thornton allowed each of us a little piece of ground. This was customary ;— but what was quite contrary to custom, he allowed us time to cultivate it. He endeavored to stimulate our industry by the promise of buying all we could produce, not at a mere nominal price, as was the fashion on other plantations, but at its full value.

I am sorry to say it, but it is not the less true, that major Thornton's people, like all slaves who have the means and the opportunity—were generally, drunkards. Our master took good care that whiskey did not interfere with our work. To be drunk before the task was finished was a high misdemeanor. But after the day's labor was over, we were at liberty to drink as much as we pleased ;—provided always, that it did not prevent us from turning out at daylight the next morning. Sunday was generally a grand Saturnalia.

Hitherto, I had scarcely been in the habit of drinking. But now I began to be eager for any thing which promised to sustain my sinking spirits, and to excite my stagnant soul. I soon found in whiskey, a something that seemed to answer the purpose. In that elevation of heart which drunkenness inspires, that forgetfulness of the past and the present, that momentary halo with which it crowns the future, I found a delight which I hastened to repeat, and knew not how to forego. Reality was to me a blank, dark and dreary. Action was forbidden ; desire was chained ; and hope shut out. I was obliged to find relief in dreams and illusions. Drunkenness, which degrades the freeman to a level with the brutes, raises, or seems to raise the slave, to the dignity of a man. It soon became my only pleasure, and I indulged it to excess. Every day, as soon as my task was finished, I hastened to shut myself up with my bottle. I drank in solitude, —for much as I loved the excitement of drunkenness,

I could not forget its beastliness and insanity, and I hated to expose my folly to the sight of my fellow servants. But my precautions were not always successful. In the phrensy of excitement I sometimes forgot all my sober precautions, undid the bolts I had carefully fastened, and sought the company I most desired to shun.

One Sunday, I had been drinking, till I was no longer the master of my own actions. I had left my house, and gone to seek some boon-companions with whom to protract the revel and increase its zest. But I was unable to distinguish one object from another, and after straggling off for some distance, I sunk down, almost insensible, upon the carriage way, which led towards major Thornton's house.

I had grown a little more sober, and was endeavoring to rally my thoughts and to recollect where I was, and what had brought me there, when I saw my master riding up the road, with two other gentlemen. They were all on horseback; and as drunk as I was, I saw at a glance, that my master's two companions, were very much in the same predicament. The manner in which they reeled backward and forward in their saddles was truly laughable; and I expected every moment to see them come tumbling to the ground. I made these observations as I lay upon the road, without once thinking where I was, or recollecting the danger I was in of being ridden over. They had come quite near before they noticed me. By that time I was sitting up, and my master's drunken companions took it into their heads, to jump their horses

over me. Major Thornton did his best to prevent
them; one he succeeded in stopping,—but the other
evaded his attempt to sieze the bridle, swore that the
sport was too pretty to be lost, put spurs to his horse,
and brought him up to the leap.

But the horse had no fancy for this sort of sport.
When he saw me before him, he started back, and his
drunken rider came tumbling to the ground. The
others dismounted and went to his assistance. Before
he was well upon his feet, he begged major Thornton's attention, and forthwith commenced a very grave
lecture on the indecency of allowing servants to get
drunk, and to lie about the plantation—particularly
across the roads, frightening gentlemen's horses, and
putting the necks of their riders into jeopardy. " Especially you, major Thornton, who pretend to be a pattern
for all of us. By God, sir, if you did as you ought to
do, every time one of the damned fellows had the insolence to get drunk, you would tie him up and give
him forty lashes. That 's the way I do, on my plantation."

My master was so very fond of setting forth his
method of farming, and his plan of plantation-disci-
pline, that he did not always stop to consider whether
his auditors were drunk or sober. The present opportunity was too good to be lost, and rubbing his
hands together, he answered, with a half-smile, and a
very sagacious look,—"but, my dear sir, you must
know it is a part of my plan to let my servants
drink as much as they please, so that it does not interfere with their tasks. Poor fellows! it serves to keep

11

them out of mischief, and soon makes them so stupid they are the easiest creatures in the world to manage." Here he paused a minute, and assuming the look, which a man puts on, who thinks he is going to urge an unanswerable argument—" Besides," he added, " if one of these drinking fellows happens to take a huff and runs away, the very first thing he does, is to get drunk, so that you seldom have any difficulty in catching him."

Though I was still too much under the influence of whiskey, to be capable of much muscular motion, I had so far recovered my senses as to comprehend perfectly, all that my master was saying ; and no sooner had he finished, than, drunk as I was, I made a resolution to drink no more. I was not yet so far lost, as to be able to endure the idea, of being myself the instrument of my own degradation. My resolution was well kept ; for I have seldom tasted spirits since that day.

CHAPTER XVI.

IT is the lot of the slave, to be exposed, in common with other men, to all the calamities of chance and all the caprices of fortune. But unlike other men, he is denied the consolation of struggling against them. He is bound hand and foot ; and his sufferings are aggravated ten fold, by the bitter idea that he is not allowed to help himself, or to make any attempt to escape the blow, which he sees impending over him. This idea of utter helplessness, is one of the most distressing in nature,—but it is one of those miseries with which the slave must early learn to be familiar.

Major Thornton, by over exertion and imprudent exposure, brought on a fever, which in a short time, assumed a very unfavorable aspect. It was the first time he had been sick for many years. The alarm and terror, which the news of his danger excited at Oakland, was very great. Every morning and evening, we collected about the house to learn how our master did ; and mournful were the faces, and sad the hearts, with which we heard the bitter words, " no better." The women, at Oakland, had always been treated with peculiar indulgence, such as their sex and weakness demands,—but demands so often without obtaining it. Major Thornton's illness gave an instance how full of gratitude is the female heart, and at what a trifling expense, one may purchase its most zealous affection.

All the women, on the place, were anxious to be employed, in some way, in ministering to the comfort of their suffering master. The most disagreeable duties were eagerly performed ; and if ever man was tenderly and assiduously nursed, it was major Thornton. But all this care, all our sympathy, our sorrow and our terrors, were of no effect. The fever raged with unabated fury, and seemed to find new fewel in the strength of the patient's constitution. But that fewel was soon exhausted, and in ten days, our master was no more.

When his decease became known, we looked upon each other in silent consternation. A family of helpless orphans, from whom death had just snatched their last surviving parent, could not have felt a greater destitution. Tears rolled down the cheeks of the men ; and the cries and lamentations of the women were truly distressing.. His old nurse, in particular, wept and would not listen to any consolation. She had good reason. At his father's death she had been sold, with the other property, to satisfy the creditors. But major Thornton had re-purchased her, out of his very first earnings ; he had made her the head-servant of his household, and had always treated her with great tenderness. The old woman loved him like her own child, and lamented her " dear son Charly," as she called him, with all the pathetic energy of a widowed and childless mother.

We all attended the funeral, and followed our dead master to the grave. The hollow sound of the earth as it fell upon the coffin, was echoed back from every bosom ; and when this last sad office was finished, we stood over the grave, and wept together. Doubt not the sincerity of our sorrow ! It was for ourselves we were lamenting.

Major Thornton was never married ; and he left no children whose rights the laws acknowledged. If he had intended to make a will, his sudden death prevented him ; and his property passed to a troop of cousins for whom, I suspect, he did not entertain any great affection. At all events, I had never seen any of them at Oakland, nor could I learn from the other servants, that either of them had ever made a visit there. It was thus that we became the property of strangers, who had never seen us, and whom we had never seen.

These heirs-at-law were poor as well as numerous, and seemed very eager to turn all the property into money, so as to get their several shares with the least possible delay. An order of court, or whatever the legal process may be called, was soon obtained ; and the sale of the slaves was advertised to take place at the county court-house. The agent to whom the care of the estate was intrusted made the necessary preparations. Of course it was not thought expedient that we should know what was going on, or what our new owners intended to do with us. The secret was carefully kept lest some of us should run away.

The day before that which had been appointed for the sale, we were collected together. The able bodied men and women were handcuffed and chained in a string. A few old grey headed people and the younger children were carried in a cart. The rest of us were driven along like cattle—men, women and children

11*

together. Three fellows on horse-back, with the usual
equipment of long whips, served at once, as guards
and drivers.

I shall not attempt to describe our affliction. It
would be but the repetition of an oft-told tale. Who
has not read of slave-traders on the coast of Africa ?
Whose heart has not ached at picturing the terrors
and despair of the kidnapped victims ? Our case was
much the same. Many of us had been born and reared at Oakland, and all looked upon it as a home—nay
more, as a city of refuge, where we had always been
safe from gratuitous insults and aggressions. From
this home, we were how snatched away, without a moment's warning ; and were driven chained to the slave-
market to be sold to the highest bidder.

Is it strange that we were reluctant to go ? Had
we been setting out, of our own accord, to seek our
our fortunes, we could not have broken, all at once, all
the ties that bound us to Oakland, without some throbs
of natural grief. What then, must have been our anguish to leave it as we did ?

But the tears of the men, the sobs of the women,
and the cries and terrors of the poor children, availed us nothing. Our conductors cracked their whips
and made a jest of our lamentations. Our sorrowful
procession moved slowly on ; and many a sad lingering look, we cast behind us. We said nothing ;
and our melancholy reflections were only interrupted
by the curses, shouts, and loud laughter of our drivers.

We lodged, that night, by the road side ; our drivers sleeping and keeping watch by turns. The next

day, we reached the county court-house, and at the appointed hour, the sale began. The company was not very numerous, and the bidders seemed extremely shy. Many of our late master's neighbors were present. One of them remarked that several of us were fine stout fellows, but, for his part, he should be afraid to buy any of the Thornton hands, for we had been so spoilt by our late master's foolish indulgence, that one of us would be enough to spread discontent through a whole neighborhood. This speech was received with evident applause, and it had its intended effect. The auctioneer did his best, and harangued most eloquently upon our healthy, sound and plump condition. "As to the over-indulgence, that gentleman speaks about," he observed, " a good cow-hide and strict discipline will soon bring them into proper subordination ;—and from what I have heard of that gentleman's own management, he is the very person who ought to buy them." A slight titter ran through the company, at this sally of the auctioneer's, but it did not seem to make the bidding much brisker. We went off at very moderate prices. Most of the younger men and women, and a large proportion of the children were bought by a slave-trader, who had come on purpose to attend the sale. It was very difficult to get a bid for several of the old people. Mr Thornton's nurse, who, as I have mentioned, had been his house-keeper, and a person of no little consequence at Oakland, was knocked off for twenty dollars. She was bought by an old fellow, well known in the neighborhood for his cruelty to his servants. He shook his head as the auctioneer's hammer struck the table, grinned an ugly smile, and said he believed the gal was yet able to handle a hoe ; —any how, he would get one summer's work out of her. The old lady had scarcely held up her head since the death of her master ; but she forgot all her sorrows, she forgot even to deplore the lot that seemed to await her, in her anger at being sold at so small a price. She turned to her purchaser, and with an indignant air, told him that she was both younger and stronger than folks thought for, and assured him that he had made the best bargain of any of the company. The old fellow chuckled, but said nothing. It was very easy to read his thoughts. He was evidently resolving to hold the old woman to her word.

Some of the old and decrepid slaves could not be sold at all. They were not worth purchasing, and nobody would bid. I do not know what became of them.

The slave-dealer who had purchased most of the children, declined buying such of the mothers as were past the age of child-bearing. The parting of these mothers from their children, was a new scene of misery and lamentation. The poor things snatched a little while before, from the home of their birth and their infancy, and now, torn from the mothers that bore and nursed them, clasped their little hands, and shrieked with all the unrestrained vehemence of infant agony. The mothers wept too, but their grief was more subdued. There was one old women, the mother, she said, of fifteen children. One little girl, about ten or twelve years old, was all that remained to her. The others had been sold and scattered, she knew not whither. She was now to part from her youngest and only remaining child. The little girl clung to her mother's dress with all the terror of one who was about to be kidnapped, and her screams and cries might have touched a heart of stone. Her new master snatched the child away, hit her a cut with his whip, and bade her hold her damned clatter. A slave-trader, however he may have the exterior of a gentleman, is in fact, the same ferocious barbarian, whether on the coast of Guinea, or in the heart of the "Ancient Dominion."

When our new master had completed his purchases, he prepared to set out with his drove. He was one of a slave-dealing firm, whose head quarters were at the city of Washington, the seat of the federal government, and the capital of the United States of America. It was to this place that he intended to carry us. The whole purchase was about forty head, consisting in nearly equal proportions of men, women and children. We were joined in couples by iron collars about our necks, which were connected by a link of iron. To these connecting links, a heavy chain was fastened, extending from one end of the drove to the other. Besides all this, the right and left hands of every couple were fastened together by hand-cuffs, and another chain passed along these fastenings. The collars about our necks, with their connecting chain, might have been thought perhaps, under ordinary circumstances, a sufficient security; but as our new master had heard from major Thornton's neighbors,

who were present at the sale, that we were "a set of
very dangerous fellows," he thought it best, as he said,
to omit no *reasonable* means of security.

The drove was presently put in motion. Our purchasers, with two or three assistants, rode beside us on
horseback, armed with whips, as usual. The journey
was slow, sad and wearisome. We traveled without
any good will ; the poor children harrassed with the
weight of their chains, and unaccustomed to fatigue ;
and all of us, faint for want of food;—for our new master was an economist, who spent as little on the road,
as possible.

I will not dwell upon the tedious monotony of our
sufferings and our journey. Suffice it to say, that after
traveling for several days, we crossed the noble and
wide-spreading Potomac, and late at night, began to
enter the federal city. Perhaps I ought to say, the place
where the federal city was to be,—for Washington,
at that time, seemed only a straggling village, scattered
over a wide extent of ground, and interspersed with
deserted fields, overgrown with bushes. There were
some indications however, of the future metropolis.
The Capitol, though unfinished, was rearing its spacious walls in the moon-light, and gave promise of a
magnificent edifice. Lights gleamed from the windows.
The Congress perhaps was in session. I gazed at the
building with no little emotion. " This," said I to
myself, " is the head-quarters of a great nation,—the
spot in which its concentrated wisdom is collected, to
devise laws for the benefit of the whole community,—
the just and equal laws of a free people and a great

democracy !"—I was going on with this mental soliloquy, when the iron collar about my neck touched a place from which it had rubbed the skin, and as I started with the pain, the rattling of chains reminded me, that ' these just and equal laws of a free people and a great democracy' did not avail to rescue a million* of bondmen from hopeless servitude ; and the cracking of our drivers' whips told too plainly that within a stone's throw of the Temple of Liberty —nay, under its very portico—the most brutal, odious and detestable tyranny found none to rebuke or to forbid it.   What sort of liberty is it whose chosen city is its slave-market?—and what that freedom which permits the bravado insolence of a slave-trading aristocracy to lord it in the very halls of her legislation ?

We passed up the street, which led by the Capitol, and presently arrived at the establishment of Savage, Brothers & Co, our new masters.   Half an acre of ground, more or less, was enclosed with a wall some twelve feet high, well armed at the top, with iron spikes and pieces of broken bottles.   In the centre of the enclos-

---

* The slaves in the United States are now nearly two millions and a half.   It ought perhaps to be added, that by the federal constitution the general government has no right to interfere with the question of slavery in the States.   The legislature of each State is the sole judge of that question, within its own limits.   Slavery however, is still tolerated within the District of Columbia, which includes the city of Washington, over which Congress has an exclusive right of legislation. It is to be hoped that the people of the free States will not be deterred by the insolent and ferocious spirit of the slave-holders, from doing themselves the justice to abolish slavery wherever it is within their power.   EDITOR.

ure, was a low brick building of no great size, with a
few narrow, grated windows, and a stout door, well
secured with bars and padlocks. This was the establishment, which was used by Messrs. Savage, Brothers
& Co as a ware-house, in which they stowed away
such slaves, as they purchased from time to time, in
the neighboring country, to be kept till they were ready to send them off in droves, or to ship them to the
South. In common with all the slave-trading gentry,
Messrs. Savage, Brothers & Co had the free use of
the city prison; but this was not large enough for the
scale on which they carried on operations; so they
had built a prison of their own. It was under the
management of a regular jailer, and was very much
like any other jail. The slaves were allowed the liberty of the yard during the day time; but at sun set,
they were all locked up promiscuously in the prison.
This was small and ill ventilated; and the number that
was forced into it, was sometimes very great. While
I was confined there, the heat and stench were often
intolerable; and many a morning, I came out of it
with a burning thirst and a high fever.

The states of Maryland and Virginia claim the honor
of having exerted themselves for the abolition of the
African slave trade. It is true they were favorable to
that measure,—and they had good reasons of their own
for being so. They gained the credit of humanity, by
the same vote that secured them the monopoly of a
domestic trade in slaves, which bids fair to rival any
traffic ever prosecuted on the coast of Africa. The
African traffic, they have declared to be piracy, which

the domestic slave-trade flourishes in the heart of their own territories, a just, legal and honorable commerce !

The district of Columbia, which includes the city of Washington, and which is situated between the two states above mentioned, has become, from the convenience of its situation, and other circumstances, the centre of these slave-trading operations,—an honor which it shares however, with Richmond and Baltimore, the chief towns of Virginia and Maryland. The lands of these two states have been exhausted by a miserable and inefficient system of cultivation, such as ever prevails where farms are large and the laborers enslaved. Their produce is the same with the productions of several of the free states north and west of them ; and they are every day, sinking faster and faster, under the competition of free labor to which they are exposed.

Many a Virginian planter can only bring his revenue even with his expenditures, by selling every year, a slave or two. This practice, jocularly, but most significantly known, as ' eating a negro'—a phrase worthy of slave-holding humanity—is becoming every day, more and more common. A very large number of planters have ceased to raise crops with the expectation of profit. They endeavor to make the produce of their lands pay their current expenses ; but all their hopes of gain are confined to the business of raising slaves for the southern market ; and that market is as regularly supplied with slaves from Virginia, as with mules and cattle from Kentucky.

But the slave-trade in America, as well as in Africa,

12

carries with it the curse of depopulation ; and, together with the emigration which is constantly going on, has already unpeopled great tracts of country in the lower part of Virginia, and is fast restoring the first seats of Anglo-American population to all their original wildness and solitude.　Whole counties almost, are grown up in useless and impenetrable thickets, already retenanted with deer and other wild game, their original inhabitants.

CHAPTER XVII.

WE were driven into the prison-yard, through a stout gate well studded with iron nails.　The heavy padlocks of the prison-door were unfastened, and we were thrust in, without further ceremony.　A faint glimmer of moon-light stole in at the narrow and grated windows of the prison ; but it was some time before I was able to distinguish one object from another. When at length, my eyes had accommodated themselves to the faintness of the light, I found myself crowded into the midst of perhaps a hundred human beings,—most of them young men and women between the ages of eighteen and twenty-four,—who were closely packed on the·bare floor, half naked, and many of them extremely filthy.

A considerable number had started up at our entrance, and they now began to crowd about us, and to inquire who we were, and whence we came. They seemed glad of anything to break the monotony of their confinement. But wearied and fatigued, we were in no humor for talking ; and sinking down upon the floor of our prison, notwithstanding the poisonous stench, and the confined and impure atmosphere, we were soon buried in profound slumbers. Sleep is the dearest solace of the wretched ; and there is this sweet touch of mercy in it, that it ever closes the eyes of the oppressed, more willingly than those of the oppressor. I hardly think that any member of the firm of Savage, Brothers & Co slept so soundly that night, as did the most unquiet of their newly purchased victims.

Day came—the prison-door was unlocked, and we were let out into the enclosure about it. The scanty allowance of corn-bread which the penuriousness of our wealthy but economical masters allowed us, was doled out to each. My meal finished, I sat down upon the ground, and observed the scene about me. With a few exceptions, the prisoners were collected in groups, some containing two or three, and others a much larger number. The men were more numerous than the women, though the females had received a considerable addition from our party. The acquaintance of these new comers was eagerly sought for, and they were constantly receiving solicitations to enter into temporary unions, to last while the parties remained together. Most of the women whom we found in the prison, had already formed connections of this sort.

These courtships,—if so they should be called,—were still going on, when a tall young fellow, with a very quizzical face, produced a three stringed fiddle, and after preluding for a few moments, struck up a lively tune. The sound of the music soon drew a large group about him, who provided themselves with partners and began a dance. As the fiddler warmed to his business, he played faster and faster, and the dancers, amidst laughs and shouts and boisterous merriment, did their best to keep up with the tune.

It is thus that men, whenever their natural sources of enjoyment fail them, betake themselves to artificial excitements. Too often, we sing and dance, not because we are merry, but in the hope to become so ; and merriment itself is seldomer the expression and the evidence of pleasure, than the disguise of weariness and pain,—the hollow echo of an aching heart.

But the entire company did not join the dancers. As it happened, it was Sunday ; and a part of them seemed to entertain conscientious scruples about dancing on that, and for ought I know, upon any other day. The more sober part of the company gradually collected together in the opposite corner of the prison-yard ; and a sedate young man, with a handsome and intelligent face, mounted upon the head of an empty barrel which happened to be standing there, and taking a hymn book from his pocket struck up a Methodist psalm. His voice was sweet and clear, and his singing far from disagreeable. He was soon joined by several others ; and as the chorus swelled, the sound of the psalmody almost drowned the scraping of the fiddle and the laughter of the dancers. I observed too, that several of the dancing party, cast their eyes, from time to time wistfully towards the singers ; and before the psalm was half finished, several of the females had stolen softly away, and mingled in the group collected about the preacher. The singing being ended, he began to pray. His hands were clasped, and raised towards heaven, and he spoke with a ready fluency, and a natural earnestness and unction, not always heard from a regular clergyman in a cushioned pulpit. Tears ran down many a face ; and sighs and groans almost drowned the voice of the speaker. These perhaps, were mere practiced responses, as artificial, and as little sincere, as the drawl of the parish clerk in the English church service. And yet in some cases, they had every appearance of being genuine bursts of natural feeling,—an involuntary tribute to the eloquence and fervor of the speaker.

Next followed the exhortation. The text was from Job ; and the preacher began upon the trite subject of patience. But like all ignorant and illiterate speakers, he soon deserted his original topic, and ran on from one thing to another, with very little of method or connection. Now and then, some sparks of sense were struck out ; but they were speedily quenched in a flood of absurdity. It was a strange farrago ;—but it

12*

was delivered with a volubility, an earnestness and a force, which produced a strong effect upon the hearers. It was not long before he had worked them up to a pitch of excitement, which far surpassed that of the dancers in the opposite corner. Indeed, the dancing group grew thinner and thinner, and the squeak of the fiddle sounded weaker and weaker, till at last the fiddler threw down his instrument, and with his remaining adherents hastened to swell the audience of a performer whose powers so much out-matched his own.

As the sermon proceeded, the groans and cries of mercy and amen, grew louder and more frequent; and several, overcome by their feelings, or wishing or affecting to be so, fell flat upon the ground, and screamed and shouted as if they had been possessed by evil spirits. So strong was the contagion, and so powerful the sympathetic infectiousness of this spiritual intoxication, that I,—a mere looker on,—felt a strong impulse to rush among the crowd, and to shriek and shout with the rest. The paroxysm was now at its height, and the speaker was almost exhausted by his vehement gesticulation, when stamping his foot, with more than common energy—he burst in the head of the barrel and tumbled headlong among his auditors.

This unlucky accident instantly converted the cries and groans of his hearers, into shouts of irrepressible laughter; and they seemed to pass all at once, from a state of the utmost terror and solemnity, into outrageous and uncontrolable merriment. The fiddler crept out from amidst the hurly burly, caught up his fiddle, and struck up a lively air,—I forget the name of it, but

I recollect very well that it contained some allusion to the disaster of his rival. The dance was renewed ; while the preacher, with a few of his more attached hearers, slunk away mortified and disheartened. The dancers grew more boisterous, and the fiddler played his best ; till at last the party had fairly tired themselves out, and were too much exhausted to keep it up any longer.

Men born and bred in slavery, are not men but children. Their faculties are never permitted to unfold themselves ; and it is the aim of their masters, and the necessary effect of their condition, to keep them in a state of perpetual imbecility. Tyranny is ever hostile to every species of mental developement, for its great object is to keep its victims in a state of ignorance and degradation, and therefore of helplessness.

I soon made myself acquainted with a number of my fellow prisoners, and entered into conversation with them. Some of them had been in the jail a fortnight, and others longer. I presently discovered that they considered their confinement as a sort of holyday. They had nothing to do ;—and not to be compelled to work seemed, for them, the supreme idea of happiness. As to being confined within the walls of a prison,—they had the liberty of the yard, and it was just as agreeable being shut up within four brick walls as to be prisoner on a plantation, forbidden to go beyond the line of its zig-zag fences. Then they had no overseer to harrass them, and nothing to do but to dance and sleep. Nothing was wanted but a little whiskey, and even that was not always wanting. They seemed anxious to drown all

memory of the past, and all dread of the future, and to
bask without concern, in the sunshine of their present
felicity.

CHAPTER XVIII.

I had been in jail ten days or a fortnight, when Messrs Savage, Brothers & Co selected from their ware-
house a cargo of slaves for the Charleston market.   I
was one of the number ; and with some fifty others,
was loaded on board a small vessel bound for that port.
The captain's name was Jonathan Osborne.   He was
a citizen of Boston, and the vessel, the brig Two
Sallys, belonged to that port, and was the property of
a rich and respectable merchant.

The people of the northern States of the American
Union, talk finely upon the subject of slavery, and
express a very proper indignation at its horrors.   Yet
while the African slave trade was permitted, their merchants carried it on ;—and these same merchants do
not always refuse to employ their vessels in the domestic slave trade,—a traffic not one iota less base and
detestable.

Northern statesmen have permitted slavery where no

constitutional objections prevented them from abol-
ishing it ; the courts and lawyers of the North
scrupulously fulfil to the utmost letter, the constitutional obligation to restore to the Southern master,
the victim who has escaped his grasp, and fled to the
' free States,' in the vain hope of protection ; whilst
the whole North looks calmly on and tamely suffers
the Southern slave-holders to violate all the provisions
of that same constitution, and to imprison, torture, and
put to death, the citizens of the North without judge or
jury, whenever they imagine that such severities can
contribute, in the slightest degree, to the security of
their slave-holding tyranny. Nay more,—many of the
Northern aristocrats, in the energy of their hatred for
democratical equality, seem almost ready to envy,
while they affect to deplore, the condition of their
Southern brethren. And yet the northern States of the
union dare to assert that they are undefiled by the stain
of slavery. It is a vain, false boast. They are partners in the wrong. The blood of the slave is on their
hands, and is dripping, in red and gory drops, from the
skirts of their garments.

Before leaving the prison, we were supplied with
handcuffs, those usual badges and emblems of servitude, and having reached the wharf, we were cram-
med together, into the hold of the vessel, so close that
we had hardly room to move, and not room enough
either to lie or sit with comfort. The vessel got under
way soon after we came on board, and proceeded
down the river. Once or twice a day, we were suffered to come on deck, and to breathe the fresh air for a

few minutes ; but we were soon remanded to our dungeon in the hold.   The mate of the vessel seemed to
be a good natured young man, and disposed to render
our condition as comfortable as possible ; but the captain was a savage tyrant, worthy of the business in
which he was engaged.

We had been on our voyage a day or two, and had
already cleared the river, and were standing down the
bay, when I became excessively sick.   A burning
fever seemed raging in my veins.   It was after sunset ;
the hatches was closed down ; and the heat of the narrow hold, in which we were confined, and which was
more than half filled up with boxes and barrels, became
intolerable.   I knocked against the deck, and called
aloud for air and water.   It was the mate's watch.
He came forward to ascertain what was the matter,
and bade the men unfasten the hatches and lift me on
deck.   I snatched the bason of water which he gave
me, and though brackish and dirty, it seemed to my
feverish taste the most delicious of drinks.   I drained
it to the bottom and called for more ;—but the mate,
who feared perhaps that excessive drinking might aggravate my disorder, refused this request.   I wanted
air as much as water.   This he did not refuse me ;
and I was lying on the deck, imbibing at every pore
the cool breeze of the evening, when the captain came
up the companion-way.

He no sooner saw the hatches off, and me lying
on the deck, than he stepped up to his mate with a
clenched fist and a face distorted with passion, and ad-

dressed him with " How dare you take off the hatches
after sundown, without my orders?"

The mate attempted an apology, and began with
saying that I was taken suddenly sick, and had called
for assistance ;—but without waiting to hear him out,
the brutal captain rushed by, and hitting me a kick,
precipitated me headlong, into the hold, upon the
heads of my companions. Without stopping to inquire, whether or not my neck was broken, he bade
his men replace and secure the hatches. Luckily I
sustained but little injury ; though I came within an
inch of having my scull broken against one of the
beams. The water I had drank, and the cool air I
had breathed, abated my fever, and I soon began to
grow better.

In the course of the next day, we passed the capes of
the Chesapeake, and entered the great Atlantic. We
stood to the southward and eastward, and were making rapid way, when it came on to blow a furious
gale. The tossing and pitching of the ship was terrible indeed to us poor prisoners, confined in the dark
hold, and expecting, at every burst of thunder, that the
vessel was breaking in pieces. The storm continued
to increase. The noise and tumult on deck, the
creaking of the rigging, the cries of the seamen, and
the sound of cracking spars, and splitting canvass added to our terror. Pretty soon, we found that the
hold was filling with water, and an alarm was given that
the vessel had sprung a-leak. The hatches were opened, and we were called on deck. Our handcuffs were
knocked off, and we were set to work at the pumps.

I could not tell whether it was night or morning; for the gale had now lasted a good while, and since it began, we had not been suffered to come on deck. However it was not totally dark. A dim and horrid glimmer, just sufficient to betray our situation, and more terrible perhaps than total darkness, was hovering over the ocean. At a distance, the huge black waves, crested with pale blue foam, seemed to move on like monsters of the deep; nor when nearer, did they lose any of their terrors. Now we sunk into a horrid gulf, between two watery precipices, which swelled on either side, black, and frowning, and ready to devour us; and now, lifted on the top of a lofty wave, we viewed all around, a wild and fearful waste of dark and stormy waters. It was a terrible sight for one who had never seen the sea before; and as I gazed upon it, half stupified with terror, little did I think that this same fierce and raging element, was to prove hereafter, my best and surest friend!

The brig was almost a total wreck. Her foremast was gone by the board; and she was lying too on the starboard tack, under a close reefed main-top-sail. These are terms which, at that time, I had never heard. It was long afterwards that I learned to use them. But the whole scene remains as distinct upon my memory as if it had been painted there. Notwithstanding all our efforts, the leak gained upon us; and the captain soon made up his mind that it would be impossible to keep the vessel afloat. Accordingly he made his preparations for quitting her. He and his mates were armed with swords and pistols; and cutlasses were put into the hands of two or three of the crew. The long boat had been washed overboard ; but they had succeeded in securing the jolly boat, which they now lowered away and dropped into the water under the vessel's lee. The crew were already embarking, before we well understood what they were about ;—but as soon as we comprehended that they were going to desert the ship, we rushed frantickly forward, and demanded to be taken on board. This they had expected, and they were prepared for it. Three or four pistol shots were fired among us, and several of us were severely wounded by the sailors' cutlasses. At the same time, they cried to us to stand back, and they would take us on board as soon as all things were ready. Terrified and confused, we stood a moment doubting what to do. The sailors improved this interval to jump on board,—" cast off" shouted the captain,—the seamen bent to their oars, and the boat was fast quitting the vessel, before we had recovered from our momentary hesitation.

We raised a shout, or rather a scream of terror, at finding ourselves thus deserted ; and three or four poor wretches, on the impulse of the moment, sprang into the water, in the hope of reaching the boat. All but one sunk instantly in the boiling surge ; he, a man of herculean frame, springing with all the effort of a death-struggle, was carried far beyond the rest, and rising through the billows, found himself just behind the boat. He stretched out his hand and caught the rudder. The captain was steering. He drew a pistol and fired it at the head of the swimmer. We heard a

13

scream above all the noise of the tempest. It was
only for a moment ; he sunk, and we saw him no more.

It is impossible to convey any adequate idea of the terror and confusion which now prevailed on board.   The
women, now screaming, now praying, were frantic with
fear.   Four or five poor fellows lay about the deck
bleeding and desperately wounded.   Death seemed to
ride upon the storm, and to summon his victims. The
vessel still lay with her head to windward ; but the
spray dashed over her continually, and every now and
then, she shipped a sea which set the decks a-float
and drenched us in salt water.   It occurred to me, that
unless the pumps were kept going, the vessel would
soon fill and carry us to the bottom.   I called about
me, such of the men as seemed to be most in their
senses, and endeavored to explain to them our situation ; but they were stupified with terror, and would
not or could not understand me.   As a last resource, I
rushed forward, crying—" pump my hearties, pump for
your lives." This was the phrase which the captain and
his mates had continually repeated, as they stood over
us and directed our labor.   The poor creatures seemed
to obey as if instinctively, this voice of command.
They collected about me and began to work the pumps.
If it had no other good effect, at least it served to
call off our attention from the horrors with which we
were surrounded.   We plyed our work till one of the
pumps was broken and the other choked and rendered
useless.   By this time the storm had abated, and the
vessel, notwithstanding all our fears to the contrary,
still rode the waves.

It grew lighter by degrees. Presently the clouds began to break away, and to drive in large and misty masses along the sky. Occasionally the sun broke out, and after a considerable dispute, whether it were rising or setting, we concluded it must be some four or five hours past sunrise.

As soon as the women had recovered from the first paroxysm of their terror, they gave such care as they could, to the poor sufferers, who had been wounded. They had bound up their wounds and had collected them together on the quarter deck. One poor fellow who had been shot through the body with a pistol ball, was much worse hurt than the others. His wife was supporting his head on her lap, and trying to cool his parched lips with a cup of water. She was standing by him, or rather clinging to him, at the moment he was wounded. She had caught him in her arms as he fell, had dragged him from the press, and from that moment seemed to forget all the horrors of our situation, in her incessant efforts to soothe his pains. Her affectionate care had proved of little avail. The struggle was now almost over. In a little while, he expired in her arms.

When she found that he was dead, her grief which she had controled and suppressed so long, burst forth in all its energy. Her female companions gathered about her,—but the poor woman was beyond the reach of consolation.

Some of us now ventured below, and took the liberty of overhauling the steward's stores. Every thing was more or less damaged with salt water ; but we lighted upon a cask or two of bread, which was tolerably dry, and which sufficed to furnish us a sumptuous repast.

We had not finished it, before we discovered a vessel standing towards us. As she approached, we waved fragments of the tattered sails, and shouted for assistance. Having run down pretty near us, she hove too, and sent a boat on board. When the boat's crew had mounted over the brig's side, they seemed utterly amazed at the scene which her decks presented. I stepped forward, and explained to the officer the nature of our situation ;—that we were a cargo of slaves bound from Washington to Charleston, and that the vessel and her lading had been deserted by the crew ; that contrary to every expectation, we had succeeded in keeping her afloat, but that the pumps were out of order and she was again filling.

The mate hastened back to his own ship and soon returned with the captain and the carpenter. After examining and consulting together, they determined to put a part of their own crew on board the brig and to navigate her into Norfolk, to which port they were bound, and which was the nearest harbor. The carpenter was set at work stopping her leaks and repairing her pumps. Her new crew set up a jury foremast, out of such materials as they found on board. She was soon in sailing order, and they shook the reefs out of her main-top-sail and put her before the wind.

The vessel which had rescued us, was the Arethusa, of New York, Charles Parker, master ; and lest we might need assistance, she slackened sail and kept us company. Before night, we made the land and a pilot came on board. The next morning we anchored in the harbor of Norfolk. I must be excused from describing the town, as I had no opportunity to see it ; for we were hurried off, and locked up in the jail for safe keeping.

CHAPTER XIX.

WE remained in jail some three weeks, before any body condescended to inform us why we were kept there, or what was to become of us. We now learned that captain Parker and his crew had libelled the Two Sallys and her cargo for salvage ; and that the Court had ordered the libelled property to be sold at auction, for the joint benefit of the owners and salvors. This was all Greek to us. I had not the most distant idea what was meant by ' libelling for salvage,' and I hardly think that any of the others understood it better than I. Nobody took the trouble to explain it to us ;—it was enough for us to understand, that we were to be sold, the why and the wherefore, it was thought of no consequence for slaves to know.

13*

As I had already been twice sold at public auction, the thing had lost its interest and its novelty. I was tired of the confinement of the prison ; and as I knew that I must be sold at last, I was as ready to take my chance now as ever.

The sale was much like other sales of slaves. There was only one circumstance about it, that seemed worthy of particular notice. The wounded men, though they were not yet cured,—indeed two of the four were hardly thought out of danger,—were to be sold among the rest. " Damaged articles," the auctioneer observed, " which he was willing to dispose of at a great discount." The four were offered in one lot,—" like so many broken frying pans," said one of the spectators ;—" but for my part, I have no fancy for speculating either in broken frying pans, wounded slaves, or sick horses." A physician who was present, was advised to purchase. " If they should happen to die," said his adviser, " they would be quite useless to any body else, but you might find some use for their dead bodies." Various other jests equally pointed and brilliant, were thrown out by others of the company, and were received with shouts of laughter, that contrasted a little harshly, with the sad, woe-begone faces, and low moans of the wounded men, who were brought to the place of sale on little pallets, and who lay upon the ground, the very pictures of sickness and distress.

This jocular humor had reached a high pitch, when it was rather suddenly checked, by a tall fine looking man, who had more the air and manners of a gentleman than the greater part of the company. He observed, with a tone and a look of some severity, that in his opinion, selling men upon their death-beds was no laughing matter. He immediately made a bid quite beyond any thing that had been offered, and the auctioneer pronounced him to be the purchaser. I hoped this same gentleman might have purchased me also ;— but as soon as he had given some directions about the removal of the wounded men, he left the place of sale. Perhaps I had no reason to regret it. This gentleman, for ought I could tell, had acted, as an hundred other slave-buyers might have done, from a momentary impulse of humanity, which disgusted him, it is true, with the brutality of the rest of the company, but which in all likelihood, was neither strong nor steady enough to render his treatment of his servants much different from that of his neighbors. Such temporary fits of humanity and good nature, are occasionally felt by every body ; but they are no guarantee whatever, against an habitual disregard of the rights and feelings of those, who are not allowed to protect themselves, and who are protected neither by the laws nor by public opinion.

I was purchased by an agent of Mr James Carleton, of Carleton-Hall, in one of the northern counties of North Carolina ; and was presently sent off with two or three of my companions, for the plantation of our new master.

After a journey of four or five days, we arrived at Carleton-Hall. It was like the residences of so many other American planters,—a mean house, with no great signs about it, either of ornament or comfort.

At a short distance from the house, was the servants' quarter,—a miserable collection of ruinous cabins, crowded together without any order, and almost concealed in the vigorous growth of weeds, that sprung up around and among them.

Soon after our arrival, we were carried into the presence of our new master, who examined us one by one, and inquired into our several capabilities. Having learned that I had been raised a house-servant, and being pleased, as he said, with my manners and appearance, he told me he would take me into the house to supply the place of his man John, who had become so confirmed a drunkard, that he had been obliged to turn him into the field.

I was well enough pleased with this arrangement; for in general, those slaves who are house servants, are infinitely better off than those who are employed in field labor. They are better fed, and better clothed, and their work is much lighter. They are sure of the crumbs that fall from their master's table; and as the master's eyes and those of his guests would be offended by a display of dirt and rags in the dinning room, house servants are comfortably clothed, not so much, it is true, on their own account, as for the gratification of their owner's vanity. As it is a matter of ostentation to have a house full of servants, the labor becomes light when divided among so many. Sufficient food, comfortable clothing, and light work are not to be despised; but the circumstance which principally contributes to make the condition of the house servant more tolerable than that of the field hand, is of a different description. Men, and especially women and children, cannot have any thing much about them, be it a dog, a cat, or even a slave, without insensibly contracting some interest in it and regard for it; and it thus happens that a family servant often becomes quite a favorite, and is at length regarded with a feeling that bears some faint and distant resemblance to family affection.

This is the most tolerable—in fact, the only tolerable point of view—in which slavery can be made to present itself; and it has been, by steadily fixing their eyes on a few cases of this sort, and as steadily, closing them to all its intrinsic horrors and enormities, that some bold sophists have mustered courage to make the eulogium of slavery.

Yet this best condition of a slave,—that I mean of a household servant,—is not seldom, almost too miserable for endurance. If there are kind masters and good natured mistresses, it happens too often, that the master is a capricious tyrant, and the mistress a fretful scold. The poor servant is exposed, every hour of his life, to a course of harsh rebukes, and peevish chidings, which are always threatening to end in the torture of the lash, and which to a person of any spirit or sensibility, are more annoying than even the lash itself. And all this is without hope or chance of remedy. The master and the mistress indulge their bad humor without restraint. No fear of 'warning' puts any curb upon them. The slave is theirs; and they can treat him as they please. He cannot help himself; and there is no one to help him.

Mr Carleton, while he entertained most of the notions of his brother planters, differed from the greater
part of them in one striking particular. He was a
zealous presbyterian, and very warm and earnest, in
the cause of religion. Had any one told him, that
to hold men in slavery was a high-handed offence
against religion and morality, what would have been his
answer ? Would his heart have responded to the truth
of a sentiment so congenial to every more generous
emotion and better feeling ? I am much afraid it would
have been otherwise with him. I fear he would have
answered much like those of his brother slave-holders,
who made no pretensions whatever to peculiar piety.
With a secret consciousness of his criminality, but
with a fixed determination never to admit it, he would
have worked himself into a violent passion ; talked of
the sacred rights of property,—more sacred in a slave-
holder's estimation than either liberty or justice ; and
declaimed against impertinent interference in the affairs
of other people,—a topic, by the way, which is very
seldom much insisted upon, except by those whose
affairs will hardly bear examination.

Mr Carleton, though a zealous presbyterian, had,
as I have said, most of the feelings and notions of his
brother planters. It thus happened, that his character,
his conversation and his conduct were full of strange
contrasts, and were forever presenting an odd, incon-
gruous mixture of the bully and the puritan. I use the
word bully for want of a better,—not exactly in its
most vulgar sense, but intending to signify by it, a
certain spirit of bravado and violence,—a disposition

to settle every disputed point by the pistol, so common, I might almost say universal, in the southern States of America. Mr Carleton with all his piety, talked as familiarly of shooting people, as if he had been a professed assassin.

As I had the honor of waiting upon Mr Carleton's table, and the pleasure and advantage of listening every day to his conversation, I soon came to understand his character perfectly,—as perfectly at least as it was possible for any body to understand so very inconsistent a character. He had family prayers, night and morning, with the most punctilious regularity. He prayed long and fervently, and on his bended knees. He was particularly earnest in his petitions for the universal spread of the gospel; he asked most devoutly, that as all men were creatures of the same God, they might speedily become children of the same faith. Yet not only the plantation slaves were never invited to join in this family worship, but even the house-servants were excluded. The door was shut;—and at the very moment when the devout Mr Carleton professed to prostrate himself in the dust before his Creator, he felt too strongly the sense of his own superiority, to permit even his house-hold servants to participate in his devotions !

But for all this, Mr Carleton evidently had the cause of religion very much at heart, and seemed ready to spend and be spent in the service. There were very few clergymen in the part of the country in which he resided, and his zeal frequently led him to supply the gap, by acting as an exhorter. Indeed there was

scarcely a Sunday that he did not hold forth somewhere in the neighborhood. Within ten miles of
Carleton-Hall, in different directions, there were as
many as three churches, wretched, ruinous little buildings, that looked more like deserted barns than places
of public worship. All of these Mr Carleton had
caused to be repaired,—principally at his own expense,
and in each of them he preached occasionally. But
he did not consider a church as indispensable to an
exhortation. During the summer, he frequently held
meetings in some shady grove, or by the side of some
cool spring ; and in the winter, sometimes in his own
house, and sometimes in the houses of his neighbors.
He was generally pretty sure of a considerable audience. That part of the country was thinly inhabited,
and the people had but few amusements. They were
glad of any occasion of assembling together, and
seemed to care very little whether it were a preaching
or a frolic. Besides, Mr Carleton was really an
agreeable speaker ; and the earnestness and vehemence
of his manner were well calculated to attract an audience.

A very considerable proportion of his hearers were
slaves ;—for though he did not judge it expedient to
allow them to become partakers in his private devotions, he had no objection to their swelling his audience,
and giving a sort of eclat to his public performances.
Indeed, towards the end of his discourses, he would
often condescend to introduce a few sentences for their
particular benefit. The change which took place in his
manner when he came to this part of his sermon was

sufficiently obvious. The phrase, 'dear brethren,' which in the earlier part of it, he was forever repeating, was now suddenly dropped. The preacher assumed a condescending, patronizing air, and briefly and dryly informed those of his hearers, 'whom God had appointed to be servants,' that their only hope of salvation was in patience, obedience, submission, diligence and subordination. He warned them earnestly, against thieving and lying, their 'easily besetting sins;' and enforced at some length the great wickedness and folly of being discontented with their condition. All this was applauded by the masters as very orthodox doctrine, and very proper to be preached to servants. The servants themselves received it, with an outward submission, to which their hearts gave the lie. Nor is it very strange, considering the doctrines which he preached to them, that the greater part of Mr Carleton's converts among the slaves, were hypocritical fellows, who made their religion a cloak for their roguery. There was in fact, much truth in the observation of one of Mr Carleton's neighbors, that most of the slaves, in that part of the country, had no religion at all, and that those who pretended to have any were worse than the others. And how could it be otherwise, when in the venerable name of religion, they had preached to them a doctrine of double-distilled tyranny, —a doctrine which not content with now and then a human victim, demanded the perpetual sacrifice of one half the entire community ?

Alas christianity ! What does it avail,—thy concern for the poor,—thy tenderness for the oppressed,

14

—thy system of fraternal love and affection! The serpent knows how to suck poison from the harmless nature of the dove. The tyrants of every age and country, have succeeded in prostituting christianity into an instrument of their crimes, a terror to their victims, and an apology for their oppressions! Nor have they ever wanted time-serving priests and lying prophets to applaud, encourage, and sustain them!

However little the slaves might relish Mr Carleton's doctrines,—of which indeed their own hearts instinctively made the refutation,—they were very fond of attending upon his performances. It was some relief to the eternal monotony of their lives; and it gave them an opportunity of getting together after the meeting was over, and having a frolic among themselves. This recreation, which it afforded to the servants, was in my opinion, the best effect of Mr Carleton's labors; though certain gentlemen, who dreaded every assembly of slaves, as a source of discontent and conspiracy, were very earnest in the condemnation of his meetings, under the hypocritical pretence of being shocked at the violations of the Sabbath, of which they furnished the occasion!

Mr Carleton was president of a Bible society, and was very anxious and earnest about the universal diffusion of the Bible. I soon found out however, that besides myself, there was not a single slave on his plantation, nor indeed in all the neighborhood, who knew how to read:—and what was more, I learned that Mr Carleton was extremely unwilling to have any of them taught.

There is connected with this subject, a point of
view, in which the system of domestic slavery that
prevails in America, exhibits itself as out-braving all
other tyrannies, and betraying a demoniac spirit almost
too horrid to be thought of.   Mr Carleton believed,
and the immense majority of his fellow countrymen
believe also, that the Bible contains a revelation from
God of things essential to man's eternal welfare.   In
this belief, and animated by a lofty spirit of philanthropy, they have formed societies—and of one of
these Mr Carleton was president ; and contribute their
money—as Mr Carleton did very liberally, to dissem-
inate the Bible through the world, and to put this
divine and unerring guide into the possession of every
family.   But while they are so zealous to confer this
inestimable treasure on all the world beside, they sternly
withhold it from those, of whom the law has made them
the sole guardians.   They withhold it from their slaves,
—of whom, to use their own hypocritical cant, God
has appointed them the natural protectors,—and in so
doing, by their own confession, they voluntarily and
knowingly expose those slaves, to the danger of eternal
punishment !   To this awful danger, they voluntarily
and knowingly expose them, lest, should they learn to
read, they might learn at the same time, their own
rights, and the means of enforcing them.

What outrage upon humanity was ever equal to this ?
Other tyrannies have proceeded all lengths against
man's temporal happiness ; and in support of their evil
dominion, have hazarded every extreme of temporary
cruelty ;—but what other tyrants are recorded in all the

world's history, who have openly and publicly confessed,
that they prefer to expose their victims to the imminent
danger of eternal misery, rather than impart a degree
of instruction, which might, by possibility, endanger
their own unjust and usurped authority ?   Can any
one calmly consider the cool diabolism of this avowal,
and believe it is men who make it ? Men too, who
seem in other matters, not destitute of the common
feelings of good will ;—men who talk about liberty,
virtue, and religion, and who speak even of justice and
humanity !

Were I inclined to superstition, I should believe
they were not men, but rather demons incarnate ;—
evil spirits who had assumed the human shape, and
who falsely put on a semblance of human feelings, in
order the more secretly and securely to prosecute their
grand conspiracy against mankind. I should believe
so, did I not know that the love of social superiority,
that very impulse of the human heart, which is the
main-spring of civilization and the chief source of all
human improvement, is able, when suffered to work on,
uncontrolled by other more generous emotions, to
corrupt man's whole nature, and to drive him to acts
the most horrid and detestable. When to the cor-
ruptest form of this fierce passion, is joined a base
fear, at once cowardly and cruel, what wonder that man
becomes a creature to be scorned and hated ?—To be
pitied rather ; the maniac can hardly be held accounta-
ble for the enormities to which his madness prompts
him, even though that madness be self-created.

However diabolical the tyranny may be esteemed,

which to secure its usurped authority, is ready to sacrifice both the temporal and eternal happiness of its victims, it is no doubt well adapted to accomplish the end at which it aims ; namely, its own perpetuation. But it is necessary to go one step further. The slaveholders ought to recollect, that all knowledge is dangerous ; and that it is impossible to give the slaves *any* instruction in christianity, without imparting to them some dangerous ideas. It matters not that the law prohibits the teaching them to read. Oral instruction is as dangerous as written ; and the catechism is nothing but a Bible in disguise. Let them go on, then, and bring their work to a glorious completion. Let them prohibit at once, all religious instruction. They must come to this at last. Let me tell them, that the time is past, in which Mr Carleton's doctrine of passive obedience is all that a religious teacher has to utter. There is another spirit abroad ; and that spirit will penetrate, wherever religious instruction opens the way for it. Now-a-day it is impossible to hail the slave as a christian brother, without first acknowledging his rights as a fellow-man.

14*

CHAPTER XX.

I had not been long in Mr Carleton's service, before
I discovered, that a pretty sure way of getting into his
good graces, was to be a great admirer of his religious
performances, and a devout attendant upon such of them
as his servants might attend.   There never was a person less inclined by nature to hypocrisy than myself.
But craft and cunning are the sole resource of a slave ;
and I had long ago learned to practice a thousand arts,
which, at the same time that I despised them, I often
found extremely useful.

For these arts, I now had occasion ; and I plied my
flattery to such good purpose, that I soon gained the
good will of my master, and before long, was duly established in the situation of confidential servant.   This
was a station of very considerable respectability ; and
next to the overseer, I was decidedly the most conse-
quential person on the place.   It was my duty to attend
specially upon my master, to ride about with him to
meetings, carry his cloak and Bible, and take care
of his horse ;—for among other matters Mr Carleton
was a connoisseur of horses, and he did not like to trust
his, to the usual blundering negligence of his neighbors'
grooms.

Pretty soon, my master found out my accomplish-
ments of reading and writing—for I inadvertently betrayed a secret, which I had determined to keep to
myself.   At first he did not seem to like it ; but as he

could not unlearn me, he soon determined to turn these
acquirements of mine to some account. He had a
good deal of writing, of one sort and another ; and he
set me to work as copier. In my character of secre-
tary, I was often called upon, when my master was
busy, to write passes for the people. This raised my
consequence extremely ; and my fellow servants soon
begun to look upon me, as second only to ' master'
himself.

Mr Carleton was naturally humane and kind-hearted;
and though his sudden out-breaks of impatience and
fretfulness were often vexatious enough, still if one
humored him, they were generally soon over ; and as if
he reproached himself for not keeping a better guard
over his temper, they were often followed by an affa-
bility and indulgence greater than usual. I soon learned
the art of managing him to the best advantage, and
every day I rose in his favor.

I had a good deal of leisure ; and I found means to
employ it both innocently and agreeably. Mr Carleton
had a collection of books very unusual for a North Carolina planter. This library must have contained between two and three hundred volumes. It was the
admiration of all the country round ; and contributed
not a little, to give its owner the character of a great
scholar, and a very learned man. My situation of confidential servant, gave me free access to it. The
greater part of the volumes treated of divinity, but
there were some of a more attractive description ; and
I was able to gratify occasionally and by stealth, for I
did not like to be seen reading any thing but the Bible,

that taste for knowledge which I had imbibed when a child, and which all the degradations of servitude, had not utterly extinguished. All things considered, I found myself much more agreeably situated, than I had been since the death of my first master.

I wish, both for their sakes and his own, that all the rest of Mr Carleton's slaves had been as well off and as kindly treated as myself. The house servants, it is true, had nothing to complain of, except indeed, those grievous evils, which are inseparable from a state of servitude, and which no tenderness or indulgence on the part of the master, can ever do away. But the plantation hands—some fifty in number—were very differently situated. Mr Carleton, like a large proportion of American planters, had no knowledge of agriculture, and not the slightest taste for it. He had never given any attention to the business of his plantation ;—his youth had been spent in a course of boisterous dissipation ; and since his conversion, he had been entirely devoted to the cause of religion. Of course his planting affairs and all that related to them were wholly in the hands of his overseer, who was shrewd, plausible, intelligent and well acquainted with his business ;—but a severe task-master,—bad tempered,—and if all reports were true, not very much over-burdened with honesty. Mr Warner, for this was the overseer's name, was engaged on terms which however ruinous to the planter and his plantation, were very common in Virginia and the Carolinas. Instead of receiving a regular salary in money, he took a certain proportion of the crop. Of course, it was his interest to make the largest crop possible, without any regard whatever to the means used to make it. What was it to him though the lands were exhausted, and the slaves worn out with heavy tasks and unreasonable labors ? He owned neither the lands nor the slaves, and if in ten or twelve years,—and for something like that time he had been established at Carleton-Hall,—he could scourge all their value out of them, the gain was his, and the loss would be his employer's. This desirable consummation, he seemed pretty nearly arrived at. The lands at Carleton-Hall, were never cultivated, it is likely, with any tolerable skill ; but Mr Warner had carried the process of exhaustion to its last extremity. Field after field had been ' turned out' as they call it—that is, left uncultivated and unfenced, to grow up with broom-sedge and persimmon bushes, and be grazed by all the cattle of the neighborhood. Year after year, new land had been opened, and exposed to the same exhausting process, which had worn out the fields that had been already abandoned ;—till at last, there was no new land left upon the plantation.

Mr Warner now began to talk about throwing up his employment ; and it was only by urgent solicitations, and a greater proportion of the diminished produce, that Mr Carleton had prevailed upon him to remain another year.

But it was not the land only, that suffered. The slaves were subjected to a like process of exhaustion ; and what with hard work, insufficient food, and an irregular and capricious severity, they had become discontented, sickly and inefficient. There never was a

time that two or three of them, and sometimes many
more, were not runaways, wandering in the woods ;
and hence originated further troubles, and fresh severity.

Mr Carleton had expressly directed, that his servants should receive an allowance of corn, and especially of meat, which in that part of the world was
thought extremely liberal ; and I believe, if the allowance had been faithfully distributed, the heartiest man
upon the place would have received about half as much
meat as was consumed by Mr Carleton's youngest
daughter,—a little girl some ten or twelve years old.
But if the slaves were worthy of belief, neither Mr
Warner's scales nor his measure were very authentic ;
and according to their story, so much as he could
plunder out of their weekly allowance, went to increase
his share in the yearly produce of the plantation.

Once or twice, complaints of this sort had been carried to Mr Carleton ; but without deigning to examine
into them, he had dismissed them as unworthy of notice.
Mr Warner, he said, was an honest man and a christian,—indeed it was his christian character that had
first recommended him to his employer ;—and these
scandalous stories were only invented out of that spite
which slaves always feel against an overseer, who compels them to do their duty.   It might be so ;—I cannot
undertake positively to contradict it.   Yet I know that
these imputations upon Mr Warner's honesty were not
confined to the plantation, but circulated pretty freely
through the neighborhood ; and if he was not a rogue,
Mr Carleton, by an unlimited, unsuspicious and unwise
confidence, did his best to make him so.

Whether the slaves were cheated or not, of their allowance, there is no dispute, that they were worked hard and harshly treated. Mr Carleton always took sides with his overseer, and was in the habit of maintaining that it was impossible to get along on a plantation without frequent whipping and a good deal of severity ;—and yet, as he was naturally good natured, it gave him pain to hear of any very flagrant instance of it. But he was much from home ; and that kept him ignorant, to a great degree, of what was going on there ; —and for the rest, the overseer was anxious to save his feelings, and had issued very strict orders, which he enforced with merciless severity,—that nobody should run to the House with tales of what was done upon the plantation. By this ingenious device, though a very common one, Mr Warner had every thing in his own way. In fact, Mr Carleton had as little control over his plantation as over any other in the county ; and he knew just as little about it.

When my master was a young man, he had betted at horse-races and gambling-tables, and spent money very freely in a thousand foolish ways. Since he had grown religious he had dropped these expenses, but he had fallen into others. It was no small sum that he spent every year, upon Bibles, church repairs, and other pious objects. For several years his income had been diminishing ; but without any corresponding diminution of his expenses. As a natural consequence, he had become deeply involved in debt. His overseer had grown rich, while he had been growing poor. His lands and slaves were mortgaged, and he began to be plagued by the sheriff's officer. But these perplexities did not cause him to forego his spiritual labors, which he prosecuted, if possible, more diligently than before.

I had now been living with him some six or seven months, and was completely established in his favor, when one Sunday morning, we set off together for a place about eight miles distant, where he had not preached before since I had been in his service. The place appointed for the meeting, was in the open air. It was a pretty place though, and well adapted to the purpose, being a gentle swell of ground over which were thinly scattered a number of ancient, and wide-spreading oaks. Their outstretched limbs formed a thick shade, under which there were neither weeds nor undergrowth, but something more like a grassy lawn, than is often to be seen in that country. Near the top of the swell, somebody had fixed up some rude benches ; and partly supported against one of the largest trees, was a misshapen little platform, with a chair or two upon it, which seemed intended for the pulpit.

Quite a troop of horses and as many as ten or twelve carriages were collected at the foot of the swell ; and the benches were already occupied by a considerable number of people. The white hearers however, were far outnumbered by the slaves, who were scattered about in groups, most of them in their Sunday dresses, and many of them very decent looking people. A few however, were miserably ragged and dirty ; and there was quite a number of half-grown children, with hardly a rag to hide their nakedness.

My master seemed well pleased with the prospect of so large an audience. He dismounted at the foot of the hill, if a rise so gentle deserved the name, and delivered his horse into my charge. I sought out a convenient place in which to tie the horses ; and as I knew the services would not begin immediately, I sauntered about, looking at the equipages and the company. While I was occupied in this way, a smart carriage drove up. It stopped. A servant jumped from behind, opened the door and let down the steps. An elderly lady, and another about eighteen or twenty, occupied the back seat. On the front seat, was a woman whom I took to be their maid, though I could not see her distinctly. Something called off my attention and I turned another way. When I looked again, the two ladies were walking up the hill and the maid was on the ground, with her back towards me, taking something from the carriage. A moment after, she turned round, and I knew her. It was my Cassy,—it was my wife.

I sprang forward and caught her in my arms. She recognized me at the same moment ; and uttering a cry of surprise and pleasure, she would have fallen had I not supported her. She recovered herself directly, and bade me let her go, for she had been sent back for her mistress' fan, and she must make haste and carry it to her. She told me to wait though,—for if she could get leave she would come back again immediately. She tripped up the hill, and overtook her mistress. I could see by her gestures, the eagerness with which

15

she urged her request. It was granted,—and in a moment she was again at my side. Again I pressed her to my bosom, and again she returned my embrace. Once more I felt what it was to be happy. I took her by the hand and led her to a little wood, on the opposite side of the road. Here was a thick young growth where we could sit, screened from observation. We sat down upon a fallen tree ; and while I held her hands fast locked in mine, we asked and answered a thousand questions. My history, since our separation, has been told already. Here follows a summary of hers.

END OF VOL. I.

THE

SLAVE:

OR

MEMOIRS OF ARCHY MOORE.

ALL men are by nature equally free and independent, and have certain IN-HERENT RIGHTS, of which, when they enter into society, they cannot by any compact deprive or divest their posterity, viz: the enjoyment of life and liberty, with the means of acquiring and possessing property, and pursuing happiness and safety. *Virginia Bill of Rights, Art. I.*

VOLUME II.

BOSTON:
JOHN H. EASTBURN, PRINTER.

1836.

MEMOIRS.

CHAPTER I.

It seemed to be with great reluctance, that the poor girl carried back her recollection to that terrible day, which had separated us, as we then thought, forever. She hesitated,—and seemed half ashamed, and almost unwilling to speak of what had followed after that separation. I pitied her,—and great as was my curiosity, if my feelings on that occasion deserve so trifling a name, I could almost have wished her to pass over the interval in silence. Distressing doubts and dreadful apprehensions crowded upon me, and I almost dreaded to hear her speak. But she hid her face in my bosom, and murmuring in a voice half choked with sobs, " my husband must know it,"—she began her story.

She was already, she said, more than half dead with fright and horror, and the first blow that colonel Moore struck, beat her senseless to the ground. When she came to her senses, she found herself lying on a bed, in a room which she did not recollect ever to have seen before. She rose from the bed as well as her bruises would allow her ;—for she did not move without difficulty. The room was prettily furnished ; the bed was hung with curtains, neat and comfortable ; a dressing table stood in one corner ; and there was all the usual furniture of a lady's bed-chamber,—but it was not like any room in the house at Spring-Meadow.

She tried to open the doors of which there were two,—but both were fastened. She endeavored to get a peep from the windows, in the hope that she might know some part of the prospect. But she could only discover that the house seemed to be surrounded by trees ; for the windows were guarded on the outside by close blinds, which were fastened in some way she did not understand, so that she could not open them. This fastening of the doors and windows, satisfied her that she was held a prisoner, and confirmed all her worst suspicions.

As she passed by the dressing table, she caught a look at the glass. Her face was deadly pale;—her hair fell in loose disorder over her shoulders, and looking down, she saw stains of blood upon her dress, but whether her own or her husband's she could not tell. She sat down on the bed-side ; her head was dizzy and confused, and she scarcely knew whether she was awake or dreaming.

Presently one of the doors opened, and a woman entered. It was Miss Ritty,* as she was called among the servants at Spring-Meadow, a pretty, dark-complexioned damsel, who enjoyed at that time, the sta-

* Henrietta.

tion and dignity of colonel Moore's favorite. Cassy's heart beat hard, while she heard some one fumbling at the lock. When the door opened she was glad to see that it was only a woman, and one whom she knew. She ran towards her, caught her by the hand, and begged her protection. The girl laughed, and asked what she was afraid of. Cassy hardly knew what answer to make. After hesitating a moment, she begged Miss Ritty to tell her where she was, and what they intended to do with her.

" It is a fine place you 're in," was the answer, " and when master comes, you can ask him what is to be done with you." This was said with a significant titter, which Cassy knew too well how to interpret.

Though Miss Ritty had evaded a direct answer to her inquiry, it now occurred to her where she must be. This woman, she recollected, occupied a small house,—the same that once had been inhabited by Cassy's mother and by mine,—at a considerable distance from any other on the plantation. It was surrounded by a little grove which almost hid it from view, and was very seldom visited by any of the servants. Miss Ritty looked upon herself, and was in fact regarded by the rest of us, as a person of no little consequence ; and though she sometimes condescended to make visits, she was not often anxious to have them returned. Cassy, however, had been once at her house. There were two little rooms in front, into which she was freely admitted ; but the room behind was locked, and it was whispered among the servants, that colonel Moore kept the key, so that even Miss Ritty herself

did not enter it except in his company.   This perhaps
was scandal ; but Cassy recollected to have noticed
that the windows of this room were protected against
impertinent curiosity, by close blinds on the outside ;
and she no longer doubted where she was.

She told Miss Ritty as much, and inquired, if her
mistress knew of her return.

Miss Ritty could not tell.

She asked if her mistress had got another maid in
her place.

Miss Ritty did not know.

She begged for permission to go and see her mistress ; but that, Miss Ritty said, was impossible.

She requested that her mistress might be told where
she was ; and that she wished very much to see her.
Miss Ritty said that she would be glad to oblige her,
but she was not much in the habit of going to the
House, and the last time she was there, Mrs Moore
had spoken to her so spitefully, that she was determined never to go again, unless she were absolutely obliged to.

Having thus exhausted every resource, poor Cassy
threw herself upon the bed, hid her face in the bed-
clothes, and sought relief in tears.

It was now Miss Ritty's turn.   She patted the poor
girl on the shoulder, bade her not be down-hearted,
and unlocking a bureau which stood in the room, she
took out a dress which she pronounced to be mighty
handsome.   She bade Cassy get up and put it on, for
her master would be coming presently.   This was
what Cassy feared ; but she hoped, if she could not

escape the visit, at least to defer it. So she told Miss Ritty that she was too sick to see any body ; she absolutely refused to look at her dresses, and begged to be allowed to die in peace. Miss Ritty laughed when she spoke of dying ; yet she seemed a little alarmed at the idea of it, and inquired what was the matter.

Cassy told her that she had seen and suffered enough that day, to kill any body ; that her head was sick and her heart was broken, and the sooner death came to her relief the better. She then mustered courage to mention my name, and endeavored to discover what had become of me. Miss Ritty again shook her head and declared that she could give no information.

At this moment the door opened, and colonel Moore came in. He had a haggard and guilty look. The flush which overspread his face, when she had last seen him, was wholly gone ; his countenance was pale and ghastly. She had never seen him look so before, and she trembled at the sight of him. He bade Ritty begone ; but told her to wait in the front room as perhaps he might need her assistance. He bolted the door, and sat down on the bed by Cassy's side. She started up in terror, and retired to the farthest corner of the room. He smiled scornfully, and bade her come back and sit down beside him. She obeyed ;—for however reluctant, she could do no better. He took her hand, and threw one arm about her waist. Again she shrank from him and would have fled ; but he stamped his foot impatiently, and in a harsh tone, bade her be quiet.

For a moment he was silent;—then changing his manner, he summoned up his habitual smile, and began in that mild, gentle, insinuating tone, in which he was quite unsurpassed. He plied her with flattery, soft words and generous promises. He reproached her, but without any harshness, for her attempts to evade the kindness he intended her. He then spoke of me ; but no sooner had he entered on that subject than his voice rose, his face became flushed again, and he seemed in manifest danger of loosing his temper.

She interrupted him, and besought him to tell her how I did and what had become of me. He answered that I was well enough ; much better than I deserved to be ; but she need give herself no further thought or trouble on that score, for he intended to send me out of the country as soon as I was able to travel, and she need not hope nor expect ever to see me again.

She throw herself at his feet and begged that she might be sent off and sold with me. He affected to be greatly surprised at this request, and inquired why she made it. She told him, that after all that had happened, it were better that she should not live any longer in his family ;—beside, if she were sold at the same time, the same person might buy her that bought her husband. That word, husband, put him into a violent passion. He told her that she had no husband, and wanted none ; for he would be better than a husband to her. He said that he was tired of her folly, and with a significant look, he bade her not be a fool, but to leave off whining and crying, be a good girl, and do as her master desired ; was it not a servant's duty to obey her master ?

She told him that she was sick and wretched, and begged him to leave her. Instead of doing so, he threw his arms about her neck, and declared that her being sick was all imagination, for he had never seen her look half so handsome.

She started up ;—but he caught her in his arms, and dragged her towards the bed. Even at that terrible moment her presence of mind did not forsake her. She exerted all her strength, and succeeded in break-away from his hateful embraces. Then summoning up all her energies, she looked him in the face, as well as her tears would allow her, and striving to command her voice, " Master,—Father," she cried, " what is it you would have of your own daughter ?"

Colonel Moore staggered as if a bullet had struck him. A burning blush overspread his face ; he would have spoken, but the words seemed to stick in his throat. This confusion was only for a moment. In an instant he recovered his self-possession, and with out taking any notice of her last appeal, he merely said, that if she was really sick, he did not wish to trouble her. With these words he unbolted the door, and walked out of the room.

She heard him talking with Miss Ritty ; and he had been gone but a few moments, before she entered. She began with a long string of questions about what colonel Moore had said and done ; but when Cassy did not seem inclined to give her any answer, she laughed, and thanked her, and told her she need not trouble herself, for she had been peeping and listening at the key-hole, the whole time. She said, she could not imagine, why Cassy made such a fuss. In a very young girl it might be excusable ; but in one as old as she was, and a married woman too, she could not understand it. Such is the morality, and such the modesty to be expected in a slave !

The poor girl was in no humor for controversy ; so she listened to this ribaldry without making any answer to it. Yet even at this moment, a faint ray of hope began to display itself. It occurred to her, that if Miss Ritty could be made sensible of the risk she ran in aiding to create herself a rival, she would not be pleased at the prospect of being perhaps supplanted in a situation, which she seemed to find so very agreeable. This idea appeared to offer some chance of gaining over Miss Ritty to aid her in escaping from Spring-Meadow; and at once, she resolved to act upon it. It was necessary to be cautious and to feel her way, lest by piqueing the girl's pride, she might deprive herself of all the advantage to be gained from working upon her fears.

She approached the subject gradually, and soon placed it in a light, in which, it was plain, her companion had never viewed it. When it was first suggested to her, she expressed a deal of confidence in her own beauty, and affected to have no fears ;—yet it soon became obvious, that notwithstanding all her boasting, she was a good deal alarmed. Indeed it was quite impossible for her, to look her anticipated rival in the face, and not to be so. Cassy was well pleased to see the effect of her suggestions ; and began to entertain some serious hopes of once more making her escape.

It was, to be sure, a miserable, and most probably an ineffectual resource, this running away. But what else could she do ? What other hope was there of escaping a fate which all her womanly and all her religious feelings taught her to regard with the utmost horror and detestation ? This was her only chance ; she would try it, and trust in God's aid to give her endeavors a happy issue.

She now told Ritty distinctly, how she felt, what she intended, and what assistance she wanted. Her new confederate applauded her resolution. "Certainly, if colonel Moore was really her father, that did make a difference ; and her being a methodist might help to account for her feelings, for she knew that sort of folks were mighty strict in all their notions."

But though Miss Ritty was ready enough to encourage and applaud, she seemed very reluctant to take any active part in aiding and abetting an escape, which though apparently it tended to promote her interests, might end, if her agency in it were discovered, in bringing her into danger and disgrace.

Several plans were talked over, but Miss Ritty had some objection to all of them. She preferred any thing to the risk of being suspected by her master, of plotting to defeat his wishes. As they found great difficulty in fixing upon any feasible plan, it was agreed at last, in order to gain time, to give out that Cassy was extremely sick. This indeed was hardly a fiction; —for nothing but the very critical nature of her situation had enabled the poor girl to sustain herself against the shocks and miseries of the last four and twenty hours. Ritty undertook to pursuade her master, that the best thing he could do, was to let her alone till she got better. She would promise to take her into training in the mean time, and was to assure colonel Moore, that she did not doubt of being soon able to convince her, that it was both her interest and her duty, to comply with her master's wishes.

So far things went extremely well. They had hardly arranged their plan, before they heard colonel Moore's step in the outer room. Ritty ran to him, and succeeded in pursuading him to go away without any attempt to see Cassy. He commended her zeal, and promised to be governed by her advice. The next day a circumstance happened which neither Cassy nor Ritty had anticipated, but which proved very favorable to their design. Colonel Moore was obliged to set off for Baltimore, without delay. Some pressing call of business, made his immediate departure indispensable. Before setting out, however, he found time to visit Miss Ritty, and to enjoin upon her to keep a watchful eye upon Cassy, and to take care and bring her to her senses, before his return.

If Cassy was to escape at all, now was her time. She soon hit upon a scheme. Her object was, to screen Ritty from suspicion as much as to favor her own flight. Luckily the same arrangement might be made to accomplish both purposes. Cassy could only escape through the door or out of the windows. Escaping through the door was out of the question, be-

cause Ritty had the key of it, and was supposed to be
sleeping or watching, or both together, in the front
room. The escape then must be by the windows.
These did not lift up as is commonly the case, but
opened upon hinges on the inside. The blinds by
which they were guarded on the outside were slats
nailed across the window-frames and not intended to
be opened. These must be cut or broken, and as they
were of pine, this was a task of no great difficulty. Ritty brought a couple of table knives, and assisted in cutting them away,—though according to the story she
was to tell her master, she was sleeping all the time,
most soundly and unsuspiciously, and Cassy must have
secretly cut away the slats with a pocket-knife.

Early in the evening of colonel Moore's departure,
every thing was ready, and Cassy was to sally forth as
soon as she dared to venture. Ritty agreed not to
give any notice of her escape till late the next day.
This delay she could account for by the plea of not
being able to find the overseer, and by a pretended un-
certainty as to whether it would be colonel Moore's
wish, that the overseer should be informed at all about
the matter. At all events, they hoped that no very
vigorous pursuit would be made until colonel Moore's
return.

Cassy now made ready for her departure. She felt
a pang at the idea of leaving me ;—but as Ritty could
not or would not tell her what had become of me, and
as she knew, that separated and helpless as we were,
it was impossible for us to render each other any assistance, she rightly judged, that she would best serve me,

and best comply with my wishes, by adopting the only plan, that seemed to carry with it any likelihood of preserving herself from the violence she dreaded.

Cassy had supplied herself from Ritty's allowance, with food enough to last for several days. It was now quite dark, and time for her to go. She kissed her hostess and confederate, who seemed much affected at dismissing her on so lonely and hopeless an adventure, and who freely gave her what little money she had. Cassy was a good deal touched at this unexpected generosity. She let herself down from the window, bade Ritty farewell, and summoning up all her resolution and self-command, she took the nearest way across the fields, towards the high-road. This road was little traveled except by the people of Spring-Meadow and one or two other neighboring plantations, and at this hour of the evening, there was little danger of meeting any body, except perhaps a night-walking slave, who would be as anxious as herself to avoid being seen. There was no moon,—but the glimmer of the star-light served to guide her steps. She felt no apprehension of losing her way, for she had frequently been in the carriage with her mistress, as far as the little village at the court-house of the county ; and it was hither, that in the first instance, she determined to go.

She arrived there, without having met a single soul. As yet there were no signs of morning. All was still, save the monotonous chirpings of the summer insects, interrupted now and then by the crowing of a cock or the barking of a watch-dog. The village consisted of a dilapidated court-house, a black-smith's shop, a tav-

ern, two or three stores, and half a dozen scattered
houses. It was situated at the meeting of two roads.
One of these she knew, led into the road that ran towards Baltimore. She had flattered herself with the
idea of reaching that city, where she had many acquaintances, and where she hoped she might find protection and employment. Her chance of ever getting
there was very small. Baltimore was some two or
three hundred miles distant; and she did not even
know which of the roads that met at the court-house
she ought to take. She could not inquire the way,
beg a cup of cold water, or even be seen upon the
road, without the greatest danger of being taken up
as a run-away, and carried back to the master from
whom she was flying.

After hesitating for some time, she took one of the
roads that offered themselves to her choice, and walked
on with vigor. The excitement of the last day or two
seemed to give her an unnatural strength, for after a
walk of some twenty miles, she felt fresher than at
first. But the light of the morning dawn, which began
to show itself, reminded her that it was no longer safe
to pursue her journey. Close by the road side was a
friendly thicket, the shrubs and weeds all dripping with
the dew. She had gone but a little way among them,
when she found them so high and close as to furnish a
sufficient hiding-place. She knelt down, and destitute
as she was of human assistance, she besought the aid
and guardian care of Heaven. After eating a scanty
meal,—for it was necessary to husband her provisions,
—she scraped the leaves together into a rude bed, and

composed herself to sleep. The three preceding nights she had scarcely slept at all,—but she made it up now, for she did not wake till late in the afternoon.

As soon as evening closed in, she started again, and walked as vigorously as before. The road forked frequently ; and she had no means of determining which of the various courses she ought to follow. She took one or the other, as her judgment, or rather as her fancy decided ; and she comforted herself with the notion, that whether right or wrong in her selections, at all events, she was getting further from Spring-Meadow.

In the course of the night she met several travelers. Some of them passed without seeming to notice her. She discovered some at a distance and concealed herself in the bushes till they had passed. But she did not always escape so easily. More than once, she was stopped and questioned,—but luckily she succeeded in giving satisfactory answers. Indeed there was nothing in her complexion, especially in the uncertain light of the evening, that would clearly indicate her to be a slave ; and in answering the questions that were put to her, she took care to say nothing that would betray her condition. One of the men who questioned her, shook his head, and did not seem satisfied ; another, sat on his horse and watched her till she was fairly out of sight ; a third told her, that she was a very suspicious character ;—but all three suffered her to pass. She was the less liable to interruption, because in Virginia, the houses of the inhabitants are not generally situated along the public roads. The planters usually prefer to build at some distance from the high way,—and the roads, passing along the highest and most barren tracts, wind their weary length through a desolate, and what seems almost an uninhabited country. When morning approached again, she concealed herself as before, and waited for the return of night to pursue her journey.

She proceeded in this way for four days, or rather nights, at the end of which time her provisions were entirely exhausted. She had wandered she knew not whither,—and the hope of reaching Baltimore, which at first had lightened her fatigue, was now quite gone. She knew not what to do. To go much further without assistance was scarcely possible. Yet should she ask any where for food or guidance, though she stood some chance perhaps of passing for a free white woman, still her complexion, and the circumstance of her travelling alone, might cause her to be suspected as a run-away, and very probably, she would be stopped, put into some jail, and detained there, till suspicion was changed into certainty.

She was traveling slowly along, the fifth night, exhausted with hunger and fatigue, and reflecting upon her unhappy situation, when descending a hill, the road came suddenly upon the banks of a broad river. There was no bridge ; but a ferry boat was fastened to the shore, and close by was the ferry house, which seemed also to be a tavern. Here was a new perplexity. She could not cross the river without calling up the ferry people or waiting till they made their appearance, and this would be exposing herself at once

to that risk of detection which she had resolved to defer to the very last moment.   Yet to turn back and seek
another road seemed to be an expedient equally desperate.   Any other road, which did not lead in a direction opposite to that which she wished to follow, would
be likely to bring her again upon the banks of the same
river ; and as she could not live without food, she
would be soon compelled to apply somewhere for assistance, and to face the detection she was so anxious
to avoid.

   She sat down by the road side, resolved to wait for
the morning and to take her chance.   There was a
field of corn near the house, and the stalks were covered with roasting ears.   She had no fire, nor the means
of kindling one, but the sweet milky taste of the unripe
kernels served to satisfy the cravings of hunger.

   She had chosen a place where she could observe
the first movements about the ferry house.   The
morning had but just dawned, when she saw a man
open the door and come out of it.   He was black, and
she walked boldly up to him, and told him that she
was in great haste and wished to be taken across the
ferry immediately.   The fellow seemed rather surprised at seeing a woman, a traveler, alone, and at that
hour of the morning ;—but after staring at her a minute
or two, he appeared to recollect that here was an opportunity of turning an honest penny, and muttering
something about the earliness of the hour, and the ferry
boat not starting till after sunrise, he offered to take
her across in a canoe, for half a dollar.   This price
she did not hesitate to pay ; and the fellow no doubt,

put it into his own pocket, without ever recollecting to
hand it over to his master, or to mention a word to
him about this early passenger.

They entered the boat, and he paddled her across.
She did not dare to ask any questions, lest she should
betray herself, and she did her best to quiet the curiosity of the boatman, who however, was very civil and
easily satisfied. Having landed on the opposite shore,
she traveled on a mile or two further. By this time
it was broad day-light and she concealed herself as
usual.

At night, she set out again. But she was faint with
hunger, her shoes were almost worn out, her feet were
swollen and very painful, and altogether, her situation
was any thing but comfortable. She seemed to have
got off the high-way, and to be traveling some cross-
road, which wound along through dreary and deserted
fields, and appeard to be very little frequented. All
that night, she did not meet a single person or pass a
single house. Painful as was the effort, she still struggled to drag along her weary steps; but her spirits
were broken, her heart was sinking, and her strength
was almost gone. At length the morning dawned;
but the wretched Cassy did not seek her customary
hiding-place. She still kept on in hopes of reaching
some house. She was now quite subdued; and chose to
risk her liberty, and even to hazard being carried
back to Spring-Meadow and subjected to the fearful
fate from which she was flying, rather than perish with
hunger and fatigue. Sad indeed it is, that the noblest
resolution and the loftiest stubbornness of soul is com-

pelled so often to yield to the base necessities of animal nature, and from a paltry and irrational fear of death,—of which tyrants have ever known so well to take advantage,—to sink down from the lofty height of heroic virtue, to the dastard submissiveness of a craven and obedient slave !

She had not gone far before she saw a low mean looking house by the road side. It was a small building of logs, blackened with age, and not a little dilapidated. Half the panes or more, were wanting in the two or three little windows with which it was provided, and their places were supplied by old hats, old coats, and pieces of plank. The door seemed dropping from its hinges ; and there was no enclosure of any kind about the house, unless that name might properly be given to the tall weeds with which it was surrounded. Altogether, it showed most manifest signs of thriftless and comfortless indolence.

She knocked softly at the door, and a female voice, but a rough and harsh one, bade her come in. There was no hall or entry ; the out-door opened directly into the only room ; and on entering, she found it occupied by a middle aged woman, barefooted, and in a slovenly dress, with her uncombed hair hanging about a haggard and sun-burnt face. She was setting a rickety table, and seemed to be making preparations for breakfast. The house had but one room, of which one side was almost wholly taken up by an enormous fire place. A fire was burning in it, and the corn cakes were baking in the ashes. In the opposite corner was a low bed, on which a man, the master of the family most likely, lay still a-sleep, undisturbed by the cries and clamors of half-a-dozen brats, who had been tumbling and bawling about the house, unwashed, uncombed and half naked, but who were seized with sudden silence, and slunk behind their mother, at the sight of a stranger.

The woman pointed to a rude sort of stool or bench, which seemed the only piece of furniture in the nature of a chair, which the house contained, and asked Cassy to sit down. She did so ; and her hostess eyed her sharply, and seemed to wait with a good deal of curiosity to hear who she was, and what she wanted. As soon as Cassy could collect her thoughts, she told her hostess that she was traveling from Richmond to Baltimore to see a sick sister. She was poor and friendless, and was obliged to go on foot. She had lost her way, and had wandered about all night, without knowing where she was, or whither she was going. She was half dead, she added, with hunger and fatigue, and wanted food and rest, and such directions about the road, as might enable her to pursue her journey. At the same time she took out her purse, in order to show that she was able to pay for what she wanted.

Her hostess, notwithstanding her rude and poverty-stricken appearance, seemed touched with this pitiful story. She told her to put up her money ; she said she did not keep a tavern, and that she was able to give a poor woman a breakfast, without being paid for it.

Cassy was too faint and weak to be much in a humor for talking ; besides, she trembled at every word, less she might drop some unguarded expression that

would serve to betray her. But now that the ice was
broken, the curiosity of her hostess could not be kept
under. She overwhelmed her with a torrent of questions, and every time Cassy hesitated, or gave any
sign of confusion, she turned her keen grey eyes upon
her, with a sharp and penetrating expression that increased her disorder.

Pretty soon the ash-cakes were baked, and the other
preparations for breakfast were finished, when the woman shook her good man roughly by the shoulder, and
bade him bestir himself. This connubial salutation
roused the sleeper. He sat up on the bed and stared
about the room with a vacant gaze; but the redness
of his eyes, and the sallow paleness of his face, seemed to show thst he had not quite slept off the effects of
the last night's frolic. The wife appeared to know
what was wanting; for she forthwith produced the
whiskey-jug, and poured out a large dose of the raw
spirit. Her husband drank it off with a relish, and
with a trembling hand, returned the broken glass to his
wife, who filled it half full and emptied it herself.
Then turning to Cassy, and remarking, that, " a body
was fit for nothing till they had got their morning bit-
ters," she offered her a dram, and seemed not a little
astonished at its being declined.

The good man then began leisurely to dress himself;
and had half finished his toilette before he seemed to
notice that there was company in the house. He now
came forward and bade the stranger good morning.
His wife immediately drew him aside, and they began
an earnest whispering. Now and then they would

both look Cassy in the face, and as she was conscious
that she must be the subject of their conversation, she
began to feel a good deal of embarrasment, which she
was too little practised in deceit to be able to conceal.
This matrimonial conference over, the good woman
bade Cassy draw up her stool and sit down at the
breakfast table. The breakfast consisted of hot corn-
cakes and cold bacon, a palatable meal enough in any
case, but which Cassy's long starvation made her look
upon as the most delicious she had ever eaten. Sweet
indeed, ought to be that mess of pottage, for which
one sells the birthright of freedom !

She ate with an appetite which she could not restrain ; and her hostess seemed a good deal surprised
and a little alarmed, at the rapidity with which the
table was cleared. Breakfast being finished, the man
of the house began to question her. He asked her
about Richmond, and whether she knew such and such
persons, who, as he said, were living there. Cassy had
never been in Richmond, and knew the town only by
name. Of course, her answers were very little to the
purpose. She blushed and stammered and held down
her head, and the man completed her confusion by
telling her, that it was very plain she had not come
from Richmond, as she pretended ; for he was well acquainted with the place, and it was clear enough, from
her answers, that she knew nothing about it. He told
her that it was no use to deny it ;—her face betrayed
her ;—and he reckoned, if the truth was told, she
was no better than a run-away. At the sound of this
word, the blood rushed into her face, and her heart

sunk within her. It was in vain, that she denied, protested, and entreated. Her terror, confusion and alarm only served to give new assurance to her captors, who seemed to chuckle over their prize, and to amuse themselves with her fright and misery, very much as a cat plays with the mouse it has caught.

He told her that if she were in fact a free woman, there was not the slightest ground for alarm. If she had no free papers with her, she would only have to lie in jail till she could send to Richmond and get them. That was all!

But that was more than enough for poor Cassy. No proofs of freedom could she produce ; and her going to jail would be almost certain to end in her being restored to colonel Moore, and becoming the wretched victim of his rage and lust. That fate, must be deferred as long as possible, and there seemed but one way of escaping it.

She confessed that she was a slave, and a run-away; but she positively refused to tell the name of her master. He lived, she said, a great way off; and she had run away from him not out of any spirit of discontent or disobedience, but because his cruelty and injustice were too great to be endured. There was nothing she would not choose rather than to fall into his hands again ; if they would only save her from that,— if they would only let her live with them, she would be their faithful and obedient servant as long as she lived.

The man and his wife looked at each other and seemed pleased with the idea. They walked aside and talked it over. Nothing appeared to deter them from accepting her proposal, at once, but the fear of being detected in harboring and detaining a run-away. Cassy did her best to quiet these apprehensions ; and after a short struggle, avarice and the dear delight of power triumphed over their fears, and Cassy became the property of Mr Proctor ; for so the man was named. His property, as he might speciously argue, by her own consent,—a ten times better title, than the vast majority of his countrymen could boast.

To prevent suspicions among the neighbors, it was agreed that Cassy should pass for a free woman, whom Mr Proctor had hired ; and as this gentleman had been so fortunate as to have been initiated into the art and mystery of penmanship, an accomplishment somewhat rare among the ' poor white folks' of Virginia, in order that Cassy might be prepared to answer impertinent questions, he gave her free-papers, which he forged for the occasion.

It was a great thing to have escaped returning to Spring-Meadow. But for all that, Cassy discovered, that her present situation would not prove very agreeable. Mr Proctor was the descendant and representative of what, at no distant period, had been a rich and very respectable family. The frequent division of a large estate, which nobody took any pains to increase, while all diminished it by idleness, dissipation and bad management, had left Mr Proctor's father in possession of a few slaves and a considerable tract of worn-out land. At his death, the slaves had been sold to pay his debts, and the land, being divided

among his numerous children, had made Mr Proctor
the possessor of a few barren acres. But though
left with this miserable pittance, he had been brought
up, in the dissipated and indolent habits of a Virginian
gentleman ; the land he owned, which was so poor
and worthless that none of his numerous creditors
thought it worth their while to disturb him in the possession of it, still entitled him to the dignity of a free-
holder and a voter ; and he felt himself as much above,
what is esteemed in that country, the base and degraded condition of a laborer, as the richest aristocrat in
the whole state. He was as proud, as lazy, and as
dissipated as any of the nabobs, his neighbors ; and
devoted the principal part of his time to gambling,
politics and drink.

Luckily for Mr Proctor, his wife was a very notable
woman. She boasted no patrician blood ; and when
her husband began to talk, as he often did, about
the antiquity and respectability of his family, she
would cut him short by observing, that she thought
herself full as good as he was,—but for all that, her ancestors had been 'poor folks' as far back as any body
knew any thing about them. If the question between
aristocracy and democracy were to be settled by the
experience of the Proctors, the plebeians, most un-
doubtedly, would carry the day ; for while her husband
did little or nothing but frolic, drink and ride about the
country, Mrs Proctor plowed, planted and gathered in
the crop. But for her energy and industry, it is much
to be feared that Mr Proctor's aristocratic habits would

have soon made himself and his family a burden upon the county.

Cassy's services were a great accession to this establishment. Her new mistress seemed resolved to make the most of them, and the poor girl before long, was almost completely broken down, by a degree and a kind of labor to which she was totally unaccustomed. Two or three times a week, at least, Mr Proctor came home drunk ; and on these occasions, he bluster-ed about, threatened his wife, and beat and abused his children without any sort of mercy. Cassy could hardly expect to come off better than they did ;—indeed his drunken abuse would have become quite intolerable, if the energetic Mrs Proctor had not known how to quell it. At first, she used mild meas-ures, and coaxed and flattered him into quiet ; but when these means failed, she would tumble him into bed, by main strength, and compel him to lie still by the terror of the broom-stick.

It was nothing but the wholesome authority, which Mrs Proctor exercised over her husband, that pro-tected Cassy against what she dreaded even more than Mr Proctor's drunken rudeness. Whenever he could find her alone, he tormented her with solicitations of a most distressing kind ; and nothing could rid her of his importunities, except the threat of complaining to Mrs Proctor. But her troubles did not end even here. Mrs Proctor listened to her complaints, thanked her for the information, and said she would speak to Mr Proctor about it. But she could not imagine that a slave could possibly be endowed with the slightest

particle of that virtue, of which the free women of
Virginia boast the exclusive possession. Full of this
notion, she judged it highly improbable, whatever merit
Cassy might pretend to claim, that she had actually resisted the importunities and solicitations of so very se-
ducing a fellow as Mr Proctor ; and filled with all the
spite and fury of female jealousy, she delighted herself
with torturing and tormenting the object of her suspicions. Mrs Proctor, with all her merit, had one
little foible which, most likely she had adopted out of
compliment to her husband. She thought a daily dram
of whiskey necessary to keep off the fever and
ague ; and when through inadvertance, as sometimes
would happen, she doubled the dose, it seemed to give
a new edge to the natural keenness of her temper. On
these occasions, she plied both words and blows with a
fearful energy ; and though perhaps it were difficult to
say which of the two was most to be dreaded, both
together they were enough to exhaust the patience of a
saint.

Poor Cassy could discover no means of delivering
herself from this complication of miseries, under which
she was ready to sink, when she was most unexpect-
edly relieved, by the unsolicited interference of a couple
of Mr Proctor's neighbors. They were men of leisure
like him ; like him too, they were of good families, and one of them had received an excellent education, and was more or less distantly connected with
several of the most distinguished people in the state.
But a course of reckless dissipation had long ago stripped them of such property as they had inherited,

and reduced them to live by their wits ; which they exercised in a sort of partnership, principally on the race-course and at the gaming table.

These two speculating gentlemen were on terms of intimacy with Mr Proctor, and they knew that he had a free woman, for such they supposed Cassy to be, living at his house. In common with most Virginians, they considered the existence of a class of freed people as a great social annoyance, and likely enough in the end, seriously to endanger those ' sacred rights of property,' in defence of which there is nothing, which a true-born son of liberty ought not to be proud to undertake. Instigated doubtless, by such patriotic notions, these public-spirited persons judged that they would be rendering the state a service,—to say nothing of the money they might put into their own pockets,—by applying to this great political evil, so far at least as Cassy was a party to it, a remedy, which the doctrines of more than one of the Virginian statesmen, and the spirit of more than one of the Virginian statutes would seem fully to sanction. In plain English, they resolved to seize Cassy and sell her for a slave !

The business of kidnapping is one of the native fruits of the American system of slavery ; and is as common, and as well organized in many parts of the United States, as the business of horse-stealing is, in many other countries. When they take to stealing slaves, the business of these adventurers becomes very hazardous ; but while they confine themselves to stealing only free people, they can pursue their vo-

cation with comparatively little danger. They may
perhaps inflict some trifling personal wrong ;—but according to the doctrines of some of the most popular
among the American politicians, they are doing the public no inconsiderable service ; since, in their opinion,
nothing seems to be wanting to render the slave-holding states of America a perfect paradise, except the
extermination of the emancipated class. It was no
doubt, by some such lofty notions of the public good,
that Cassy's friends were actuated. At all events,
those sophistries which tyranny has invented to justify
oppresssion, are as much an apology for them as for
any one else.

As far as Cassy could learn, their scheme was pretty
much as follows. They invited Mr Proctor to a
drinking frolic, and as soon as the whiskey had reduced him to a state of insensibility, a message was sent
to his wife that her husband was taken dangerously ill,
and that she must instantly come to his assistance.
Notwithstanding a few domestic jars, Mr and Mrs
Proctor were a most loving couple ; and the good
woman, greatly alarmed at this unexpected news, immediately set out to visit her husband. The conspira-
tors had followed their own messenger, and were concealed in a thicket close to the house watching for her
departure. She was hardly out of sight, before they
rushed into the field where Cassy was at work, bound
her hand and foot, put her into a sort of covered waggon or carry-all which they had provided for the occasion, and drove off as fast as possible. They traveled
all that day, and the following night. Early the next

morning, they reached a small village where they met
a slave-trader with a gang of slaves, on his way to
Richmond. The gentlemen-thieves soon struck up a
bargain with the gentleman slave-trader ; and having
received their money, they delivered Cassy into his
possession.

He seemed touched with her beauty and her distress, and treated her with a kindness which she hardly
expected from one of his profession. Her shoes and
clothes were nearly worn out. He bought her new
ones,—and as she was half dead with fatigue, terror
and want of sleep, he even went so far as to wait a day
at the village in order that she might recover a little
before setting out, on the journey to Richmond.

But she soon found that she was expected to make
a return for all these favors. When they stopped for
the night, at the end of the first day's journey, she received an intimation that she was to share the bed of
her master ; and directions were given to her how
and when to come there. These directions she saw
fit to disregard. In the morning her master called
her to account. He laughed in her face, when she
spoke of the wickedness of what he had commanded,
and told her he did not want her to be preaching any
of her sermons to him. He would excuse her disobedience this time ; but she must take very good care
not to repeat it.

The next evening she received directions similar to
those which had been given her the day before ; and
again she disobeyed them. Her master, who had
been drinking and gambling half the night, with some

boon companions whom he found at the tavern, enrag-
ed at not finding her in his room as he had expected
sallied forth in pursuit of her. Luckily he was too
drunk to know very well where he was going. He
had gone but a few steps from the tavern door, before he
stumbled over a pile of wood, and injured himself very
seriously. His cries soon brought some of the tavern's people to his assistance. They carried him to his
room, bound up his bruises, and put him to bed.

It was late the next morning before he was able to
rise ; but he was no sooner up than he resolved to
take ample vengeance for his disappointment and his
bruises. He came hobbling to the tavern door, with a
crutch in one hand and a whip in the other. He had
all his slaves paraded before the house, and made two
of the stoutest fellows among them hold Cassy by the
arms, while he plied the whip. Her cries soon collected the idlers and loungers, who seem to constitute the principal population of a Virginian village.
Some inquired the cause of the whipping, but without
seeming to think the question of consequence enough
to wait for an answer. It seemed to be the general
opinion that the master was tipsy, and had chosen
this way to vent his drunken humors ; but whether
drunk or sober, nobody thought of interfering with his
‘ sacred and unquestionable rights.’ On the contrary,
all looked on with unconcern, if not with approbation ;
and the greater number seemed as much pleased with
the sport, as so many boys would have been, with
the baiting of an unlucky cat.

Just in the midst of this proceeding, a handsome

traveling carriage drove up to the door. There were two ladies in it, and they no sooner saw what was going on, than with that humanity, so natural to the female heart, that not even the horrid customs and detestable usages of slave-holding tyranny can totally extinguish it, they begged the brutal savage to leave beating the poor girl, and tell them what was the matter. The fellow reluctantly dropped the lash, and answered in a surly tone, that she was an insolent disobedient baggage, not fit to be noticed by two such ladies, and that he was only giving her a little wholesome correction. However, this did not seem to satisfy them ; and in the mean time the carriage steps were let down and they got out. Poor Cassy was sobbing and crying and scarcely able to utter a word ; her hair had fallen down over her face and shoulders ; and her cheeks were all stained with tears. Yet even in this situation, the two ladies seemed struck with her appearance. They entered into conversation with her, and soon found that she had been bred a ladies' maid, and that her present master was a slave-trader. These ladies, it seemed, had been traveling at the north ; and while on their journey, had lost a female servant by a sudden and violent attack of fever. They were now on their return to Carolina ; and the younger of the two, suggested to her mother, for such their relation proved to be, to buy Cassy to supply the place of the maid they had lost. The mother started some objections to purchasing a stranger, about whom they knew nothing, and who had been sold by her former owner, they knew not for what reasons. But when Cassy's

tears and prayers and supplications, were added to the
entreaties of her daughter, she found herself quite unable to resist ; and she sent to ask the man his price.
He named it.   It was a high one ;—but Mrs Montgomery, for that was the lady's name, was one of those
people, who when they have made up their minds to
do a generous action, are not easily to be shaken from
their purpose. She took Cassy into the house with
her, ordered the trunks to be brought in, and told the
man to make out his bill of sale. The purchase was
no sooner completed, than her new mistress took
Cassy up stairs and soon fitted her with a dress better
becoming her new situation, than did the coarse gown
and heavy shoes for which she was indebted to the
generosity of her late master.

Cassy was dressed, the bill of sale was delivered,
and the money paid, when Mrs Montgomery's brother
and traveling companion rode up. He rallied his sister not a little, on what he called her foolish propensity
to interfere between other people and their servants ;
he took her to task rather severely, for the imprudence
of her purchase, and the high price she had paid ; and
he told her with a smile and a shake of the head, that
one time or other, her foolish confidence and generosity would be her ruin. Mrs Montgomery took her
brother's raillery all in good part ; the carriage was
ordered, and they proceeded together on their journey.

The ladies with whom Cassy had come to the meeting, were Mrs Montgomery and her daughter. They
lived some ten miles from Carleton-Hall. So near
had Cassy and myself been to each other for six long

months or more, without knowing it. Cassy spoke of her mistress with the greatest affection. Her gratitude was unbounded ; and she seemed to find a real pleasure and enjoyment in serving a benefactress who treated her with a gentle and uniform kindness, not often exerted even by those who are capable of momentary acts of the greatest generosity.

As Cassy finished her story, she threw her arms about my neck, leaned her head upon my bosom, and looking me in the face, while the tears were streaming from her eyes, she heaved a sigh, and whispered that she was too, too happy ! With such a mistress, and restored, so unexpectedly to the arms of a husband, whom, fondly as she loved him, she feared to have lost forever, what more could she desire !

Alas poor girl !—she forgot that we were slaves ;— and that the very next day might again separate us, subject us to other masters, and renew my tortures and her miseries !

CHAPTER II.

BEFORE we had half finished what we had to say to each other, the movement of the people on the hill-side informed us that the morning's religious services were over. Never before had one of my master's sermons seemed so short to me. We hastened towards the spot; I to receive my master's orders, and Cassy to attend upon her mistress. As we came near the rural pulpit, I observed Mr Carleton in conversation with two ladies, who proved to Mrs Montgomery and her daughter. We stopped at a little distance from them. Miss Montgomery looked around, and seeing us standing together, she beckoned to Cassy, and pointing to me, she inquired if that was the husband, who had put her into such a flutter that morning? This question drew the notice of the other two, and my master seemed a little surprised at seeing me in this new character. " What's this Archy" he said, " what is the meaning of all this? It is the first I ever heard of your being married. You don't pretend to claim that pretty girl there for your wife?"

I replied that she was indeed, my wife, though it was now some two years or more, since we had seen or known any thing of each other. I added, that I had never mentioned my marriage to him, because I had despaired of ever seeing my wife again; and now, it was nothing but the merest accident that had brought us together.

" Well Archy if she is your wife, I don't know how I can help it, though I suppose I shall have you spending half your time at Poplar-Grove ;—is not that what your place is called Mrs Montgomery ?"

She said it was ;—and after a moment's pause, observed, that too little respect, she feared, was often paid to the matrimonial connexions of servants. For her part, she could not but regard them as sacred ; and if Cassy and myself were really married, and I was a decent, civil fellow, she had no objection to my visiting Poplar-Grove, as often as Mr Carleton would permit me.

My master undertook to answer for my good behavior ; and turning to me, he bade me bring up the horses. I made all the haste I could ; but before I returned, Mrs Montgomery was gone, and Cassy with her. We mounted, and had already taken the road to Carlton-Hall, when my master seemed to recollect that I had just found a wife from whom I had been long separated ; and it began to occur to him, that possibly we might take some pleasure in being indulged with a little of one another's company. He gave me joy of my discovery, with an air half serious, half jocose,—as if in doubt whether a slave were properly entitled to a master's serious sympathy,—and remarked, in a careless tone, that perhaps I would like to spend the remainder of the day at Poplar-Grove.

As I knew that Mr Carleton had much real goodness of heart, I had long since learned to put up with

his cavalier manner ; and however little I might be
pleased with the style in which he made the offer, the
matter of his present proposal was so much to my
fancy, that I eagerly caught at it. He took his pencil
from his pocket, and wrote me a pass ; I asked and
received such directions as he could give me about the
way ; and putting spurs to my horse, I soon overtook
Mrs Montgomery's carriage, which I followed to Poplar-Grove.

This was one of those pretty, and even elegant country seats, which are sometimes seen, though very seldom, in Virginia and the Carolinas; and which may serve
to prove that the inhabitants of those states, notwithstanding their almost universal negligence of such matters, are not totally destitute of all ideas of architectural
beauty and domestic comfort. The approach to the
house was through a broad avenue of old and venerable oaks. The buildings had the appearance of considerable antiquity ; but they were in perfect repair,
and the grounds and fences were neat and well kept.

As the ladies left the carriage I came up. I told
Mrs Montgomery that my master had given me leave
to visit my wife, and I hoped she would have no objection to my spending the afternoon there.

Mrs Montgomery answered, that Cassy was too
good a girl to be denied any reasonable indulgence ;
and as long as I behaved well she would never make
any objection to my coming to see her. She put me
several questions about our marriage and separation ;
and the softness of her voice and the unassuming gen-

tleness of her manner, satisfied me that she was an amiable and kind-hearted woman.

No doubt, through the broad extent of slave-holding America, there are many amiable women, and good mistresses. Yet how little does their kindness avail! It reaches only here and there. It has no power to alleviate the wretchedness or to diminish the tortures of myriads of wretches, who never hear a voice softer than the overseer's, and who know no discipline milder than the lash.

The house servants at Poplar-Grove, were treated with kindness and even with indulgence, and were much attached to the family ; but as happens in so many other cases, the situation of the field hands was extremely different. Some three years before, Mrs Montgomery, by her husband's death, and the will which he left, became the owner and sole mistress of the estate. Upon this occasion, her good nature, and her sense of justice, prompted her to extend the same humane system to the management of the plantation, which she had always acted upon, in the government of her own house-hold. During her husband's life, the servant's quarter had been three miles or more from the House ; and as the slaves were never allowed to come there, unless they were sent for, Mrs Montgomery saw scarcely any thing of them, and knew very little of their wants and grievances, and next to nothing of the general management of the estate. Indeed she spent the greater portion of every year, in visiting her relations in Virginia, or in trips to the northern cities ; and when at home, her husband's manifest disinclination to her having any thing to do with those matters, had always prevented her from meddling in any way, with the plantation affairs.

But when her husband was dead, and the plantation and slaves had become her own property, she could not reconcile herself to the idea of taking no thought, concern or care for the welfare and well-being of more than an hundred human creatures, who toiled from morning to night for her sole benefit. She resolved upon a total change of system ; and ordered the servant's quarter to be removed near the house, so that she might be able to go there daily and have an opportunity of inspecting and relieving the wants and grievances of her servants.

She was shocked at the miserable pittance of food and clothing which her husband had allowed them, and at the amount of labor which he had exacted. She ordered their allowances to be increased, and their tasks to be diminished. Several instances of outrageous severity having reached her ears, she dismissed her overseer and procured a new one. The servants no sooner discovered that their mistress had interested herself in their welfare, than she was overwhelmed with petitions, appeals and complaints. One wanted a blanket, another a kettle, and a third, a pair of shoes. Each asked for some trifling gift, which it seemed very hard to refuse ; and every request that was granted was followed by half-a-dozen others, equally trifling and equally reasonable. But before the end of the year, these small items amounted to a sum sufficient to swallow up half the usual profits of the plantation. Scarcely a day passed, that Mrs Montgomery was not pestered with complaints about the severity of her new overseer ; and the servants were constantly coming to her to beg off from some threatened punishment. Two or three instances in which the overseer was checked for the tyrannical manner in which he exercised his authority, only served to increase this annoyance. She was perplexed with continual appeals, as to which she found it next to impossible to get at the truth ; since the overseer always told one story and the servants another. The second overseer was dismissed ; a third threw up his place in disgust ; and a fourth, who resolved to humor the indulgent disposition of his employer, suffered the hands to take their own course and to do pretty much as they pleased. Of course they did not care to work, while they had the choice of being idle. Every season, since Mrs Montgomery had commenced her experiments, the crop had fallen lamentably short ; but this year, there was scarcely any crop at all.

Her friends now thought it time to interfere. Her brother, whom she loved, and for whose opinion and advice she entertained a high regard, had all along, remonstrated against the course she was pursuing. He now spoke in a more decided tone. He told her, that the silly notions she had taken up about the happiness of her slaves, would certainly ruin her. Where was the need of being more humane than her neighbors ?— and what folly could be greater than to reduce herself and her children to beggary in the vain pursuit of a sentimental and impracticable scheme ?

Mrs Montgomery defended herself and her conduct
with great earnestness. She pleaded her duty towards
those unhappy beings whom God had placed in her
power and under her protection. She even went so
far as to hint at the injustice of living in luxury upon
the fruits of forced labor; and she spoke with much
feeling of the savage brutality of overseers and the torture of the lash. Her brother replied, that such talk
was very pretty, and generous, and philanthropic, and
all that ; and while it went no further than talk, he had
not the least objection to it. But pretty and philanthropic as it was, it would not make either corn or tobacco. She might talk as she pleased ; but if she expected to live by her plantation, she must manage it
like other people. Every body who knew any thing
about the matter would tell her, that if she wished to
make a crop she must keep a smart overseer, put a
whip into his hands, and give him unlimited authority
to use it. If she would do this, she might justly call
herself the mistress of the plantation ; but as long as she
followed her present plan, she would be no better than
the slave of her own servants ; and her philanthropy
would end in their being sold for debt, and her being
left a beggar.

These warm remonstrances made a deep impression
upon Mrs Montgomery. She could not deny that the
plantation had produced scarcely any thing since she
had come into possession of it ; and she was conscious
that after all her labors in their behalf, her servants
were discontented, idle and insubordinate. However,
she did not feel inclined to yield the point. She still

maintained that her ideas on the mutual relation of
master and servant, were the obvious dictates of justice and humanity, which no one could despise or
overlook, who made any pretensions to virtue or to
conscience. She argued that the system, which she
was attempting to introduce, was a good one; and that
nothing was wanting except an overseer who had sense
enough to carry it into judicious operation. Possibly
there was something of truth in this. If she could
have found a man like major Thornton, and made an
overseer of him, she might perhaps have succeeded.
But such men are seldom found any where, and in
slave-holding America, very seldom indeed. Take
the American overseers together, and they are the
most ignorant, intractable, stupid, obstinate, and self
willed race that ever existed. What could a woman
do, who could only act through assistance of this sort,
and who had the prejudices of the whole neighborhood
actively excited against her? Things went on from
bad to worse. The ready money which her husband
had left her was all spent, and her affairs soon became
so entangled and embarrassed, that she was obliged to
call upon her brother for assistance. He refused in
the most positive manner, to have any thing to do with
the business, unless she would surrender to him the
sole and exclusive management of her affairs. To
these hard terms, after a short and ineffectual struggle,
she was obliged to consent.

He immediately took the plantation into his own
hands. He removed the cabins to their former situation; revived the old rule that no servant should ever

go to the House unless specially sent for ; reduced
them to their former allowance of food and clothing ;
and engaged an overseer on the express condition that
Mrs Montgomery should never listen to any complaints
against him, or intermeddle, in any way, with his
management of the plantation.

Within the first month after this return to the old
system, near one third of the working hands ran away.
Mrs Montgomery's brother told her, that this was no
more than might be expected ; for the rascals had been
so spoiled and indulged as to render them quite impatient of the necessary and wholesome severity of plantation discipline. After long searching, and a good
deal of trouble and expense, the run-aways, except
one or two, were finally recovered ; and Poplar-Grove,
under its new administration, passed by degrees to its
ancient routine of whipping and hard labor. Once in
awhile, notwithstanding all the pains that were taken to
prevent it, some instance of severity would reach the
ear of Mrs Montgomery ; and in the first burst of indignant feeling, she would sometimes declare, that the
narrowest poverty would be far better, than the wealth
and luxury for which she was indebted to the whip of
the slave-driver. But the first burst of generous passion was no sooner over, than she acknowledged to
herself, that to think of giving up the luxury to which
she had been accustomed from her infancy, was out
of the question. She strove to escape from the
knowledge, and to banish the recollection of injustice
and cruelty, which her heart condemned, but which
she lacked the power, or rather the spirit, to remedy.

She fled from a home, where she was forever haunted by the spectre of that delegated tyranny, for which, however she might attempt to deny or disguise it, she could not but feel herself responsible ; and while her slaves toiled beneath the burning sun of a Carolina summer, and smarted under the lash of a stern and relentless overseer, she attempted to drown the remembrance of their wrongs in the dissipations and gaieties of Saratoga or New York.

But she was obliged to spend a part of the year at Poplar-Grove ; and with all her care, she could not always save her feelings from some rude brushes. Of this I had a striking instance on my first visit. One of her plantation hands had been so far indulged by the overseer, who, by the way, was a very rigid presbyterian, as to receive a pass to attend Mr Carleton's meeting. After the meeting was over, his mistress happened to to see him there ; and as she wished to send a message to one of her neighbors, she called him to her, and sent him with it. It so happened that Mrs Montgomery's overseer, was at this neighbor's, when the servant arrived there with his mistress' message. The overseer no sooner saw him, than he inquired what business he had to come there, when his pass only allowed him to go to the meeting and return again. It was in vain that he pleaded his mistress' orders. The overseer said that made no difference whatever ; for Mrs Montgomery had nothing at all to do with the plantation hands ; and to impress this fact upon his memory he gave him a dozen lashes on the spot.

The poor fellow was bold enough to come to the

House, and make his complaint to Mrs Montgomery.
Nothing could exceed her anger and vexation. But
her agreement with her brother left her without a
remedy. She made the servant a handsome present ;
told him that he had been very unjustly punished ; and
begged him to go home and say nothing about it to
any body. She submitted to the mortification of making this request, in hopes of saving the poor fellow
from a second punishment. But by some means or
other, as I learned afterwards, the overseer found out
what had been going on ; and to vindicate his supreme
authority, and keep up the discipline of the plantation,
he inflicted a second whipping more severe than the
first.

Such is the malignant nature and disastrous operation of the slave-holding system, that in too many instances, the sincerest good will, and best intended efforts in the slave's behalf, end only in plunging him into
deeper miseries. It is impossible to build any edifice
of good on so evil a foundation. The whole system
is totally and radically wrong. The benevolence, the
good nature, the humanity of a slave-holder, avail as
little as the benevolence of the bandit, who generously clothes the stripped and naked traveler in a
garment plundered from his own portmanteau. What
grosser absurdity than the attempt to be humane-
ly cruel and generously unjust ! The very first act in
the slave's behalf, without which, all else is useless
and worse than useless, is—to make him free !

CHAPTER III.

I have before observed that Sunday is the slave's holiday. Where intermarriages are allowed between the slaves of different plantations, this is generally the only occasion on which the scattered branches of the same family are indulged with an opportunity of visiting each other. Many planters, who pride themselves upon the excellence of their discipline, forbid these intermarriages altogether; and if they happen to have a superabundance of men-servants, they prefer that one woman should have a half-a-dozen husbands rather than suffer their slaves to be corrupted, by gadding about among other people's plantations.

Other managers, just as good disciplinarians, and a little more shrewd than their neighbors, forbid the men only to marry away from home. They are very willing to let their women get husbands where they can. They reason in this way. When a husband goes to see his wife, who lives upon another plantation, he will not be apt to go empty-handed. He will carry something with him, probably something eatable, plundered from his master's fields, that may serve to make him welcome and render his coming a sort of festival. Now every thing that is brought upon a plantation in this way, is so much clear gain; and so far as it goes, it amounts to feeding one's people at the expense of one's neighbors!

Sunday, as I have said, is the day upon which are
paid the matrimonial visits of the slave. But Sunday
was no holiday to me ; for I was generally obliged, on
that day, to attend my master upon his ecclesiastical ex-
cursions. To make up for this, Mr Carleton allowed
me Thursday afternoons, so that I was able to visit
Cassy at least once a week.

The year that followed, was the happiest of my life ;
and with all the inevitable mortifications and miseries,
which slavery, even under its least repulsive form,
ever carries with it, I still look back to that year with
pleasure,—a pleasure that still has power to warm a
heart, saddened and embittered by a thousand painful
recollections.

Before the end of the year, Cassy made me a father.
The infant boy had all his mother's beauty ; and only
he who is a father, and as fond a husband too as I was,
can know the feelings with which I pressed the little
darling to my heart.

No !—no one can know my feelings,—no one, alas,
but he, who is, as I was, the father of a slave. The
father of a slave !—and is it true then, that this child
of my hopes and wishes, this pledge of mutual love,
this dear, dear infant of whom I am the father, is it
true he is not mine ?

Is it not my duty and my right, a right and duty
dearer than life, to watch over his helpless infancy,
and to rear him with all a father's tenderness and love,
to a manhood, that will perhaps repay my care, and in
turn, sustain and cherish me, a tottering weak old
man ?

My duty it may be; but it is not my right. A slave can have no rights. His wife, his child, his toil, his blood, his life, and every thing that gives his life a value, they are not his; he holds them all but at his master's pleasure. He can possess nothing; and if there is any thing he seems to have, it is only by a sufferance which exists but in his owner's will.

This very child, this very tender babe, may be torn from my arms, and sold to-morrow into the hands of a stranger, and I shall have no right to interfere. Or if not so; if some compassion be yielded to his infancy, and if he be not snatched from his father's embraces and his mother's bosom while he is yet all unconscious of his misery, yet what a sad, wretched, desolate fate awaits him! Shut out from every chance or hope of any thing which it is worth one's while to live for; —bred up a slave!

That single word, what volumes it does speak! It speaks of chains, of whips and tortures, compulsive labor, hunger and fatigues, and all the miseries our wretched bodies suffer. It speaks of haughty power, and insolent commands; of insatiate avarice; of pampered pride and purse proud luxury; and of the cold indifference and scornful unconcern with which the oppressor looks down upon his victims. It speaks of crouching fear, and base servility; of low, mean cunning and treacherous revenge. It speaks of humanity outraged; manhood degraded; the social charities of life, the sacred ties of father, wife and child trampled under foot; of aspirations crushed; of hope extinguished; and the light of knowledge sacriligiously

put out.   It speaks of man deprived of all that makes
him amiable or makes him noble ;   stript of his soul
and sunk into a beast.

And thou, my child, to this fate thou art born !
May heaven have mercy on thee, for man has none !

The first burst of instinctive and thoughtless pleasure, with which I had looked upon my infant boy was
dissipated forever, the moment I had recovered myself enough to recollect what he was born to.   Various
and ever changing, but always wretched and distressing
were the feelings with which I gazed at him, as he
slept upon his mother's bosom, or waking, smiled at her
caresses.   He was indeed a pretty baby;—a dear, dear
child ;—and for his mother's sake I loved him, how I
loved him !   Yet struggle as I might, I could not, for
a moment, escape the bitter thought of what his fate
must be.   Full well I knew that did he live to be a
man, he would repay my love, and justly, with curses,
curses on the father who had bestowed upon him nothing but a life incumbered and made worse than worthless, by the inheritance of slavery.

I found no longer the same pleasure in Cassy's society, which it used to afford me ;   or rather the pleasure which I could not but take in it, was intermingled
with much new misery.   I did not love her less ; but
the birth of that boy had infused fresh bitterness into
the cup of servitude.   Whenever I looked upon him,
my mind was filled with horrid images.   The whole
future seemed to come visibly before me.   I saw him
naked, chained, and bleeding under the lash ;   I saw
him a wretched, trembling creature, cringing to escape

it ; I saw him utterly debased, and the spirit of manhood extinguished within him ; already he appeared
that worthless thing,—a slave contented with his fate !

I could not bear it. I started up in a phrensy of
passion ; I snatched the child from the arms of his
mother ; and while I loaded him with caresses, I looked
about for the means of extinguishing a life, which, as
it was an emanation from my existence, seemed destined to be only a prolongation of my misery.

My eyes rolled wildly, I doubt not ; and the stern
spirit of my determination must have been visibly
marked upon my face ; for gentle and unsuspicious as
she was, and wholly incapable of that wild passion
which tore my heart, my wife, with a mother's instinctive watchfulness, seemed to catch some glimpse of
my intention. She rose up hastily, and without speaking a word, she caught the baby from my feeble and
trembling grasp ; and as she pressed it to her bosom,
she gave a look that told me all that she feared ; and
told me too, that the mother's life was bound up in that
of the child.

That look subdued me. My arms dropped powerless, and I sunk down in a sort of sullen stupor. I
had been prevented from accomplishing my purpose,
but I was not satisfied that in foregoing it, I did a father's duty to the child. The more I thought upon it—
and it so engrossed me that I could scarcely draw my
thoughts away,—the more was I convinced that it was
better for the boy to die. And if the deed did peril
my own soul, I loved the child so dearly that I did not
shrink, even at that.

But then his mother.

I would have reasoned with her ; but I knew how vain would be the labor to array a woman's judgment against a mother's feelings ; and I felt, that one tear stealing down her cheek, one look of hers, like that she gave me when she snatched the child away, would, even in my own mind, far outbalance the weightiest of my arguments.

The idea of rescuing the boy, by one bold act, from all the bitter miseries that impended over him, had shot upon my mind, like some faint struggling star across the darkness of a midnight storm. But that glimmer of comfort was now extinguished. The child must live. The life I gave him, I must not take away. No ! not though every day of it would draw new curses on my devoted head,—and those too, the curses of my child. This, this alas ! is the barbed arrow that still is sticking in my heart ; the fatal, fatal wound that nought can heal.

CHAPTER IV.

ONE Sunday morning when the boy was about three months old, two strangers unexpectedly arrived at Carleton-Hall. In consequence of their coming, some urgent business occupied my master's attention, so that he found himself obliged to give up the meeting which he had appointed for that day. I was not sorry for it; for it left me at liberty to visit my wife and child.

It was the autumn. The heat of summer had abated, and the morning was bright and balmy. There was a soothing softness in the air ; and the woods were clothed in a gay variety of colors, that almost outvied the foliage of the spring. As I rode along towards Poplar-Grove, the serenity of the sky, and the beauty of the prospect, seemed to breathe a peaceful pleasure to my heart. It was the more needed ; for I had been a good deal irritated by some occurrences during the week ; and every new indignity to which my situation exposed me, I now seemed to suffer twice over, once in my own person, and a second time, in anticipation for my child. I had set out in no very agreeable frame of mind ; but the ride, the prospect and the fine autumnal air, had soothed me into a cheerful alacrity of spirit, such as I had hardly felt for some weeks past.

Cassy welcomed me with a ready smile, and those caresses which a fond wife bestows so freely on the husband whom she loves. Her mistress, the day before, had given her some new clothes for the child, and she had just been dressing him out, to make the little fellow fit, she said, to see his father. She brought the boy and placed him on my knee. She praised his beauty ; and with her arm about my neck, she tried to trace his father's features in the baby's face. In the full flow of a mother's fond affection, she seemed unconscious and forgetful of the future ; and by a thousand tender caresses, and all the little artifices of a woman's love, she sought to make me forget it too. She had but little success. The sight of that poor, smiling, helpless and unconscious child, brought back all my melancholy feelings. Yet I could not bear to disappoint my wife's hopes and efforts ; and to make her think herself successful, I strove to affect a cheerfulness I did not feel.

The beauty of the day tempted us abroad. We walked among the fields and woods, carrying the child by turns. Cassy had an hundred little things to tell me of the first slight indications of intelligence which the boy was giving. She spoke with all a mother's fluency and fervor. I said but little ; indeed I hardly dared to speak at all. Had I once begun, I could not have restrained myself from going on ; and I did not wish to poison her pleasure, by an outpouring of that bitterness which I felt bubbling up, at the bottom of my heart.

The hours stole away insensibly, and the sun was already declining. I had my master's orders to be back that night ; and it was time for me to go. I clasped the infant to my heart. I kissed Cassy's cheek and pressed her hand. She seemed not satisfied with so cold a parting; for she threw her arms about my neck and loaded me with embraces. This was so different from her usual coy and timid manner, that I was at a loss to understand it. Is it possible that she felt some instinctive presentiment of what was going to happen? Did the thought dart across her mind, that this might be our last, our final parting?

CHAPTER V.

WHEN I got back to Carleton-Hall, I found every thing in the greatest confusion. It was not long before I was made acquainted with the cause. It seemed that some twelve months previous, Mr Carleton had found himself very much pressed for money. This had obliged him to look a little into his affairs. He found himself burdened with a load of debt of which before, he had no definite idea; and as his numerous creditors, who had been too long put off with promises, were begining to be very clamorous, he saw that some vigorous remedy was necessary. To borrow, seemed the most certain means of relief from the immediate pressure of his debts ; and he succeeded in obtaining a large loan from some Baltimore money-lenders, of which he secured the repayment by a mortgage upon his slaves, including even the house servants and myself among the number. This money he expended in satisfying several executions, which had already issued against him ; and in stopping the mouths of the most clamorous of his creditors. The money was borrowed for a year ; not with any expectation on Mr Carleton's part, of being able to repay it in that time, out of any funds of his own ; but in the hope that before the year's end, he might succeed in obtaining a permanent loan, and so be enabled to cancel the mortgage.

In this expectation, he had hitherto been disappointed ; and he was yet negociating with the persons from whom he expected to borrow, when the time of repayment, mentioned in the mortgage, expired. This happened about a month previous ; and when I got back to Carleton-Hall, I found that the strangers who had arrived that morning, were the agents of the Baltimore money-lenders, who had been sent to take possession of the mortgaged property. They had already caught as many of the slaves as they could find ; and I no sooner entered the house, than I was seized, and put under a guard. These precautions were thought necessary to prevent the slaves from running away, or concealing themselves from the agents of their new owners.

My poor master was in the greatest distress and embarrassment that could be imagined. It was in vain that he begged for delay, and proposed various terms of accommodation. The agents declared that they had no discretion in the matter ; they were instructed to get either the money or the slaves ; and in case the money was not forthcoming, to proceed with the slaves to Charleston, in South Carolina, which, at that time, was esteemed the best market for disposing of that commodity.

As to paying the money at once, that was out of the question ; but Mr Carleton hoped that he might be able in the course of a few days, if not to obtain the loan for which he was negociating, at least to get such temporary assistance as would enable him to discharge the mortgage. The agents agreed to give him twenty-four hours, but refused to wait any longer. Mr Carleton despaired of doing any thing in so short a time ; and did not think it worth his while to attempt it. The plantation hands must go ; there did not seem to be any remedy for that ; but he was very desirous to save his house servants from the slave-market, and he begged the agents not to leave him without a servant to make his bed or cook his dinner.

The agents replied that they were truly sorry for the disagreeable situation in which he found himself ; but that, since the mortgage was made, several of the slaves included in the schedule were dead ; that some of the others seemed hardly worth the sum at which they had been valued ; that the price of slaves had fallen considerably since the mortgage was made, and seemed likely to fall more ; and that every thing considered, they thought it more than doubtful whether the mortgaged property would be sufficient to satisfy the debt. However, they were desirous to indulge him as

far as their duty to their principals would allow ; and
if he would pay the value of such of the slaves as he
wished to retain, they had no objections to receive the
money instead of the servants.

Mr Carleton had not fifty dollars in the house ; but
he immediately started off to see what he could borrow
in the neighborhood. Wherever he went, he found
that the news of what had happened, had preceded
him. Besides this Baltimore mortgage, he was known
to owe many other debts ; and his neighbors generally
looked upon him as a ruined man. Of course, the
greater part of them felt no inclination to lend him
their money ; and in fact, very many of them were
not so much better off than Mr Carleton as to have
much money to lend. After riding about the greater
part of the day, he succeeded in borrowing a few
hundred dollars, on condition however, that he should
secure the repayment by a mortgage of such slaves as he
should redeem. He had returned to the house a little
before I did, and was already considering with himself
which of his slaves he should retain. He told me that
I had been a good and trust-worthy servant ; and that
he was very unwilling to part with me. But he had
not money enough to redeem us all ; and his old nurse
and her family were entitled to be retained in prefer-
ence to any of the rest of us. Not only were their
services the most essential to him, but the mother had
long been a favorite servant, her children were born
and bred in his family, and he considered it a matter of
conscience to keep them, at all events. The agents
released those of the servants whom he selected. The

rest of us were kept confined, and received notice to be ready for a start, early the next morning.

I had yet one hope. I thought if Mrs Montgomery could be informed of my situation she would certainly buy me. I mentioned it to my master. He told me not to flatter myself too much with that idea ;—for Mrs Montgomery already had more servants about her house than she had any kind of use for. However, he readily undertook to write her a note explaining my situation. It was despatched by a servant, and I waited with impatient hope for the answer.

At last the messenger returned. Mrs Montgomery and her daughter had gone that morning to visit her brother, who lived some ten miles from Poplar-Grove, and they were expected to be absent three or four days. I believe I had heard something of this in the morning ; but in my hurry, confusion and excitement, it had escaped my memory.

My last hope was now gone ; and as it went, the shock I felt was dreadful. Till that moment, I had concealed from myself, the misery of my situation. I had been familiar with calamity, but this exceeded any thing I had ever suffered. It is true, I had once before been separated from my wife; but my bodily pains, my delirium and fever had helped to blunt the agony of that separation. Now, I was torn from both wife and child !—and that too, without any thing to call off my attention, or to deaden the torture of con-scious agony. My heart swelled with impotent pas-sion, and beat as though it would leap from my bosom. My forehead glowed with a burning heat. I would

have wept ; but even that relief was denied me. The
tears refused to flow ; the fever in my brain had
parched them up.

My first impulse was, to attempt making my escape.
But my new masters were too well acquainted with
the business of legal kidnapping, to give me an opportunity. We were all collected in one of the out-
houses and carefully secured. With many of the plantation hands, this was quite an unnecessary precaution.
A large proportion of them were so sick and weary of
the tyranny of Mr Carleton's overseer, that they were
glad of any change ; and when their master made them
a farewell visit, and began to condole with them upon
their misfortune, several of them were bold enough to
tell him that they thought it no misfortune at all ; for
whatever might happen, they could not be worse
treated than they had been by his overseer.   Mr Carleton seemed not well pleased at this bold disclosure,
and took his leave of us rather abruptly ; and certainly
this piece of information could not have been very
soothing to his feelings.

At early dawn we were put into traveling order.
A waggon carried the provisions and the younger children.   The rest of us were chained together and traveled in the usual fashion.

It was a long journey, and we were two or three
weeks upon the road.   Considering that we were
slaves driven to market, we were treated on the whole,
with unexpected humanity.   At the end of the third
or fourth day's journey, the women and children were
released from their chains, and two or three days

later, a part of the men received the same indulgence.
Those of us, of whom they were more suspicious,
were still kept in irons. Our drivers seemed desirous
to enhance our value by putting us into good condition.
Our daily journey was quite moderate ; we were all
furnished with shoes, and were allowed plenty to eat.
At night we encamped by the road-side ; kindled a
large fire, cooked our hominy, and made a hut of branches to sleep under. Several of the company declared that they were never so well treated in all their
lives ; and they went along laughing and singing more
like men traveling for pleasure, than like slaves going
to be sold. So little accustomed is the slave to kindness or indulgence of any sort, that the merest trifle is
enough to put him into ecstacy. The gift of a single
extra meal is sufficient to make him fall in love even
with a slave-driver.

The songs and laughter of my companions only served to aggravate my melancholy. They observed it,
and did their best to cheer me. There never was a
kinder-hearted company, and I found some relief even
in their rude efforts at consolation ; for there is more
power in the sympathy of the humblest human creature
than the haughty children of luxury are apt to believe.
I was a favorite among the servants at Carleton-Hall,
because I had taken some little pains to be so ; for I
had long since renounced that silly prejudice and foolish pride, which at an earlier period, had kept me aloof
from my fellow servants, and had justly earned me, their
hatred and dislike. Experience had made me wiser,
and I no longer took sides with our oppressors by join-

ing them in the false notion of their own natural superiority ;—a notion founded only in the arrogant prejudice of conceited ignorance, and long since discarded
by the liberal and enlightened ; but a notion which is
still the orthodox creed of all America, and the principal, I might almost say the sole foundation, which
sustains the iniquitous superstructure of American slavery. I had made it a point to gain the good will and
affection of my fellow servants, by mixing among
them ; taking an interest in all their concerns ; and
rendering them such little services as my favor with
Mr Carleton put in my power. Once or twice indeed,
I had overstepped the mark, and got myself into very
serious trouble by letting my master know what severities his overseer inflicted. But though my attempts at
serving them were not always successful, their gratitude was not the less on that account.

When my companions observed my melancholy they
stopped their songs, and having run through their few
topics of condolence, they continued their conversation
in a subdued and moderated tone, as if unwilling to
irritate my feeling by what might seem to me, unsea-
sonable merriment. I saw, and in my heart acknowledged the kindness of their intention ; but I did not
wish that my sadness should cast a shade over what
they enjoyed as a holiday ; the only holiday perhaps
which their miserable fate would ever allow them.
I told them that nothing would be so likely to cheer
me, as to see them merry ; and though my heart was
aching and ready almost to burst, I forced a laugh, and
started a song. The rest joined in it ; the chorus

rose again loud as ever ; the laugh went round ; and the
turbulence of their merriment soon allowed me to sink
again into a moody silence.

I had the natural feelings of a man ; I loved my wife
and child.   Had they been snatched from me by death,
or had I been separated from them, by some fixed, inevitable, natural necessity, I should have wept, no
doubt, but my feelings would have been those of simple
grief, unmixed with any more bitter emotion.   But
that the dear ties of husband and father, ties so twin-
ed about my inmost heart, should be thus violently
severed, without a moment's warning, and at a creditor's caprice ; and he too the creditor of another ;
to be thus chained up, torn from my home, and driven
to market, there to be sold to pay the debts of a
man who called himself my master ;—the thoughts of
this stirred up within my soul a bitter hatred and a
burning indignation against the laws and the people
that tolerate such things ; fierce and deadly passions
which tore my heart, distracted and tormented me,
even more than my grief at the sudden separation.

But the more violent emotions ever tend to cure
themselves.   If the patient survive the first paroxysm,
his mind speedily begins to verge towards its natural
equilibrium.   I found it so.   The torture of furious
but impotent emotions at first almost overpowered me.
But my feelings softened by degrees ; till, at length,
they subsided into a dull, but fixed and settled misery ;
a misery which the impulse of temporary excitement
may sometimes make me forget, but which, like the
guilty man's remorse, is too deeply rooted to be ever
eradicated.

CHAPTER VI.

At length we arrived at Charleston, the capital of South Carolina. We spent several days in recruiting ourselves after our long journey. As soon as we had recovered from our lameness and fatigues, we were dressed up in new clothes, and fitted out to show off to the best advantage. We were then exposed for the inspection of purchasers. The women and children, pleased with their new finery, seemed to enjoy the novelty of their situation, and appeared as anxious to find a master and to bring a high price, as though the bargain were actually for their own benefit. The greater part of our company were bought up by a single purchaser, and I among the rest. We were purchased by general Carter, a man of princely fortune, indeed one of the richest planters in South Carolina ; and were immediately sent off to one of his plantations, at some distance from the city.

The lower country of South Carolina, from the Atlantic for eighty or an hundred miles inward, including more than half the state, is, with the exception I shall presently mention, one of the most barren, miserable, uninviting countries in the universe. In general, the soil is nothing but a thirsty sand, covered for miles and miles, with forests of the long-leaved pine. These tracts are called, in the expressive phrase of the country, *Pine Barrens*. For a great distance inland, these

Barrens preserve almost a perfect level, raised but a few feet above the surface of the sea. The tall, straight, branchless trunks of the scattered pines, rise like slender columns, and are crowned with a tuft of knarly limbs and long, bristly leaves, through which the breezes murmur with a monotonous sound, much like that of falling waters, or waves breaking on a beach. There is rarely any undergrowth, and the surface is either matted with the saw-palmetto, a low ever-green, or covered with a coarse and scattered grass, on which herds of half-wild cattle feed in summer, and starve in winter. The trunks of the pines scarcely interrupt a prospect, whose tedious sameness is only varied by tracts, here and there, of almost impenetrable swamp, thickly grown up with bays, water oaks, cypresses and other large trees, adown whose spreading branches and whitened trunks, the long dusky moss hangs in melancholy festoons, drooping to the ground, the very drapery of disease and death. The rivers, which are wide and shallow, swelled with the heavy rains of spring and winter, frequently overflow their low and marshy banks, and help to increase the extent of swampy ground,—the copious source of poisonous vapors and febrile exhalations. Even where the country begins to rise into hills, it preserves, for a long distance, its sterile character. It is a collection of sandy hillocks thrown together in the strangest confusion. In many places, not even the pine will grow ; and the barren and thirsty soil, is clothed only with stunted bushes of the dwarf oak. In some spots even these are wanting ; and the bare sand is drifted by the winds.

Throughout all this extent of country, of which, with all its barrenness, a great part might, and by the enterprising spirit of free labor doubtless would be, brought into profitable cultivation, there are only some small tracts, principally along the water courses, which the costly and thriftless system of slave labor has found capable of improvement. All the rest still remains a primitive wilderness, with scarcely any thing to interrupt its desolate and dreary monotony.

This description does not include the tract stretching along the sea-shore, from the mouth of the Santee to that of the Savannah, and extending in some places, twenty or thirty miles up the country. The coast between these rivers, is a series of islands ;—the famous *sea-islands* of the cotton markets ; and the main land, which is separated from these islands by innumerable narrow and winding channels, is penetrated, for some distance inland, by a vast number of creeks and inlets. The islands present a bluff shore and a fine beach towards the ocean, but the opposite sides are often low and marshy. They were originally covered with a magnificent growth of ever-green oaks. The soil is light ; but it possesses a fertility never yet attained in the dead and barren sands of the interior. These lands are protected by embankments from the tides and floods, and the fields are divided and drained by frequent dikes and ditches. Such of them as can be most conveniently irrigated with fresh water, are cultivated as rice-fields ;—the higher and dryer lands are employed in the production of the long staple, or sea-island cotton,—a species which excels every other in the length of its fibre, and almost rivals silk in strength and softness.

These beautiful districts present a strong contrast to the rest of the lower country of South Carolina. As far as the eye can stretch, nothing is to be seen but a smooth, level, highly-cultivated country, penetrated in every direction by creeks and rivers. The residences of the planters are often handsome buildings, placed on some fine swell, and shaded by a choice variety of trees and shrubbery. These houses are inhabited by their owners only in the winter. They are driven from home in the summer, partly by the tedium of a listless and monotonous indolence, and partly, by the unhealthiness of the climate, which is much aggravated by the rice cultivation. This absentee aristocracy congregates in Charleston, or dazzles and astonishes the cities and watering places of the north by its profuse extravagance and reckless dissipation. The plantations are left to the sole management of over-seers, who, with their families, form almost the only permanent free population of these districts. The slaves are ten times as numerous as the free. The whole of this rich and beautiful country is devoted to the support of a few hundred families in a lordly, luxurious, dissipated indolence, which renders them useless to the world and a burden to themselves ; and to con-tribute towards this same great end, more than an hun-dred thousand human beings are sunk into the very lowest depths of degradation and misery.

General Carter, our new master, was one of the richest of these American grandees. The plantation to which we were sent, was called Loosahachee ; and though very extensive, was but one out of several which he owned. Coming as I did from Virginia, there were many things in the appearance of the country, and in the way in which things were managed, that were entirely new to me.

I and my companions who had always been accustomed to some small quantity of meat as a relish to our corn diet, found our mere unseasoned hominy neither so palatable nor so nourishing as we could wish. Being strangers and new-comers, we had not yet learned the customs of the country ; and were quite unacquainted with many of the arts by which the Carolina slaves are enabled to eke out their scanty and insufficient allowance. Our only resource was an appeal to our master's generosity ; and it happened, that about a fortnight after we were put upon the plantation, general Carter, with several of his friends, made a flying visit from Charleston to Loosahachee, to see how the crops were coming on. This we thought to be a good opportunity to get some improvement of our fare. We did not like to ask too much, lest our request should be rejected without ceremony. Indeed, we determined to be as moderate as possible ; and after due consultation, it was resolved to petition our master for a little salt to season our hominy,—a luxury to which we had always been accustomed, but which was not included in the Loosahachee allowance, which consisted simply of corn. My companions requested me to act as spokesman ; and I readily undertook to do so.

When general Carter and his friends came near my task, I walked towards him. He asked me what I meant by leaving my work in that fashion, and inquired what I wanted. I told him that I was one of the servants whom he had lately purchased ; that some of us were born and raised in Virginia and the rest in North Carolina ; that we were not used to living upon bare hominy without any thing to give it a relish ; and that we should take it as a very great favor if he would be kind enough to allow us a little salt.

He seemed to be rather surprised at the boldness of this request, and inquired my name.

"Archy Moore," I answered.

"Archy Moore!" he cried with a sneer,—" and pray tell me how long it has been the fashion among you fellows to have double names ? You are the first fellow I ever owned, who was guilty of such a piece of impertinence ;—and a damned impertinent fellow you are. I see it in your eye. Let me beg leave to request of you, Mr Archy Moore, to be satisfied with calling yourself Archy, the next time I inquire your name."

I had taken the name of Moore, since leaving Spring-Meadow ; an assumption not uncommon in Virginia, and which is there thought harmless enough. But the South Carolinians, who of all the Americans, seem to have carried the theory and practice of tyranny to the highest perfection, are jealous of every thing

that may seem in any respect, to raise their slaves
above the level of their dogs and horses.

The words and manner of my master were sufficiently irritating, but I was not to be shuffled off in that way.
I passed over his rebuke in silence, but ventured
again, in the most respectful terms I could command,
to renew the request, that he would be pleased to allow
us a little salt to season our hominy.

" You are a damned, unreasonable, dissatisfied set of
fellows as ever I met with!" was the answer. " Why
boy, you eat me out of house and home already. It
is as much as I can do to buy corn for you. If you
want salt, is n't there plenty of sea-water within five
miles ?   If you want it, you have nothing to do but to
make it ?"

So he said ; and as they wheeled their horses and
rode away, he and his companions joined in a loud
laugh at the wit and point of his answer.

CHAPTER VII.

AMONG Mr Carleton's servants, or rather the servants that had been Mr Carleton's, but who had now become the property of general Carter, was one named Thomas. While we had lived together at Carleton-Hall, I had contracted an intimacy with him, which we still kept up. He was of unmixed African blood, with good features, a stout muscular frame, and on several accounts, a very remarkable man.

His bodily strength, and his capacity for enduring privation and fatigue, were very uncommon ; but the character of his mind was still more so. His passions were strong and even violent ; but what is very rare among slaves, he had them completely under his control ; and in all his words and actions he was as gentle as a lamb. The truth was, that when quite young, he had been taken in hand by certain methodists, who lived and labored in his neighborhood ; and so strong and lasting were the impressions which their teaching made upon him, and so completely had he imbibed their doctrines, that it seemed as if several of the most powerful principles of human nature had been eradicated from his bosom.

His religious teachers had thoroughly inculcated into a soul, naturally proud and high-spirited, that creed of passive obedience and patient long-suffering, which under the sacred name of religion, has been often found more potent than whips or fetters, in upholding tyranny and subduing the resistance of the superstitious and trembling slave.   They had taught him, and he believed, that God had made him a servant ; and that it was his duty to obey his master, and be contented with his lot.   Whatever cruelties or indignities the unprovoked insolence of unlimited authority might inflict upon him, it was his duty to submit in humble silence ; and if his master smote him on one cheek, he was to turn to him the other also.   This, with Thomas, was not a mere form of words run through with, and then forgotten. In all my experience, I have never known a man over whom his creed appeared to hold so powerful a control.

Nature had intended him for one of those lofty spirits who are the terror of tyrants, and the bold assertors of liberty.   But under the influence of his religion, he had become a passive, humble and obedient slave.   He made it a point of duty to be faithful to his master in all things. He never tasted whiskey ; he would sooner starve than steal ; and he preferred being whipped to telling a lie. These qualities, so very uncommon in a slave, as well as his cheerful obedience, and laborious industry, had gained him the good will even of Mr Carleton's overseer.   He was treated as a sort of confidential servant ; was often trusted to keep the keys and give out the allowance ;—and so scrupulously did he fulfil all that was required of him, that even the fretful caprice of an overseer had no fault to find.   He had lived at Carleton-Hall more than ten years, and in all that time, had never once been whipped.   What was most remarkable and uncommon of all, at the same time that he obtained the confidence of the overseer, Thomas had succeeded in gaining the good will of his fellow servants. There never lived a kinder-hearted, better tempered man. There was nothing he was not ready to do for a fellow creature in distress; he was ever willing to share his provisions with the hungry, and to help the weak and tired to finish their tasks. Besides, he was the spiritual guide of the plantation, and could preach and pray almost as well as his master. I had no sympathy for his religious enthusiasm, but I loved and admired the man; and we had long been on terms of close intimacy.

Thomas had a wife, Ann, by name, a pretty, sprightly, good natured girl, whom he loved exceedingly. It was a great comfort to him,—indeed he regarded it as a special interposition of Providence in his behalf, —that when carried away from Carleton-Hall they had not been separated. Never was a man more grateful or more delighted than Thomas was, when he found that both he and Ann had been purchased by general Carter. That they should fall into the hands of the same owner was all he desired; and he readily transferred to the service of general Carter all that zeal and devotion, which, as he had been taught to believe, a slave owes to his master. While all the rest of us, upon our first arrival at Loosahachee, had been complaining and lamenting over the hardness of our tasks and the poor and insufficient food which our new master allowed us, Thomas said not a word; but had worked away with such zeal and vigor, that he soon gained the reputation of being one of the best hands on the place.

Thomas' wife had an infant child but a few weeks old, who according to the Carolina fashion, was brought to her in the field to be nursed ;—for the Carolina planters, spendthrifts in every thing else, in all that regards their servants, are wonderful economists. One hot afternoon, Ann sat down beneath a tree, and took the infant from the hands of the little child herself scarcely able to walk, who had the care of it during the day. She had finished the maternal office, and was returning slowly, and perhaps rather unwillingly to her task, when the overseer rode into that part of the field. The name of our overseer was Mr Martin. He was one of those who are denominated smart fellows and good disciplinarians. He had established a rule that there was to be no loitering at Loosahachee. Walking was too lazy a pace for him; if there was any occasion to go from one part of the field to another, it was to be in a run. Ann had perhaps forgotten, at all events, she was not complying with this ridiculous piece of discipline. This was no sooner observed by the overseer, than he rode up to her ; cursed her for a lazy vagabond ; and commenced beating her over the head with his whip. Thomas happened to be working close by. He felt every stroke ten times as keenly as though it had lighted upon his own shoulders. Here was a trial too strong for the artificial principles of any creed. He moved forward as though he would go to his wife's assistance. We who were by, begged him to stop ; and told him he would only

get himself into trouble.   But the cries and shrieks of
his wife made him deaf to our entreaties ; he rushed
forward ; and before the overseer was aware, he seized
his whip, snatched it from his hand ; and demanded
what he meant by beating a woman in that way for no
offence whatever ?

To judge from Mr Martin's looks, this was a display
of spirit, or as he would call it, of insolence and insubordination, for which he was not at all prepared.   He
reined back his horse for a rod or two ;—when, seeming to recollect himself, he put his hand into his coat-
pocket and drew out a pistol.   He cocked it and
pointed it at Thomas, who dropped the whip and
turned to run.   Mr Martin fired ; but his hand shook
too much to enable him to take a very effectual aim ;
and Thomas continued his flight ; leaped the fence ;
and disappeared in the thicket by which it was bordered.

Having put the husband to flight, the overseer turned to the wife who stood by trembling and crying.
He was boiling over with rage and passion, and seemed determined to spend his fury on this helpless and
unhappy woman.   He called the driver of the gang,
and two or three other men to his assistance, and bade
them strip off her clothes.

The preparations being complete, Mr Martin commenced the torture.   The lash buried itself in her
flesh at every blow ; and as the poor wretch threw up
her gashed and gory arms, the blood ran down in
streams.   Her cries were dreadful.   Used as I had
been to similar scenes, my heart sickened and my

head grew dizzy. I longed to seize the monster by
the throat and dash him to the ground. How I restrained myself I do not know. Most sure I am, that
nothing but the base and dastard spirit of a slave could
have endured that scene of female torture and distress,
and not have interfered.

Before Mr Martin had finished, poor Ann sunk to
the ground in a state of total insensibility. He ordered us to make a litter of sticks and hoe-handles, and to
carry her to his house. We laid her down in the passage. The overseer brought a heavy chain, one end of
which he put around her neck, and the other he fastened to one of the beams. He said her fainting was
all pretence ; and that if he did not chain her, she
would be running away and joining her husband.

We were now all ordered into the woods to hunt
for Thomas. We separated and pretended to examine every place that seemed likely to conceal him ;
but with the exception of the drivers, and one or two
base fellows who sought to curry favor with the overseer, I do not believe that any of us felt any great anxiety or took much pains to find him. Not far from the
fence was a low swampy place, thickly grown up with
cane and gum-trees. As I was making my way
through it, I came suddenly upon Thomas, who was
leaning against the trunk of a large tree. He laid his
hand upon my shoulder, and asked what the overseer
had done to his wife. I concealed from him, as well
as I could, the miserable torture which had been inflicted upon her ; but I told him that Mr Martin was
all fire and fury, and that it would be best for him to

keep out of the way till his passion could subside a little. I promised to return in the evening and to bring him food. In the mean time, if he would lie close, there would be little danger that any one would find him.

We were presently called back from our ineffectual search and ordered to resume our tasks. I finished mine as quickly as I could ; hastened home, got some food ready, and went to see poor Ann. I found her lying in the passage chained as we had left her. Her low moans showed that she had so far recovered herself as to be once more sensitive to pain. She complained that the chain about her neck hurt her and made it difficult to breathe. I stooped down and was attempting to loosen it, when Mrs Martin made her appearance at the door ; she asked what right I had to meddle with the girl ; and bade me go about my business. I would have left the food I had brought ; but Mrs Martin told me to take it away again ; it would learn the wench better manners, she said, to starve her for a day or two.

I took up my little basket, and went away with a heavy heart. As soon as it grew dark, I set off to meet Thomas ; but lest my steps might be dogged by the overseer or some of his spies, I took a very round-about course. I found him near the place where I had met him before. His earnest entreaties to know the whole, drew from me the story of his poor wife's sufferings and her present situation. It moved him deeply. At intervals he wept like a child ;—then he strove to restrain himself, repeating half aloud, some

texts of scripture, and what seemed a sort of prayer.
But all would not do ; and carried away at last, by a
sudden gust of passion, forgetful of all his religious
scruples, he cursed the brutal overseer with all the energy of a husband's vengeance. Presently he recovered
his self command, and began to take fault to himself,
ascribing all the blame to his own foolish interference.
The thought that what his affection for his wife had
prompted him to do, had only served to aggravate her
sufferings, seemed to agitate him almost to distraction.
Again, the tide of passion swept all before it. His
countenance grew convulsed ; his bosom heaved ; and
he only found relief in half uttered threats and muttered execrations.

He consulted with me as to what he had better do.
I knew that the overseer was terribly incensed against
him. I had heard him say, that if such a daring act of
insolence was not most signally punished, it would be
enough to corrupt and disorder the whole neighborhood. I was aware that Mr Martin would not dare
absolutely to put him to death. But this prohibition
to commit murder is the sole and single limit to an
overseer's authority ; and I knew that he had both the
right and the will to inflict a torture compared to which
the agonies of an ordinary death-struggle would be but
trifling. I therefore advised Thomas to fly ; since
even if he were caught at last, no severer punishment
could be inflicted upon him than he would be certain
of, upon a voluntary surrender.

For a moment, this advice seemed to please him ;
and an expression of daring determination appear-

ed in his face, such as I had never seen there before.
But it disappeared in an instant. " There is Ann,"
he said, " I cannot leave her, and she, poor timid
thing, even if she were well, I could never persuade
her to fly with me. It will not do, Archy ; I cannot
leave my wife !"

What could I answer ?

I understood him well, and knew how to sympathise
with him. I could not but admit the force of his objection. Such feelings I knew it would be in vain to
combat with arguments ; indeed I could not make up
my mind to attempt it. As I had no other advice to
give, I remained silent.

Thomas seemed lost in thought, and continued for
some minutes with his eyes fixed upon the ground.
Presently he told me that he had made up his mind.
He was determined, he said, to go to Charleston and
appeal to his master.

The little I had known of general Carter, did not
incline me to put much dependence on his justice or
generosity ; but as Thomas seemed pleased with this
plan, and as it was his only chance, I applauded it.
He ate the food I had brought, and determined to set
off immediately. He had only been once to Charleston, during all the time we had been at Loosahachee ;
but as he was one of those people, who, if they have
been once to a place, find little difficulty in going a second time, I had no doubt of his finding his way to
town.

I returned to my cabin ; but I was so anxious and
uncertain about the success of Thomas, in the scheme

he had adopted, that I could not sleep. At daylight I went to my task. My anxiety acted as a stimulus upon me, and I had finished long before any of my companions. As I was passing from the field to my cabin, I saw general Carter's carriage driving up the road ; and as it passed me I observed poor Thomas behind, chained to the footman's stand.

The carriage drove up to the house. General Carter got out of it, and sent off in great haste for Mr Martin, who had taken his gun and dog early that morning, and had been beating about the woods all day, in search of Thomas. In the mean time, general Carter ordered all the hands on the plantation to be collected.

At last Mr Martin arrived. The moment general Carter saw him, he cried out—" Well sir, here is a run-away, I have brought back for you. Would you believe it ?—the fellow had the impertinence to come to Charleston with the story of his grievances ! Even from his own account of the matter, he was guilty of the greatest insolence I ever heard of. Snatching the whip from the hand of an overseer ! Things are coming to a pretty pass indeed, when these fellows undertake to justify such insubordination. The next thing we shall hear of, they will be cutting our throats. However, I stopped the scoundrel's mouth before he had said five words. I told him, I would pardon any thing sooner than insolence to my overseer. I would much sooner excuse impertinence towards myself. And to let him know what I thought of his conduct, here you see I have brought him back to you ; and I have done it myself, even at the risk of being obliged to sleep here to-night and catching the country fever. Whip the rascal well Mr Martin! whip him well! I have had all the hands collected, that they might see the punishment and take warning by it.''

Mr Martin thus invited, sprung upon his prey with a tiger's ferocity. But I have no inclination to disgust myself with another description of the horrid torment of which in America, the whip is the active and continual instrument. He who is curious in these matters, will do well to spend six months upon an American plantation. He will soon discover that the rack was a surpefluous invention; and that the whip, by those well skilled in the use of it, can be made to answer any purposes of torture.

Though Thomas was quite cut up with the lash, and whipped by two drivers till he fainted from pain and loss of blood, such was the nerve and vigor of his constitution, and the noble firmness of his mind, that he stood it like a hero, and disdained to utter any of those piercing screams and piteous cries for mercy, which are commonly heard upon the like occasions. He soon got over the effects of this discipline ; and in a few days was at work again as usual.

Not so with his wife. She was naturally of a slender constitution, and perhaps had not entirely recovered from the weakness incident upon child-birth. Either the whipping she had suffered, or her chains and starvation afterwards, or both together, had brought on a violent disorder, of which at first, she seemed to get better, but which left her suffering under a dull nervous fever, without strength or appetite, or even the desire

of recovery. Her poor baby seemed to sympathise
with its mother, and pined from day to day. At length
it died. The mother did not long survive it. She lin-
gered for a week or two. Sick as she was, she had
no attendant except a superannuated old woman who
could neither see nor hear. Thomas of course was
obliged to go to his tasks as usual. He returned one
night, and found her dead.

One of the drivers, a mean spirited fellow, and Mr
Martin's principal spy and informer, was the only person
allowed to preach at Loosahachee, and to act as the
leader in those mummeries to which the ignorant and
superstitious slaves give the name of religion. He paid
a visit to the afflicted husband, and offered his services
for the funeral. Thomas had so much natural good
sense, that he was not, like many persons of his way
of thinking, imposed upon and taken in, by every one
who chose to make use of the cant of sanctity. He
had long ago seen through this hypocritical fellow, and
learned to despise him. He therefore declined his assistance; and pointing to me "himself and his friend,"
he said, "would be sufficient to bury the poor girl."
He seemed about to add something more; but the
mention of his wife had overpowered him; his voice
choaked, his eyes filled with tears, and he was con-
strained to be silent.

It was a Sunday. The preacher soon left us; and
poor Thomas sat the whole day watching his wife's
body. I remained with him; but I knew how useless any attempt at consolation would be, and I said but
little.

Towards sun-set, several of our fellow servants came in; and they were presently followed by most of the plantation people. We took up the body and carried it to the place of burial. This was a fine smooth slope covered with tall trees. It seemed to have been long used for its present purpose. Numerous little ridges, some of them new, and others just discernable, indicated the places of the graves.

The husband leaned over the body, while we busied ourselves in the sad office of digging its last resting place. The shallow grave was soon finished. We all remained silent, in expectation of a prayer, a hymn, or some similar ceremony. Thomas attempted once or twice to begin; but his voice rattled in his throat, and died away in an inarticulate murmur. He shook his head, and bade us place the body in the grave. We did so; and the earth was soon heaped upon it.

It was already growing dark; and the burial being finished, those who had attended at it, hastened homeward. The husband still remained standing by the side of the grave. I took his arm, and with a gentle force, would have drawn him away. He shook me off, and raising his hand and head, he muttered in a low whisper, "murdered, murdered!" As he spoke these words, he turned his eyes on me. There gleamed in them, a spirit of passionate and indignant grief. It was plain that natural feeling was fast gaining the mastery over that system of artificial constraint in which he had been educated. I sympathised with him; and I pressed his hand to let him know I did so. He returned the pressure; and after a short pause, he added " blood for

blood ; is it not so, Archy ?" There was something
terrible in the slow, but firm and steady tone in which
he spoke. I knew not what to answer; nor did he
appear to expect a reply. Though he addressed me,
the question seemed intended only for himself. I took
his arm, and we walked off in silence.

CHAPTER VIII.

IT is customary in South Carolina, to allow the
slaves the week from Christmas to the new year, as
a sort of holiday. This indulgence is extended so far,
that during that week, they are, for the most part,
allowed to leave the plantations, the scenes of their
daily labors and sufferings, and to wander about in the
neighborhood, pretty much at their own will and pleasure. The high-ways present at that season, a singular appearance. The slaves of every age and sex,
collected from the populous plantations of the tide-
waters, and dressed in the best attire they have been
able to muster, assemble in great numbers, swarming
along the road, and clustering about the little whiskey-
shops, producing a scene of bustle and confusion,
witnessed only at the Christmas holidays.

Those shops are principally supported by a traffic with the slaves for stolen rice and cotton,—a traffic which all the vindictive fury of the planters, backed by an abundant legislation, has not been able to eradicate. They are the chief support, in fact, the only means of livelihood, open to a considerable portion of the lower order of the white aristocracy of the country. It is the same in Carolina as in Lower Virginia. The poor whites are extremely rude and ignorant, and acquainted with but few of the comforts of civilized life. They are idle, dissipated, and vicious ; with all that vulgar brutality of vice, which poverty and ignorance render so conspicuous and disgusting. Without land, or at best, possessing some little tract of barren and exhausted soil, which they have neither skill nor industry to render productive ; without any trade or handicraft art ; and looking upon all manual labor as degrading to freemen, and fit only for a state of servitude,— these poor white men have become the jest of the slaves, and are at once, feared and hated by the select aristocracy of rich planters. It is only the right of suffrage which they possess, that preserves them the show of consideration and respect with which they are yet treated. This right of suffrage, of which the select aristocracy are extremely anxious to deprive them, is the only safeguard of the poor whites. But for this, they would be trampled under foot without mercy ; and by force of law and legislation, would soon be reduced to a condition little superior to that of the very slaves themselves.

On the Christmas holidays which succeeded my

becoming an inhabitant of Loosahachee, a great number
of slaves, of whom, I was one, were assembled about a
little store on the neighboring high road, laughing, talking, drinking whiskey and making merry after our several fashions. While we were thus employed, I observed riding along the road, a mean looking fellow,
shabbily dressed, with a face of that disagreeable cada-
verous hue that makes the inferior order of whites in
Lower Carolina look so much like walking corpses.
He was mounted on a lean scraggy horse, whose hips
seemed just bursting through the skin, and he carried
in his hand an enormous whip, which he handled with a
familiar grace, seldom acquired except by an American slave-driver. As he passed us, I noticed that all
the slaves who had hats, pulled them off to him ; but
as I did not see any thing in the fellow's appearance
that demanded any particular respect, and as I was ignorant of the Carolina etiquette, which requires from
every slave an obsequious bearing towards every freeman, seldom expected in Virginia, I let my hat
remain upon my head. The fellow noticed it ; reined
up his jaded beast, and eyed me sharply. My complexion made him doubt whether I might not be a freeman ; my dress and the company I was in, gave him
equal grounds for supposing me a slave. He inquired
who I was ; and being told that I was one of general
Carter's people, he rode towards me with his upraised
whip, demanding why I did not take off my hat to
him ; and without waiting for an answer, he began to
lay the lash over my shoulders. The fellow was evidently drunk, and my first impulse was to take the

whip away from him.   Luckily I did not yield to this impulse; for any attempt to resist even a drunken white man, though that resistance was only in repelling the most unprovoked attack, according to the just and equal laws of Carolina, might have cost me my life.

I learned upon inquiry that this fellow had been an overseer ; but some time previous had been discharged by his employer for suspected dishonesty. Not long after, he had set up a whiskey shop about half a mile distant. From what he said to the owner of the store where we were assembled, it would seem that his shop had not been so much frequented during the holidays as he had expected ; and in beating me, he had vented his drunken spite and ill humor on the first object that gave him any thing like a pretence to exercise it.   I learned too, that this fellow whose name was Christie, was a cousin of Mr Martin, our overseer.   They had been close friends ; but had lately had a violent quarrel.   Christie had stabbed Martin ; and Martin had shot at Christie with his double-barrelled gun.   He had taken a still more effectual revenge by doing his best to stop the trade from Loosahachee to Christie's shop, which he had formerly winked at, and which had been carried on, much to Christie's benefit, by the exchange of well watered whiskey for general Carter's rice and cotton.

I no sooner heard this account of Mr Christie, than it occurred to me that I had him in my power; and at once, I resolved to make him smart in his turn, for the lashes he had inflicted upon me. It is true, I was obliged to play the part of a spy and an informer; but such low means are the only resource which the condition of servitude allows. As soon as I got home, I hastened to the overseer, and with an abundance of hypocritical pretences and professions of zeal for my master's service, I communicated to him as a great secret, the fact that Mr Christie was in the habit of trading with the hands, and buying whatever they brought him, without asking any questions.

Mr Martin said that he was well aware of it; and he would give me five dollars, if I would help him to detect Christie in the fact.

We quickly struck up a bargain. The overseer furnished me with a quantity of cotton; and I set off, one moon-light night, to pay a visit to Mr Christie's shop.

He recognized me at once, and jested a good deal, about the whipping he had given me. He thought it an excellent joke; and it best answered my purpose to appear very much of the same opinion. I found him not at all disinclined to trade, provided I would exchange my cotton for his whiskey, at the nominal price of a dollar a quart. It was not long before I paid him a second visit. That time, Mr Martin and one of his friends were posted outside the shop, at a place where they could peep between the logs and see and overhear the whole transaction.

To buy rice, cotton, or in fact any thing else of a slave, unless he produces a written permit from his master to sell it, according to the Carolina statute-book, is one of the most enormous crimes a man can commit. Mr Christie was indicted at the next court.

He was found guilty on the express testimony of Mr Martin and his companion ; and was fined a thousand dollars and sentenced to a year's imprisonment. The fine swept away what little property he had ; and how his imprisonment ended I never heard. More than one of the jurymen who convicted him, were grievously suspected of the very same practices ; but the dread of incuring fresh suspicion, or perhaps the jealous rivalry of trade, made those very fellows the most clamorous for his condemnation.

Mr Martin was so well pleased with my services in this affair,—in which he fancied I had put myself forward merely to be used as his cat's-paw,—that he took me quite into favor, and began to employ me as one of his regular spies and informers. Tyranny, whether on the great scale or the little, can only be sustained through a system of espoinage and betrayal, in which the most mean-spirited of the oppressed are turned into the tools and instruments of oppression. There are many alleviations of the wretchedness of slavery to be expected from the favor and indulgence of an overseer. Let it be remembered also, that so strong are the allurements which power holds out, that even among freemen, there are hundreds of thousands always to be found, who are ready to assist in sacrificing the dearest rights of their neighbors, by volunteering to be the instruments of superior tyrants. What then can be reasonably expected from those who have been studiously and systematically degraded ? What wonder, if among the oppressed are found the readiest and most relentless instruments of oppression ?

As I knew I could turn Mr Martin's favor to good account, I took care not to let him suspect, with what scorn and loathing I regarded the office in which he sought to employ me. But while he imagined that I was engaged heart and hand in his service, I counter-worked him more than once, by communicating his plans and stratagems to those whom he sought to entrap. This same Mr Martin, though he was absolute viceroy over more than three hundred people, was a very ignorant and a very stupid fellow. Several circumstances occurred, which with a shrewd person would have betrayed me; but I succeeded so completely in blinding Mr Martin's eyes, that he still continued to place an unlimited confidence in my fidelity. Of this, he soon gave me a new proof; for riding one day, into the field, where I was at work, and not finding matters going on just to suit him, he called out the driver of the gang, and took from him the whip, which he carried as the badge and principal instrument of his office. He then called for me; and having given me twenty or thirty lashes, according to the custom in such cases, he put the whip into my hand, appointed me driver of the gang, and bade me do the first duty of my new office upon the fellow to whose place I had succeeded.

It is under the inspection of drivers, who are appointed from among the slaves, at the will of the overseer, that the cultivation of a Carolina plantation is carried on. The overseers have learned too much of the airs and the luxurious indolence of their employers, to be willing to be riding about all day, in the hot sun, looking after the laborers. The slaves are divided into gangs, and each gang is put under the charge of a driver, who is generally selected for his cowardly and mean-spirited subserviency, and his readiness to tyrannise over and to betray his companions. The driver is entrusted with all the unlimited and absolute authority of the master himself. He receives a double allowance ; he has no task ;—his sole business is to look after his gang and see that they perform the work assigned them ; and for this purpose he takes his station in the midst of them whip in hand. When the overseer makes his appearance in the field, all the drivers collect about him to receive his orders. For the performance of the work assigned to his gang, each driver is himself responsible ; and that he may perfectly understand by what means he is to enforce its performance, the overseer usually inducts him into office by giving him a severe castigation with the very whip which he afterwards puts into his hand to be used upon his companions.

The absolute power of an overseer, is often, I ought rather to say always, shockingly abused ; but the absolute power of drivers is yet one step higher towards the perfection of tyranny. The driver faithfully copies all the arrogance and insolence of the overseer from whom he receives his commission ; and as he is always among his gang, the aggravating weight of his authority is so much the heavier. He is but one of themselves; and the slaves are naturally more impatient of his rule, than they would be of the same dominion, exercised by one belonging to what they have been taught to

regard as a superior race ; and whom, as being a freeman, they are ready to acknowledge as actually their
superior.   Besides, the drivers are far from limiting
their demands, as the overseer himself generally would
do, to the performance of the field labor.   They have
a thousand little spites to gratify ; a thousand purposes
of their own to accomplish.   They are in fact, the absolute masters of every thing which any of their gang
may happen to possess ; and the persons of the women are as much at their disposal as at that of the
overseer or the master.   Even, if by chance, a driver
should happen not to be disposed to abuse his authority,
the dread of loosing his situation, and the knowledge
that all the deficiencies of any of his subordinates will
be visited upon his head, makes him of necessity,
hasty, harsh and cruel.

Heaven is my witness that while I held the office of
driver, my great object was, to use the authority which
it gave me, to alleviate as far as I could, the misery of
my companions.   My gang consisted of the Carleton
hands, with whom I had long been connected, and
whom I looked upon as friends and fellow sufferers.
Many is the time, when I have seen one and another
fainting under his task, and unable to finish it, that I
have dropped the whip, seized the hoe, and instead of
of the stimulus of the lash, have used the encouragement of aid and assistance.   This I did repeatedly;
though Mr Martin, more than once, when he found me
so employed, expressed his disapprobation, and told
me it was no way, and would only bring the station of
driver into contempt.

But it is no part of my purpose to write an eulogium on myself; and I shall not hesitate to confess the whole truth. There were times that I abused my office;—and I verily believe that no man ever exercised an unlimited authority who did not abuse it. The consciousness of my power, made me insolent and impatient;—and with all my hatred, my hearty, experimental hatred of tyranny, the whip had not long been placed in my hands, before I caught myself in the act of playing the tyrant.

Power is ever dangerous and intoxicating. Human nature cannot bear it. It must be constantly checked, controled and limited, or it declines inevitably into tyranny. Even all the endearments of the family connexion; the tenderness of connubial love, and the heart-binding ties of paternity, seconded as they always are by the controling influence of habit and opinion, have not made it safe to entrust the head of a family with absolute power even over his own household. What terms then are strong enough in which to denounce the vain, ridiculous and wanton folly of expecting any thing but abuse where power is totally unchecked, by either moral or legal control?

CHAPTER IX.

Since the death of his wife, a remarkable change had taken place in my friend Thomas. He had lost his former air of contentment and good nature, and had grown morose and sullen. Instead of being the most willing and industrious laborer in the field, as he used to be, he seemed to have imbibed a strong distaste for work, and he slighted and neglected his task as much as possible. Had he been under any other driver than myself, his idleness and neglect would have frequently brought him into trouble. But I loved and pitied him; and I screened him all I could.

The wrongs and injuries that had been inflicted upon him since his arrival at Loosahachee, seemed to have subverted all the principles upon which he had so long acted. It was a subject on which he did not seem inclined to converse, and upon which I was unwilling to press him; but I had abundant reason to suspect that he had totally renounced the religion in which he had been so carefully instructed; and which, for so long a time, had exercised so powerful an influence over him. He had secretly returned to the practice of certain wild rites, which in his early youth, he had learned from his mother, who had herself been kidnapped from the coast of Africa, and who had been, as he had often told me, zealously devoted to her country's superstitions. He would sometimes

talk wildly and incoherently about having seen the spirit of his departed wife, and of some promise he had made to the apparition ; and I was led to believe that he suffered under occasional fits of partial insanity.

At all events, he was in most respects, an altered man. He had ceased to be the humble and obedient slave, contented with his lot, and zealously devoted to his master's service. Instead of promoting his master's interest, it seemed now to be his study and his aim to do as much mischief as possible. There were two or three artful, daring, unquiet spirits on the plantation, from whom till lately, he had kept aloof, but whose acquaintance he now sought, and whose confidence he soon obtained. They found him bold and prudent, and what was more, trusty and magnanimous ; and they soon gave place to his superiority of intellect, and acknowledged him as their leader. They were joined by some others, whose only motive was the desire of plunder, and they extended their depredations to every part of the plantation.

In this new character, Thomas still gave evidence that he was no ordinary man. He conducted his enterprises with singular address ; and when all other stratagems by which to save his companions from detection failed him, he had still one resource that proved the native nobleness of his soul. Such was the steady firmness of his mind, and the masculine vigor of his constitution, that he was enabled to do what few men could. He could brave even the torture of the lash—a torture, as I have said already, not less terrible than that of the rack itself. When every other resource failed him, he was ready to shield his companions by a voluntary confession ; and to concentrate upon himself a punishment, which he knew that some among them were too feeble and faint-hearted to endure. Magnanimity such as this, is esteemed even in a freeman the highest pitch of virtue ;—how then shall we sufficiently admire it in a slave ?

Thank God, tyranny is not omnipotent !

Though it crush its victims to the earth ; and tread them into the dust ; and brutify them by every possible invention ; it cannot totally extinguish the spirit of manhood within them. Here it glimmers ; and there it secretly burns ; sooner or later, to burst forth in a flame, that will not be quenched and cannot be kept under !

So long as I was in the confidence of Mr Martin, I was able to render Thomas essential service, by informing him of the suspicions, plans, and stratagems of the overseer. It was not long however, before I forfeited that confidence ; not because Mr Martin entertained any suspicions of my playing him false,—for it was very easy to throw dust in the eyes of so stupid a fellow,—but because I did not come up to his notions of the spirit and the duty of a driver. The season was sickly ; and as the hands who composed my gang were from a more northern climate, and not yet seasoned to the pestiferous atmosphere of a rice plantation, they suffered a good deal from sickness, and several of them were often unable to work. I had explained this to Mr Martin, and he seemed to be satisfied with my explanation ; but riding into the field one day, in a particular bad humor, and I believe, a little excited with liquor, he got into a towering rage at finding not half my gang in the field, and more than half the tasks untouched.

He demanded the reason.

I told him that the hands were sick.

He swore they had no business to be sick ; he was tired, he said, of this talk about sickness ; he knew very well it was all sham ; and he was determined to be imposed upon no longer. " If any more complaints are made of sickness, Archy, you have nothing to do but to whip the scoundrels and set them to work."

" What" said I, " if they are really sick ?"

" Sick or not sick, I tell you. If they are not sick a whipping is no more than they deserve ; and if they are, why nothing is so likely to do them good as a little blood-letting."

" In that case," said I, " you had better appoint another driver ; I should make but a poor hand at whipping sick people."

" Hold your tongue, you damned insolent blackguard. Who gave you leave to advise me or dispute my orders ? Hand me your whip, you rascal."

I did so ; and Mr Martin thereupon administered upon me a fresh infliction of that same discipline he had bestowed when he first put the whip into my hand. So ended my driver-ship ; and though I now lost my double allowance, and was obliged to turn into the field again, and perform my task like the other hands, I cannot say that I much regretted it. It was a pitiful

and sorry office, which no one but a scoundrel ever
ought to undertake.

I now united myself more closely to the party of
Thomas, and joined heart and hand in all their enter-
prizes. Our depredations became at last so considerable, that Mr Martin was obliged to establish a regular
watch, consisting of his drivers and a few of their subordinates, who kept prowling about the plantation all
night, and made it unsafe to venture into the fields.
This arrangement was hastened by a circumstance that
happened upon the plantation, about which a very
strict inquiry was instituted, but which led to no definite result. On one and the same night, general Carter's splendid plantation-seat, and his expensive rice
mills were discovered to be on fire ; and notwithstanding all efforts to save them, both were totally consumed. Several of the slaves, and Thomas among the
rest, were put to a sort of torture to make them acknowledge some participation in this house-burning.
That cruelty availed nothing. They all stoutly denied
knowing any thing about it. I was, as I have said,
very much in Thomas' confidence ; yet he never
spoke to me about this fire. As he was one of those
men who know how to keep their own secrets, I always suspected that he knew much more about the
matter, than he chose to divulge.

At all events, it was evidently a much more potent
feeling, than the mere love of plunder by which Thomas was actuated. Since his wife's death, he sometimes drank to excess ; but this was seldom, and there
never was a man more temperate in his meats and

drinks, or less fastidious than Thomas generally was. He had formerly dressed with much neatness; now he neglected his dress altogether. He did not love society; he had little intercourse with any body except with me; and it was not always that he seemed to wish even for my company. Thomas had little use for his share of the plunder; and in fact, he generally distributed it among his companions.

When the thing was first proposed, he seemed to have little inclination to extend our depredations beyond the limits of Loosahachee. But as it was no longer safe to continue them there; and as his company had rioted too long in plunder to be willing to relinquish it, Thomas yielded at last to their urgent solicitations, and led us, night after night, to the neighboring plantations. We soon pushed our proceedings so far, as to attract the notice of the overseers, whose domains we had invaded. At first, they supposed that the thieves were to be looked for at home; and numberless were the severities they exercised upon those whom they suspected. But in spite of all their cruelties, the depredations were still continued; and such was the singular art and cunning which Thomas displayed, in varying the scene and manner of our visits, that for a long time, we escaped all the traps and ambushes that were planned to detect us.

We were one night, in a rice field, and had almost filled our bags, when the watchful ear of Thomas detected a sound, as if of some one cautiously approaching. He supposed it might be the patrol, which, of late, instead of whiling away their time by the help of

a fiddle and a bottle of whiskey, had grown more active, and actually performed some of the duties of a
night watch. Under this impression, he gave a signal
for us to steal off quietly, in a certain order which he
had arranged before hand. The field was bordered on
one side, by a deep and wide river, from which it was
protected by a high embankment. We had come by
water ; and our canoe lay in the river, under the shade
of a clump of bushes and small trees which grew upon
the dike. One by one, we cautiously stole over the
bank, carefully keeping in the shade of the bushes,
and all but Thomas were already in the boat. We
were waiting for our leader, who, as usual, was the
last man in the retreat, when we heard several shouts
and cries, which seemed to indicate that he was discovered, if not taken. The sound of two musket
shots fired in rapid succession, increased our terror.
We hastily shoved the boat from the shore; and push-
ing her into the current of the flood-tide, which was
setting up the river, we were carried rapidly and silently out of sight of our landing place. The shouts were
still continued ; but they grew fainter and fainter, and
seemed to take a direction from the river. We now
put out our paddles, and plying with all our strength,
we pretty soon reached a small cove or creek, the
place where we kept our boat and at which we were
accustomed to embark. We drew the canoe on
shore, and carefully concealed it among the high grass.
Then, without taking out our rice-bags, and leaving
our shoes in the boat, we ran towards Loosahachee,
which we reached without any further adventure.

I was very anxious about Thomas; but I had scarcely thrown myself upon my bed, before I heard a light tap at the door of my cabin, which I knew to be his. I sprang up and let him in. He was panting for breath and covered with mud. Thomas said, that just as he was going to climb the embankment, he looked behind him, and saw two men rapidly approaching. They seemed to observe him just at the same moment, and called to him to stop. If he had attempted to reach the boat, it would have drawn them that way, and perhaps led to the detection of the whole company. The moment they called to him, he dropped his rice-bag, and stooping as low as he could, he pushed rapidly through the rice in a direction from the river. His pursuers raised a loud shout, and fired their muskets at him,—but without effect. He jumped several cross ditches, made for the high ground, at a distance from the river, and drew off the patrol in that direction. They pursued him closely ; but as he was very strong and active, and well acquainted with the place, he succeeded in escaping from among the ditches and embankments of the rice-field, gained the high grounds, and took a direction towards Loosahachee. But though he had distanced his pursuers, they had still kept upon his track ; and he expected that they would follow him up, and would shortly be arriving.

While Thomas was telling his adventures, he had stripped off his wet clothes, and washed off the mud with which he was covered. I furnished him with a dry suit, which he took with him to his own cabin which was close by mine. I hastened round to the

cabins of our companions and told them what visitors
to expect. The barking of all the plantation dogs
pretty soon informed us that the patrol was coming.
They had roused up the overseer, and with torches in
their hands, they entered and searched every cabin in
the quarter. But we were prepared for their visit;
we were roused with difficulty out of a deep sleep; and
seemed to be very much astonished at this unseason-
able disturbance.

The search proved to be a very useless one; but as
the patrol were certain that they had traced the fugitive
to Loosahachee, the overseer of the plantation upon
which we had been depredating, came over the next
morning to search out and punish the culprit. He
was accompanied by three other men, whom it seems
were freeholders of the district, selected with such
forms, or rather such neglect of all form, as the laws of
Carolina prescribe in such cases. Three Carolina
freeholders, selected at hap-hazard, constitute such a
court as in most other countries, would hardly be trusted with the final adjudication of any matter above the
value of forty shillings at the utmost. But in that part
of the world, they not only have the power of judging
all charges against slaves, and sentencing the accused
to death; but what the Carolinians doubtless consider
a much graver matter—the right of saddling the state
treasury with the estimated value of the culprit. This
law for refunding to the masters, nominally a part, but
what by over-valuation, usually amounts to the entire
value, of condemned slaves, deprives the poor wretches of that protection against an unjust sentence, which

otherwise they might find in the pecuniary interest of
their masters ; and leaves them without any sort of
shield against the prejudice, carelessness or stupidity
of their judges. But why should we expect any thing
like equity or fairness in the execution of laws which
themselves are founded upon the grossest wrong ? It
must be confessed, that in this matter the Americans
preserve throughout, an admirable consistency.

A table was set out in the passage of the overseer's
house ; some glasses and a bottle of whiskey were
placed upon it ; and the court proceeded to business.
We were all brought up and examined, one after the
other. The only witnesses were the patrol who had
pursued Thomas ; and they were ordered by the court
to pick out the culprits. That was rather a difficult
matter. There were between sixty and seventy men
of us ; the night had been cloudy and without a moon ;
and the patrol had only caught some hasty and uncertain glimpses of the person whom they had followed.
The court seemed rather vexed at their hesitation.
Yet perhaps it was not very unreasonable ; since they
were quite unable to agree together as to what sort a
man it was. One thought him short ; the other was
certain that he was quite tall. The first, pronounced
him a stout, well-set fellow ; the other had taken him
to be very slender.

By this time, the first bottle of whiskey was emptied, and a second was put upon the table. The court
now told the witnesses that it would not do ; they did
not come up to the mark at all ; and if they went on at
that rate, the fellow would escape altogether. Just at

this moment, the overseer of the plantation which had been plundered rode up ; and as soon as he had dismounted, he stepped forward to the relief of the witnesses. He said, that while the court was organizing, he had taken the opportunity, to ride over and examine the rice-field, in which the rogue had been started up. It was much trampled in places, and there were a great many foot-prints ; but they were all just alike, and seemed to have been made by the same person. He took a little stick from his pocket, on which he said, he had carefully marked their exact length and breadth.

Now this was a trick for detecting people, which Thomas understood very well ; and he had taken good care to be prepared for it. Our whole company were provided with shoes of the largest size we could get, and all exactly of the same pattern ; so that our tracks had the appearance of being made by a single person, and he a fellow with a very large foot.

This speech of the overseer seemed to revive the drooping hopes of the judges ; and they made us all sit down upon the ground and have our feet measured. There was a man on the plantation named Billy, a harmless, stupid fellow, wholly unconnected with us; but unluckily for him, the only one of all the slaves whose foot corresponded at all with the measure. The length of this poor fellow's foot was fatal to him. The judges shouted with one voice, and in the style of condemnation to be expected from such a court, that " they would be damned if he was not the thief." It was in vain that the poor fellow denied the charge and pleaded for mercy. His terror, confusion and surprise, only served to confirm the opinion of his guilt ; and the more he denied, and the louder he pleaded, the more positively his judges were determined against him. Without further ceremony they pronounced him guilty, and sentenced him to be hung !

The sentence was no sooner pronounced than preparations were made for his execution. An empty barrel was brought out, and placed under a tree that stood before the door. The poor fellow was mounted upon it ; the halter was put about his neck, and fastened to a limb over his head. The judges had already become so drunk as to have lost all sense of judicial decorum. One of them kicked away the barrel, and the unhappy victim of Carolina justice dropped struggling into eternity.

The execution over, the slaves were sent into the field ; while Mr Martin, with the judges and witnesses and several others whom the fame of the trial had drawn to Loosahachee, commenced a regular drunken debauch, which they kept up all that day, and the night following.

CHAPTER X.

The authority of masters over their slaves is in general a continual reign of terror. A base and dastard fear is the sole principle of human nature to which the slave-holder appeals. When it was determined to hang the poor fellow, whose fate I have described in the last chapter, his judges could not know, nor do I suppose, they much cared, whether he were innocent or guilty. Their great object was to terrify the survivers; and by an example of what they would denominate wholesome and necessary severity, to deter from any further trespasses upon the neighboring plantations. In this they succeeded; for though Thomas endeavored to keep up our spirits, we were thoroughly scared, and felt little inclination to second his boldness which seemed to grow more determined, the more obstacles it encountered.

One of our confederates in particular, was so alarmed at the fate of poor Billy, that he seemed to have lost all self control; and we were in constant fear lest he should betray us. When the first paroxysm of his terror was at its height, the evening after he had witnessed the execution, I believe he would gladly have confessed the whole, if he could have found a white man sober enough to listen to him. After a while, he grew more calm; but in the course of the day he had dropped some hints, which were carefully treasured up

by one of the drivers.   He reported them as I discovered, to the overseer ;   but Mr Martin had not yet recovered from the effects of the frolic ;   and he was too
drunk and stupid to understand a word that the driver
said to him.

We had began to get the better of our fears, when
a new incident happened, which determined us to seek
our safety in flight.   Some persons, in passing along
the river bank, had discovered our canoe, which in the
hurry of our flight, we had taken too little care to conceal.   It contained not only our bags full of rice,—for
we had not yet recovered courage enough to go after
them,—but our shoes also, all exactly of the same
size, and corresponding with the measure which had
been produced upon the trial.   Here was ample proof
that quite a number had been engaged in the scheme
of depredation ;   and as one of the company had been
traced to Loosahachee, it would be reasonable to look
for the others upon the same plantation.   Luckily I
obtained an early intimation of this discovery, by
means of one of the overseer's house-servants, with
whom I had the policy to keep up a pretty intimate
connection.   A man had arrived at the overseer's
house, his horse dripping with foam,—and with an appearance of great haste and impatience, he had asked to
see the overseer.   The moment he came in, the stranger
requested to speak with him alone ;   and Mr Martin
took his guest into another room and locked the door.
The girl, who was my spy and informant, under an
appearance of the greatest simplicity was artful and intelligent ;   and she was prompted to overhear this secret

conversation, as much by her own curiosity, as by the
suspicion that it might possibly be something, in which
I would take an interest. She contrived to conceal herself in a closet, which was separated from the room in
which the overseer and his visitor were conversing, only
by a thin partition ; and having overheard his story,
the substance of which I have already mentioned,—and
learned besides, that the court would hold a new session at Loosahachee, the day following,—she hastened
to inform me of what she had heard. She knew nothing in particular, of our affairs, but she had reason to
believe that this piece of news would not be entirely
uninteresting to me.

I informed Thomas of what she had told me.
We agreed at once, that our best chance of safety was
in flight ; and we immediately communicated our intention, and the cause of it, to the rest of our confederates. They were anxious to accompany us ; and we
all resolved to be off that very night.

As soon as evening came on, we stole away from
the plantation and gained the woods in company. As
we anticipated that a very diligent search would be
made for us, we thought it best to separate. Thomas
and myself resolved to keep together ; the others scattered and took various directions. As long as the
darkness lasted, we traveled on as rapidly as we could.
When the morning began to appear, we plunged into a
thick swampy piece of woods, and having broken
down some branches and young trees, we made as dry
a bed as we were able and lay down to sleep. We
were much fatigued with our long and rapid journey,

and slept soundly. It was past noon when we waked.
Our appetites were sharp, but we had no provisions.
Just as we were beginning to consider what course it
would be best for us to pursue, we heard the distant baying of a hound. Thomas listened for a moment, and then
exclaimed that he knew that cry. It was a famous
dog, a cross of the blood-hound, which Mr Martin had
long had in training, and upon whose performances in
tracking out run-aways he very much prided himself. The place where we were, was a thick swamp,
in which it was difficult to move, and not easy to
stand. To cross it would be impossible; and we resolved to get into the edge of it, where the ground
was harder, and the undergrowth thinner, and to continue our flight. We did so,—but the hound gained
rapidly upon us, and his baying sounded louder and
louder. Thomas drew a stout sharp knife, which he
carried in his pocket. We were now just at the border where the dry ground came down upon the swamp,
and looking behind us, across the level and open
woods, we could see the hound coming on with his
nose to the ground, and uttering at intervals a deep and
savage cry. Farther behind, but still in full view, we
saw a man on horseback, whom we took to be Mr
Martin himself.

The dog was evidently upon our track ; and following it to the place where we had first plunged into the
swamp, he disappeared from our view. But we could
still hear his clamor, which grew louder and almost
constant ; and we soon perceived by the rustling and
cracking of the underwood that he was close upon us.

At this moment we faced about and stood at bay ;—
Thomas in front, with his knife in hand, and I just behind, with a sharp and heavy lightwood knot, the best
indeed the only weapon, of which I could avail myself. Presently the dog emerged from the swamp.
The moment he saw us, he redoubled his cry, and
dashed forward foaming and open-mouthed. He made
a great leap directly at Thomas' throat, but only succeeded in seizing his left arm, which Thomas raised as
a shield against the dog's attack. At the same instant
he dealt a stroke with his knife, which penetrated to
the hilt, and both dog and man came struggling to the
ground. How the contest would have ended had
Thomas been alone, is very doubtful ; for though the
hound had already received several wounds, they only
seemed to increase his ferocity, and he still struggled to get at the throat of his antagonist. My light-
wood knot now did good service ;—two or three heavy
blows upon the dog's head laid him senseless and
sprawling on the ground.

While we had been awaiting the dog's attack, and
during the contest, we had scarcely thought of his
master ; but looking up, after it was over, we discovered that Mr Martin was already very near us. When
the dog took to the swamp, his master had followed
along upon its edge, and came suddenly upon us before
we had expected him. He pointed his gun and
called upon us to surrender. Thomas no sooner
saw the overseer, than he seemed to lose all his self-
control, and grasping his knife, he rushed directly upon
him. Mr Martin fired ;—but the buck-shot rattled

harmlessly among the trees, and as he was attempting
to wheel his horse, Thomas dashed upon him, seized
him by the arm, and dragged him to the ground.   The
horse ran frightened through the woods ; and it was in
vain that I attempted to stop him.   We looked round
in expectation of seeing some others of the huntsmen
coming up.   None were in sight ; and we seized the
opportunity to retreat, and to carry our prisoner into
the covert of the swamp.

We learned from him, that by the time the court
and their attendants arrived at Loosahachee, our flight
had been discovered, and that it was immediately resolved to raise the neighborhood, and to commence a
general search for the run-aways.   All the horses,
dogs and men that could be come at, were put into re-
quisition.   They were divided into parties, and immediately commenced beating through the woods and
swamps in the neighborhood.

A party of five or six men, with Mr Martin and his
blood-hound, had traced three of our companions into
a thick swamp, just on the bank of a river.   The pursuers dismounted, and with their guns in their hands,
they followed the dog into the thicket.   Our poor fellows were so overcome with fatigue, that they slept till
the very moment that the hound sprang in upon them.
He seized one of them by the throat and held him to
the ground.   The others ran ; and as they ran, the
pursuers fired.   One of the fugitives fell dead, horri-
bly mangled and cut to pieces with buck-shot ; the
other still continued his flight.   As soon as the dog
could be compelled to quit his hold of the man he had

seized,—which was not without difficulty and delay—
he was put upon the track of the surviving fugitive.
He followed it to the river, where he stood at fault.
The man had probably plunged in, and swam to the
other side ; but as the dog could not be made to take
the water, and as the swamp on the opposite bank was
reputed to be very soft and dangerous, no further pursuit was made ; the chase in that direction was given
up, and the poor fellow was suffered to escape for the
present.

The pursuers now separated. Two of them undertook to carry back to Loosahachee the captive they
had taken, and the other three, with Mr Martin and
his hound, were to continue the hunt in search of the
the rest of us. They learned from their captive the
place at which we had parted company, and the direction which the several parties had taken. After beating about for some time, the hound struck upon our
trail, and opened in full cry ; but the horses of Mr
Martin's companions were so broken down, that when
he began to spur on to keep up with the hound, he
soon left them far behind. Mr Martin ended his story
by advising us to go in and surrender ourselves ; giving us his word and honor as a gentleman and an overseer, that if we would offer him no further violence or
injury, he would protect us from punishment, and reward us most handsomely.

The sun was now setting. The short twilight
which follows a Carolina sunset would soon be succeeded by the darkness of a cloudy and moonless
night ; and we felt but little apprehension of being im-

mediately troubled by our pursuers. I looked at
Thomas, as if to inquire what we had better do. He
drew me aside,—having first examined the fastenings
of our prisoner, whom we had bound to a tree, by
some cords found in his own pocket, and which were
doubtless intended for a very different purpose.

Thomas paused for a moment, as if to collect his
thoughts; then pointing to Mr Martin, "Archy," he
said, "that man dies to-night."

There was a wild energy, and at the same time, a
steady coolness, in the tone in which he spoke. It
startled me ; at first I made no answer ; and as mean-
while I looked Thomas in the face, I saw there an expression of stern exultation, and a fixedness of purpose
not to be shaken. His eyes flashed fire, as he repeated,
—but in a low and quiet tone that contrasted strangely
with the matter of his speech—" I tell you Archy,
that man dies to-night. She commands it ; I have
promised it ; and now the time is come."

" Who commands it?" I hastily inquired.

" Do you ask who ? Archy, that man was the murderer of my wife."

Though Thomas and I had lived in great intimacy,
this was almost the first time, since the death of his
wife, that he had mentioned her to me in such plain
terms. He had, it is true, now and then made some
distant allusions to her ; and I recollected that on several occasions before, he had dropped some strange
and incoherent hints about an intercourse which he
still kept up with her.

The mention of his wife, brought tears into his

eyes ;—but with his hand, he wiped them hastily away, and soon recovering his former air of calm and steady determination, he again repeated, in the same low but resolute tone, " Archy, I tell you that man dies tonight."

When I called to mind all the circumstances that had attended the death of Thomas' wife, I could not but acknowledge that Mr Martin had been her murderer. I had sympathised with Thomas then, and I sympathised with him now. The murderer was in his power ; he believed himself called upon to execute justice upon him ; and I could not but acknowledge that his death would be an act of righteous retribution.

Still, I felt a sort of instinctive horror at the idea of shedding blood ; and perhaps too, there still crept about my heart some remains of that slavish fear and servile timidity, which the bolder spirit of Thomas had wholly shaken off. I acknowledged that the life of the overseer was justly forfeited ;—but at the same time, I reminded Thomas that Mr Martin had promised, if we would carry him home in safety, to procure our pardon and protect us from punishment.

A scornful smile played about the lip of my comrade while I was speaking. " Yes Archy," he answered, " pardon and protection !—and a hundred lashes, and a hanging the next day perhaps. No ! boy, I want no such pardon ; I want no pardon such as they will give. I have been a slave too long, already. I am now free ; and when they take me, they are welcome to take my life. Besides, we cannot trust him ;

—if we wished it, we cannot trust him. You know we cannot. They do not think themselves obliged to keep any promises they make us. They will promise any thing to get us in their power ; and then, their promises are worthless as rotten straw. My promises are not like theirs ; and have I not told you that I have promised it ? Yes, I have sworn it ; and I now say, once for all, that man must die to-night."

There was an energy and a determination, in his tone and manner, which overpowered me. I could resist it no longer, and I bade him do his pleasure. He loaded the gun, which we had taken from Mr Martin, and which he had held in his hand all the time we had been talking. This done, we returned to the overseer, who was sitting at the foot of the tree to which we had bound him. He looked up anxiously at us, as we approached, and inquired if we had determined to go in ?

" We have determined," answered Thomas. "We allow you half an hour to prepare for death. Make the most of it. You have many sins to repent of, and the time is short."

It is impossible to describe the look of mingled terror, amazement and incredulity, with which the overseer heard these words. One moment, with a voice of authority, he bade us untie him ; the next, he forced a laugh and affected to treat what Thomas had said, as a mere jest ; then, yielding to his fears, he wept like a child, and cried and begged for mercy.

" Have you shown it ?" answered Thomas. "Did

you show it to my poor wife ? You murdered her; and for her life you must answer with your own."

Mr Martin called God to witness, that he was not guilty of this charge. He had punished Thomas' wife, he confessed ; but he only did what his duty as an overseer demanded ; and it was impossible, he said, that the few cuts he gave her, could have caused her death.

" The few cuts !" cried Thomas. " Thank God, Mr Martin that we do not torture you as you tortured her ! Speak no more, or you will but aggravate your sufferings. Confess your crimes ! Say your prayers ! Do not spend your last moments in adding falsehood to murder !"

The overseer cowered beneath this energetic re-proof. He covered his face with his hands, bent down his head, and passed a few moments in a silence which was only interrupted by an inarticulate sob-bing. Perhaps, he was trying to prepare himself to die. But life was too sweet to be surrendered without another effort to save it. He saw that it was useless to appeal to Thomas ; but rousing himself once more, he turned to me. He begged me to remember the confidence, he had once placed in me, and the favors, which as he said, he had shown me. He promised to purchase us both, and give us our liberty, any thing, every thing, if we would only spare his life !

His tears and piteous lamentations moved me. My head grew dizzy, and I felt such a faintness and heart-sinking, that I was obliged to support myself against a tree. Thomas stood by, with his arms folded and

resting on the gun. He made no answer to the reiterated prayers and promises of the overseer. Indeed he did not seem to notice them. His eyes were fixed and he was lost in thought.

After a considerable interval, during all which the unhappy overseer continued to repeat his prayers and lamentations, Thomas roused himself. He stepped back a few paces, and raised the gun. " The half hour is out," he said ;—" Mr Martin are you ready ?"

" No ! oh no ! Spare me, spare me !—one half hour longer—I have much—"

He did not live to finish the sentence. The gun flashed ; the ball penetrated his brain, and he fell dead without a struggle.

CHAPTER XI.

WE scraped a shallow grave, in which we placed the body of the overseer. We dragged the dead hound to the same spot, and laid him with his master. They were fit companions.

We now resumed our flight,—not as some may perhaps suppose, with the frightened and conscience-stricken haste of murderers, but with that lofty feeling of manhood vindicated, and tyranny visited with a just retribution, which animated the soul of the Israelitish hero whilst he fled for refuge into the country of the Midianites ; and which burned in the bosoms of Wallace and of Tell, as they pursued their midnight flight among the friendly cliffs and freedom-breathing summits of their native mountains.

There were no mountains to receive and shelter us. But still we fled through the swamps and barrens of Carolina, resolved to put, as soon as possible, some good miles between us and the neighborhood of Loosahachee. It was more than twenty-four hours since we had tasted food ; yet such was the excitement of our minds that we did not faint, and were hardly sensible of weakness or fatigue.

We kept a northwesterly direction, steering our course by the stars, and we must have made a good distance ; for we did not once stop to rest, but pushed forward at a very rapid pace all night. Our way lay through the open piney woods, through which we could travel almost as fast as on a road. Sometimes a swamp or the appearances of a plantation, would compel us to deviate from our track, but as soon as we could, we resumed our original direction.

The darkness of the night, which for the last hour or two that it lasted, had been increased by a foggy mist, was just beginning to yield to the first indistinct grey dawn of the morning. We were passing along a little depression in the level of the pine barrens,—now dry, but in the wet season, probably the bed of a temporary stream,—looking for a place in which to

conceal ourselves, when we suddenly came upon a
man, lying, as it seemed asleep, in the midst of a
clump of bushes, with his head resting on a bag of
corn. We recognized him at once. He was a
slave belonging to a plantation next adjoining Loosahachee, with whom we had had some slight acquaintance, but who, as we were informed, had been a run-
away, for some two or three months past. Thomas
shook him by the shoulder, and he wakened in a terrible fright. We told him not to be alarmed, for we
were run-aways like himself, and very much in need of
his assistance, being half dead with hunger, and in a
country with which we were totally unacquainted.
At first the man appeared very reserved and suspicious. He feared it seemed, lest we might be de-
coys, sent out on purpose to entrap him. At last
however, we succeeded in dissipating his doubts ; and
no sooner was he satisfied with the account we gave of
ourselves, than he bade us follow him, and we should
presently have food.

With his bag of corn upon his shoulder he pursued
the shallow ravine in which we had found him, for a
mile or more, till at length it widened into what seemed a large swamp, or rather a pond grown up with
trees. We now left the ravine and followed along on
the edge of the pond for some distance, when presently our guide began wading in the water and called
to us to follow him. We plunged in ; but before going far, he laid down his bag of corn upon a fallen tree,
and going back, he carefully effaced the marks which
our footsteps had made upon the muddy edge of the

pond. He now led us forward through mud and water up to our waists, for near half a mile. The gigan-
tic trees among which we were wading, sprung up like
columns, from the surface of the water, with round,
straight, whitish-colored, branchless trunks, their leafy
tops, forming a thick canopy over head. There was
scarcely any undergrowth, except a species of enormous vines, which ran twining like great cables about
the bodies of the trees, and reaching to the very
tops, helped with their foliage to thicken the canopy above us. So effectually was the light excluded,
and so close did the trunks of the trees stand together,
that one could see but a very little way into this
watery forest.

The water began to grow deeper, and the wood
more gloomy ; and we were wondering whither our
guide was leading us, when presently we came to a little island which rose a few feet from the surface of
the water, so regular and mound-like, that it had quite
the appearance of an artificial structure. Perhaps it
was the work of the ancient inhabitants of the country,
and the site of one of their forts or fastnesses. It was
about an acre in extent, and was covered with a thick
growth of trees, quite different however, from those of
the lake by which it was surrounded, and much inferior in size and majesty. Its edges were bordered by
low shrubs and bushes, whose abundant foliage gave the
islet the appearance of a mass of green. Our guide
pointed out to us a little opening in the bushes, through
which we ascended ; and after having gained the dry
land, he led us through the thicket along a narrow and

winding path, till presently we came to a rude cabin built of bark and branches. He gave a peculiar whistle, which was answered ; and two or three men immediately made their appearance.

They seemed a good deal surprised at seeing us, and me especially, whom apparently they took for a free man. But our guide assured them that we were friends and fellow-sufferers, and led the way into the cabin. Our new hosts received us kindly ; and having heard how long we had been without food, before asking us any further questions, they hastened to satisfy our hunger. They produced beef and hominy in abundance, on which we feasted to our heart's content.

We were then called upon to give an account of ourselves. Accordingly we made a relation of our adventures,—omitting however, any mention of the fate of the overseer ; and as our guide, who knew us, could confirm a part of our story, our account was pronounced satisfactory, and we were presently admitted to the privilege of joining their fraternity.

There were six of them, besides ourselves ;—all brave fellows, who weary of daily task-work and the tyranny of overseers, had taken to the woods, and had succeeded in regaining a savage and stealthy freedom, which, with all its hardships and dangers, was a thousand times to be preferred to the forced labor and wretched servitude from which they had escaped. Our guide was the only one of them whom we had ever seen till now. The leader of the band had fled from his master's plantation in the neighborhood, with a single companion, some two or three years before.

They did not then know of the existence of this retreat ; but being sharply pursued, they had attempted to cross the pond or swamp, by which it was surrounded,—a thing, I suppose, which had never been done before. In this attempt they were fortunate enough to light upon the islet, which being unknown to any one else, had ever since served them as a secure retreat. They soon picked up a recruit or two ; and had afterwards been joined by their other companions.

Our guide, it seems, had been to a neighboring plantation to trade for corn ;—a traffic, which our friends carried on with the slaves of several of the nearest plantations. After the business was concluded, the men with whom he had been dealing, had produced a bottle of whiskey of which our guide had drank so freely, that he had not gone far on his way home, before his legs failed him. He sunk down in the place where we had found him, and fell fast asleep.

Drinking whiskey away from home, according to the prudent laws of this swamp-encircled commonwealth, was a high misdemeanor, punishable with thirty-nine lashes, which were forthwith inflicted upon our guide with a good deal of emphasis. He took it in good part though, as being the execution of a law to which he had himself assented, and which he knew was enacted as much for his own benefit, as for the benefit of those who had just now carried it into execution.

The life upon which we now entered had at least, the charm of novelty. In the day time we eat, slept,

told stories and recounted our escapes ; or employed
ourselves in dressing skins, making clothes, and cur-
ing provisions. But the night was our season of adventure and enterprize. As the autumn was coming on,
we made frequent visits to the neighboring corn fields
and potato patches, which we felt no scruples whatever in laying under severe contribution. This however was only for a month or two. Our regular and
certain supply was in the herds of half wild cattle,
which wander through the piney woods and feed upon
the coarse grass which they furnish. We killed as
many of these cattle as we needed, and their flesh cut
into long strips, we dried in the sun. Thus cured, it is
a palatable food ; and we not only kept a stock on hand
for our own consumption, but it furnished the principle
article of a constant but cautious traffic which, as I
have already mentioned, we carried on with the slaves
of several neighboring plantations.

This wild life of the woods has its privations and
its sufferings ; but it has too, its charms and its pleasures ; and in its very worst aspect, it is a thousand
and ten thousand times to be preferred to that mis-
called civilization which degrades the noble savage into
a cringing and broken spirited slave ;—a civilization,
which purchases the indolence and luxury of a single
master, with the sighs and tears, the forced and unwilling labor, the degradation, misery and despair of an
hundred of his fellow men ! Yes—there is more of
true manhood in the bold bosom of a single outlaw
than in a whole nation of cowardly tyrants and crouching slaves !

CHAPTER XII.

By the end of the winter, the herds of cattle which were accustomed to frequent our neighborhood were a good deal thinned ; and the pasturage had now become so bare and withered, that what remained of them were little better than walking skeletons, and in fact, scarcely worth the trouble of killing.

Moreover, the overseers of the neighboring plantations, were beginning to be very well aware that they were exposed to some pretty regular and diligent depredators. We learned from the slaves with whom we trafficed, that there was a good deal of talk about the rapid disappearance of the cattle ; and that preparations were making for a grand hunt in search of the plunderers.

With the double object of disappointing these preparations, and of getting among some fresh herds of cattle, it was resolved that five of us should make an excursion to a considerable distance, while the other two remained at home and kept close.

One of our number undertook to lead us into the neighborhood of a plantation beyond the Santee, on which he had been raised. He knew all the country about it perfectly well. There were several good hiding places he said, in which we could conceal ourselves in the day time ; and the extensive woods and wastes furnished a good range and abundance of cattle.

We set off under his guidance, and kept on for several days, or nights rather, in a northwardly direction. On the fifth or sixth evening of our journey, we started soon after sun-set, and having traveled till a little past midnight, through a country of abrupt and barren sand-hills, our guide told us that we were now in the neighborhood into which he intended to carry us. But as the moon had gone down, and it was cloudy and quite dark, he was rather uncertain as to the precise place we were at; and we should do best, he said, to camp where we were, till day-light, when he would lead us to some better place of concealment.

This advice was very acceptable;—for by this time, we were way-worn, tired and sleepy. We kindled a fire, cooked the last of the provisions we had brought with us, and having appointed one of our number to keep watch, the rest of us lay down and were soon fast asleep.

I, at least, was sleeping soundly, and dreaming of poor Cassy and our infant child, when my dream was interrupted, and I was roused from my slumbers, by what seemed a discharge of fire-arms and a gallopping of horses. I sprang upon my feet, hardly knowing whether I was awake. At the same moment, my eye fell upon Thomas, who had been sleeping beside me, and I perceived that his clothes were all stained with blood. He had already gained his feet; and without stopping to hear or see any thing further, we sprung together into the nearest thicket, and fled for some time, we scarcely knew where or why. At last, Thomas cried out that he could go no further. The bleeding of his wounds had weakened him much, and they were now growing stiff and painful. The morning was just beginning to dawn. We sat down upon the ground and endeavored to bind up his wounds the best we were able. A ball or buck-shot had passed through the fleshy part of his left arm, between the shoulder and elbow. Another shot had struck him in the side,—but as far as we could judge, had glanced on one of his ribs and so passed off without doing any mortal injury. These wounds had bled profusely and were now very painful. We bound them up the best we could; and looking round we found a little stream of water with which to wash away the blood, and quench our thirst.

Thus recruited and refreshed, we began to consider which way we should turn and what we were to do. We did not dare to go back to the camp where we had slept; indeed we were very doubtful whether we were able to do so; for the morning had been dark, and we had fled with heedless haste, taking very little note of our direction. Our island retreat was at the distance of some seven or eight days journey; and as we had traveled in the night, and not always in precisely the same direction, it would be no very easy matter to find our way back again. However, Thomas prided himself upon his woodmanship, and though he had not observed the course of our journey quite so closely as he could have wished, he still thought that he might succeed in finding the way back.

But his wounds were too recent, and he felt too weak, to think of starting off immediately. Besides it was already broad day-light ; and we had the best of reasons for traveling only by night. So we sought out a thicket in which we concealed ourselves till night-fall.

As the evening came on, Thomas declared that he felt much better and stronger ; and we resolved to set out at once, on our return. In the first place however, we determined to make an attempt to find the camp of the preceding night, in hopes that some of our companions might have escaped as well as ourselves, and that by some good luck, we might chance to fall in with them.

After wandering about for some time, at length we found the camp. Two dead bodies, stiff and bloody, lay by the extinguished embers of the fire. They seemed to have been shot dead as they slept, and scarcely to have moved a limb. The bushes about were stained and spattered with blood ; and by the moon-light, we tracked the bloody flight of one of our luckless companions for a considerable distance. This must have been our sentinel, who had probably dropped asleep, and thus exposed us to be surprised.

Perhaps he might be lurking some where in the bushes, wounded and helpless. This thought emboldened us. We shouted and called aloud. But our voices echoed through the woods, and died away unanswered. We returned again to the camp, and gazed once more upon the distorted faces of our dead companions. We could not bare to leave them unburied. I hastily scraped a shallow trench, and there we placed them. We dropped a tear upon their grave, and sad, dismayed, dejected, we set out upon our long, weary and uncertain journey.

CHAPTER XIII.

WE traveled slowly all that night, and soon after the morning dawn, we concealed ourselves again, and laid down to sleep. Thomas' wounds were much better, and seemed disposed to heal. The hurt in his side was far less dangerous than we had at first supposed, and as the pain had subsided, he was now able to sleep.

We slept well enough, but awoke weak and faint for want of food ; for it was now some twenty-four hours since we had tasted any. The sun was not yet down ; yet we resolved to set out immediately, in hopes that day-light might point out to us something with which to satisfy our hunger.

After traveling a considerable distance through the woods, just as the sun was setting, we struck into a road. This road we determined to follow, in hopes that it might presently lead us into the neighborhood of some farm-house near which we might light upon something eatable. It was an unlucky resolve ; for we had

not gone above half a mile, when just upon the crest of
a short hill, we suddenly came upon three travelers on
horseback, whom the undulations of the road had concealed from us, till we were within a few yards of each
other.

Both parties were mutually surprised. The travelers reined up their horses and eyed us sharply. Our
appearance might well attract attention. Our clothes,—
such as we had,—were torn and ragged. Instead of
shoes, we wore a kind of high moccasins, made of un-
tanned ox-hide ; we had caps of the same material ;
and the dresses of both of us, especially of Thomas,
were spattered and stained with blood.

They took me for a free man, and one of them
called out " Hallo, stranger, who are you and where
are you going ?—and whose fellow is that you have
along ?"

I did my best to take advantage of my color, and to
seem what they took me for. But this I soon found
would not avail ; for though at first, they did not seem
to entertain a suspicion that I was a slave, yet our appearance was so strange, that they questioned me very
closely. As I had no very definite idea where we
were, and was totally unacquainted with the neighborhood, I was not at all able to hit upon appropriate answers to the numerous questions they put me ; and my
statements soon grew confused and contradictory.
This served to excite their suspicions ; and while
I was attending to the questions of the one who
acted as chief spokesman, another of the company
suddenly sprang from his horse, and seizing me by the

collar, swore that I was either a run-away or a negro-stealer. The other two jumped down in a moment; and while one of them caught me by the arm, the other attempted to seize Thomas.

He eluded this attempt and turned to run. He had gone but a little distance, when looking back and seeing me on the ground, he forgot at once, his wounds, his weakness and his own danger. He grasped his staff, and rushed to my rescue. They had throttled me till I was powerless and almost insensible ; and while one of them still held me to the ground, the other stood up to meet Thomas, who as he turned short about, had struck his pursuer to the earth, and now came on to my relief, with his staff uplifted. His new antagonist was both strong and active. He succeeded in avoiding the stroke of Thomas' cudgel, and immediately closed with him. Thomas had but little use of one arm ; and his strength was much reduced by loss of blood and long fasting ; but he struggled hard and was already getting the upper hand, when the fellow whom he had knocked down at the commencement of the fight, regained his senses, and came to the assistance of his companion. Both together, they were too much for him ; and they soon got him down and bound his hands. They did the same with me ; and one of them having produced a piece of rope from his saddle-bags, they made halters of it, which they put about our necks and by the application of their whips, they compelled us to keep up with their horses.

In about half an hour, we came to a mean and for-lorn-looking cabin, by the road-side. It appeared to be a sort of inn, or tavern ; and here we were to lodge. The only persons about the house seemed to be the landlady herself and a little daughter some ten or twelve years old. The whole appearance of the place bore evident marks of discomfort and poverty. Our captors had no sooner provided for their horses, than they called for chains ;—trace-chains they said, or in fact any thing in the shape of a chain, would answer their purpose. But much to their disappointment, the land-lady declared that she had nothing of the sort. How-ever she procured some old rope ; and having secured us as effectually as they could, they made us sit down in the passage.

The landlady told them, that in all probability, we were run-aways ; for the neighborhood had lately been much troubled by them. A company of five or six men, she said, had gone out two or three nights since on purpose to hunt up the rascals, and had unexpect-edly come upon quite a party, asleep in the woods around a fire.

The gang seemed too large to be easily taken, but it was resolved that the fellows should not escape ; espe-cially as the man whose slaves they were supposed. to be, and who was one of the party, openly declared that he had rather they were all shot, than to have them wandering about the country useless to him and mis-chievous to his neighbors.

The company separated and each man approached from a different point. Upon a given signal, all fired ; and then putting spurs to their horses, they rode off and returned home each by himself. Nobody had

stopped to see what execution was done ; but as the
men were all good shots, it was supposed that most of
the run-aways were either killed or desperately wounded ; and as our clothes were bloody, and one of us
was hurt, she thought it likely, she said, that we belonged to that same gang.

It appeared in the course of the conversation between the landlady and her guests, that the murderous
kind of attack to which our companions had fallen victims, but which had been intended for another party of
run-aways, is an operation occasionally practised in
lower Carolina, when a party of slave-hunters falls in
with a gang of fugitive slaves too large to be easily
arrested.

The dispersion of the attacking party, and each one
shooting and returning by himself is only the effect of
an ancient and traditionary prejudice. By the law of
Carolina, the killing a slave is regarded as murder ; and
though probably, this law was never enforced, and
would doubtless be treated by a jury of modern slave-
holders, as an old-fashioned and fanatical absurdity, there
still lingers, in the breasts of the people, some remains
of horror at the idea of deliberate bloodshed, and a sort
of superstitious apprehension of the possible enforce-
ment of this antiquated law. To blind-fold their own
consciences, and to avoid the possibility of a judicial
investigation, each man of an attacking party takes care
to see none of the others when they fire ; and no one
goes to the place to ascertain how many have been
killed or disabled. The poor wretches who are not so
fortunate as to be shot dead upon the spot, are left to

the lingering torments of thirst, fever, starvation and festering wounds ; and when at length they die, their skeletons lie bleaching in the Carolina sun, proud proofs of slave-holding civilization and humanity.

While our captors were at supper, the little girl, the landlady's daughter, came to look at us, as we lay in the passage. She was a pretty child, and her soft blue eyes filled with tears as she looked upon us. I asked her for a little water. She hastened to get it for us ; and inquired if we did not want something to eat. I told her that we were half dead with hunger ; and she no sooner heard it, than she hastened away and soon returned with a large cake of bread.

Our arms were bound so tight that we were utterly helpless, and the little girl broke the bread and fed us with her own hand.

Is not this one instance enough to prove that nature never intended man to be a tyrant ? Avarice, a blind lust of domination, the false but specious suggestions of ignorance and passion combine to make him so ; and pity at length, is banished from his soul. It then seeks refuge in the woman's heart ; and when the progress of oppression drives it even thence, as sad and hesitating, it prepares to wing its way to heaven, still it lurks and lingers in the bosom of the child !

By listening closely to the conversation of the travelers,—for by this time the landlady had produced a jug of whiskey, and they had become very communicative,—we learned that we were within a few miles of the town of Camden, and on the great northern road leading from that town into North Carolina. Our

captors it seemed, were from the upper-country.
They had not passed through Camden, but had struck
into this road very near the place where they met us.
They were traveling into Virginia to purchase slaves.

After discussing the question at considerable length,
they concluded to delay their journey for a day or
two, and to take us to Camden, in hopes to find
our owner and obtain a reward for apprehending us ;
or if nobody should claim us immediately, they could
lodge us in jail, advertise us in the newspapers, and
give further attention to the business upon their return.

By this time, the whiskey jug was emptied, and the
travelers made preparations for sleeping. There were
but two rooms in the house. The landlady and her
daughter had one ; and some beds were prepared for
the guests, in the other. We were carried into their
room ; and after again lamenting that the landlady
could not furnish them with chains, they carefully examined and retightened the ropes with which we were
bound, and then undressed and threw themselves upon
their beds. They were probably fatigued with their
journey, and the whiskey increased their drowsy inclination ; so that before long, they all gave evident
tokens of being in a sound slumber.

I envied them this happiness ; for the tightness of
my bonds, and the uneasy position in which I was
obliged to lie, prevented me from sleeping. The moon-
beams shone in at the window, and made every object
distinctly visible. Thomas and myself were lamenting
in whispers, our wretched condition, and consulting
hopelessly together, when we saw the door of the room

cautiously and silently opening. In a moment, the landlady's little daughter made her appearance. She came towards us with noiseless steps, and one hand raised, as if motioning to us to be silent. In the other, she held a knife ; and stooping down she hastily cut the cords by which we were bound.

We did not dare to speak ; but our hearts beat hard, and I am sure our looks expressed the gratitude we felt. We gained our feet with as little noise as possible, and were stealing towards the door, when a new thought struck Thomas. He laid his hand upon my shoulder to draw my attention, and then began to pick up the coat, shoes, and other clothes of one of our captors. At once I understood his intention, and imitated his example. The little girl seemed astonished and displeased at this proceeding, and motioned to us to desist. But without seeming to understand her gestures, we gained the door with the clothes in our hands ; and passing out of the passage, we walked slowly and cautiously for some distance, taking good heed, lest the sound of our footsteps might give an alarm. In the mean time, the little girl patted the house dog on the head, and kept him quiet. When we had gained a sufficient distance we started upon a run, which we did not give over till we were fairly out of breath.

As soon as we had recovered ourselves a little, we stripped off our ragged dresses, and hid them in the bushes. Luckily the clothes which we had brought off in our flight, fitted us very tolerably, and gave us a much more respectable and less suspicious appearance. We now went on, for two or three miles till we came to a road that crossed the one upon which we were traveling, and ran off towards the south.

In all this time, Thomas had said nothing ; nor did he scarcely seem to notice my remarks, or to hear the questions, which, from time to time, I put to him. When we came to the cross-road, he suddenly stopped, and took me by the arm. I supposed that he was going to consult with me, as to the course which we should take ; and great was my surprise to hear him say, " Archy, here I leave you."

I could not imagine what he intended, and I looked at him for an explanation.

" You are now," he said, "on the road to the north. You have good clothes, and as much learning as an overseer. You can readily pass for a free man. It will be very easy to get away to those free states of which I have heard you speak so often. If I go with you, we shall both be stopped and questioned. We shall be pursued ; and if we keep together, and follow this road, we shall certainly be taken. It is a great way to the free states, and I have little chance and no hope of ever getting there ; and if I did, what should I gain by it ? I will try the woods again and do as I can. I shall be able to get back to our old place ; —but you, Archy, you can do better. You are sure of getting away to the north. Go, my boy, go, and God bless you."

I was deeply moved ; and it was some time before I was able to reply. The thoughts of escaping from my

present situation of danger and misery, to a land where
I could bear the name, and enjoy the rights of a freeman, flashed upon my mind with a radiant and dazzling
brightness that seemed almost to blot out every other
feeling. Yet still my love for Thomas, and the gratitude I owed him, glimmered through these new hopes;
and a low voice from the very centre of my heart bade
me not to desert my friend. After too long a pause,
and too much hesitation, I began to answer him. I
spoke of his wounds; of our sworn friendship; and of
the risk he so lately run in my behalf; and insisted that
I would stay with him to the last.

I spoke, I fear, with too little of zeal and earnestness. At least, all that I said, only seemed to confirm
Thomas in his determination. He replied that his
wounds were healing; and that he was already almost
as strong as ever. He added, that if I stayed with
him, I might do myself much harm without the chance
of doing him any good. He pointed along the road,
and in an energetic and commanding voice, he bade
me follow it, while he should take the cross-road towards the south.

When Thomas had once made up his mind, there
was a firmness in the tone with which he spoke, sufficient often to overawe the most unwilling. At the
present moment, I was but too ready to be prevailed
upon. He saw his advantage and pursued it. " Go
Archy," he repeated, " go;—if not for your own
sake, go for mine ! If you stay with me, and are
taken, I shall never forgive you for it."

Little by little, my better feelings yielded; and at

last I consented to the separation. I took Thomas by the hand, and pressed him to my heart. A nobler spirit never breathed ;—I was not worthy to call myself his friend.

"God bless you, Archy," he said, as he left me. I stood watching him as he walked rapidly away ; and as I looked, I was ready to sink into the earth with shame and mortification. Once or twice, I was just starting to follow him ; but selfish prudence prevailed, and I held back. I watched him till he was out of sight, and then resumed my journey. It was a base desertion, which not even the love of liberty could excuse.

CHAPTER XIV.

I walked on as fast as I was able, till after day-light, without meeting a single individual, or passing more than two or three mean and lonely houses. Just as the sun was rising, I gained the top of a considerable hill. Here there was a small house by the road side, and a horse saddled and bridled was tied to a tree near by. The animal was sleek and in good condition ; and from the cut of the saddle-bags I took him to belong

to some doctor, who had come thus early to visit a
patient. It was a tempting opportunity. I looked
cautiously this way and that, and seeing nobody, I
unfastened the horse, and jumped into the saddle. I
walked him a little distance, but presently put him into
a gallop, that soon carried me out of sight of the house.

This was a very lucky acquisition; for as I was
upon the same road, which the travelers from whom I
had escaped would follow as soon as they resumed
their journey, I was in manifest danger of being over-
taken and recognized. As I found that my horse had
both spirit and bottom, I put him to his speed, and
went forward at a rapid rate. My good luck did not
end here; for happening to put my hand into the pocket
of my new coat, I drew out a pocket-book, which
beside a parcel of musty papers, I found on examining
it a little, to contain quite a pretty sum of money in
bank notes. This discovery gave a new impulse to
my spirits, which were high enough before; and I
pushed on all day without stopping, except now and
then to rest my horse in the shade of a tree.

Towards evening I got a supper and corn for my
horse at a little hedge tavern; and waiting till the moon
rose, I set out again. By morning, my horse was
completely broken down and gave out entirely.
Thankful for his services thus far,—for according to
my reckoning he had carried me upwards of a hundred
miles in the twenty-four hours,—I stripped off his
saddle and bridle and turned him into a corn-field to
refresh himself. I now pursued my journey on foot;
for I feared if I kept the horse, the possession of him

might perhaps get me into difficulty ; and in fact, he was so jaded and worn out that he would be of very little use to me. I had got a good start upon the travelers, and I did not doubt that I could get on as fast upon foot, as they would on horseback.

Before sunset, I arrived at a considerable village. Here I indulged myself in a hearty meal, and a good night's sleep. Both were needed ; for what with watching, fasting, and fatigue, I was quite worn out. I slept some ten hours and awoke with new vigor. I now resumed my journey which I pursued without much fear of interruption ; though I judged it prudent to stop but seldom, and to push forward as rapidly as possible. I kept on through North Carolina and Virginia ; crossed the Potomac into Maryland ; and avoiding Baltimore, I passed on into Pennsylvania, and congratulated myself that at last I trod a soil, cultivated by freemen.

I had gone but a very few miles, before I perceived the difference. In fact, I had scarcely passed the slave-holding border, before the change became apparent. The spring was just opening, and every thing was beginning to look fresh, green, and beautiful. The nicely cultivated fields, the numerous small enclosures, the neat and substantial farm-houses, thickly scattered along the way, the pretty villages and busy towns, the very roads themselves, which were covered with wagons and travelers,—all these signs of universal thrift and comfort, gave abundant evidence that at length I saw a country where labor was honorable and where every one labored for himself. It was an exhilarating

and delightful prospect, and in strong contrast with all
I had seen in the former part of my journey, in which
a wretched and lonely road had led me on through a
vast monotonous extent of unprofitable woods, deserted
fields grown up with broomsedge and mullen, or fields
just ready to be deserted, gullied, barren and with all
the evidences upon them of a negligent, unwilling and
unthrifty cultivation. Here and there I had passed a
mean and comfortless house ; and once in fifty miles, a
decaying, poverty-stricken village, with a court house,
and a store or two, and a great crowd of idlers collected
about a tavern door ; but without one single sign of
industry or improvement.

I was desirous of seeing Philadelphia ; but that city,
so near the slave-holding border, I feared might be infected with something of the slave-holding spirit ; for
the worst plagues are the most apt to be contagious. I
passed by, without passing through it, and hastened on
to New York. I crossed the noble Hudson and entered the town. It was the first city I had ever seen ;
at least, the first one worthy to be called a city ; and
when I beheld the spacious harbor crowded with shipping ; the long lines of ware-houses, the numerous
streets, the splendid shops, and the swarming crowds
of busy people, I was astonished and delighted with
the new idea which all this gave me of the resources of
human art and industry. I had heard of such things
before, but to feel, one ought to see.

I did nothing for three or four days, but to wander
up and down the streets looking, gazing, and examining
with an almost insatiable curiosity. New York at that

time, was far inferior, to what it must by this time,
have become ; and the commercial restrictions which
then prevailed must have tended to diminish its business and its bustle.   Yet to my rustic inexperience,
the city seemed almost interminable ; and the rattling
of the drays and carriages over the pavements, and the
crowds of people in the streets, far exceeded all my
previous notions of the busy confusion of a city.

I had been in New York but two or three days, and
was standing one forenoon by a triangular grass-plot,
near the centre of the town, gazing at a fine building
of white marble, which one of the passers-by told me
was the City Hall, when suddenly I felt my arm rudely
seized.   I looked round, and with horror and dismay,
I found myself in the gripe of general Carter,—the
man who in South Carolina had called himself my
master ; but who, in a country that prided itself in the
title of a Free State, ought no longer to have had any
claim upon me.

Let no one be deceived by the false and boastful
title which the northern states of the American Union
have thought fit to assume.   With what justice can
they pretend to call themselves Free States, after having
made a bargain with the slave-holders, by which they
have bound themselves to deliver back again, into the
hands of their oppressors, every miserable fugitive who
takes refuge within their territory ?   The good people
of the free states have no slaves themselves.   Oh no !
Slave-holding they confess, is a horrible enormity.
They hold no slaves themselves ; they only act as bum-
bailiffs and tip-staves to the slave-holders !

My master,—for so even in the free city of New York I must continue to call him,—had seized me by one arm, and a friend of his held me by the other. He called me by name ; and in the hurry and confusion of this sudden surprise, I forgot for a moment, how impolitic it was for me to appear to know him. A crowd began to collect about us. When they heard that I was seized as a fugitive slave, some of them appeared not a little outraged at the idea that a white man should be subject to such an indignity. They seemed to think that it was only the black whom it was lawful to kidnap in this way. Such indeed is the untiring artfulness of tyranny that it is ever nestling even in the bosoms of the free ; and there is not one prejudice, the offspring as all prejudices are, of ignorance and self-conceit, of which it has not well learned how to avail itself.

Though several of the crowd did not scruple to use very strong expressions, they made no attempt to rescue me ; and I was dragged along towards that very City Hall which I had just been admiring. I was carried before the sitting magistrate ; some questions were put and answered ; some oaths were sworn, and papers written. I had not yet recovered from the first confusion of my seizure ; and this array of courts and constables was a horrid sort of danger to which I was totally unaccustomed, so that I scarcely know what was said or done. But to the best of my recollection the magistrate declined acting on the question ; though he consented to grant a warrant for detaining me in prison, till I could be taken before some other tribunal.

The warrant was made out, and I was delivered over to an officer. The court-room was filled with the crowd, who had followed us from the street. They collected close about us, as we left the court-room ; and I could see by the expression of their faces, and the words which some of them dropped, that they were very well inclined to favor my escape. At first, I seemed all submission to the officer ;—but we had gone but a very few steps, when with a sudden spring I tore myself from his grasp, and darted among the crowd, which opened to give me a passage. I heard noise, confusion and shouts behind me ; but in a moment, I had cleared the enclosure in which the City Hall stood, and crossing one of the streets by which it was bounded, I dashed down a narrow and crooked lane. The people stared at me as I ran, and some shouted stop thief ! One or two seemed half inclined to seize me ; but I turned one short corner and then another, and finding that I was not pursued, I soon dropped into a walk.

For this escape I return my thanks, not to the laws of New York, but to the good will of her citizens. The secret bias and selfish interest of the law-makers, often leads them wrong ; the unprompted and disinterested impulses of the people, are almost always right. It is true that the artful practice and cunning instigation of the purchased friends and bribed advocates of oppression, joined to the interest which the thieves and pick-pockets of a great city always have in civil tumult and confusion, may now and then succeed in exciting the young, the ignorant, the thoughtless, and the depraved to acts of violence in favor of tyranny. But

so congenial to the human heart is the love of freedom,
that it burns not brighter in the souls of sages and
of heroes, than in the bosoms even of the most ignorant and thoughtless, when not quenched by some excited prejudice, base passion, or sinister influence.

In my previous wanderings about the town, I had
discovered the road that led northwardly out of it ; and
I soon turned in that direction, determined to shake
off from my feet, the very dust of a city, where I had
been so near falling back again into the wretched condition of servitude.

I traveled all that day,—and at night, the inn-keeper,
at whose house I lodged, told me that I was in the
state of Connecticut.   I now pursued my flight for
several days, through a fine hilly and mountainous country, such as I had never seen before.   The nobleness
of the prospect, the craggy rocks, and rugged hills,
contrasted finely with the excellent cultivation of the
valleys, and the universal thrift and industry of the
inhabitants.   Where freedom nerves the arm, it is in
vain that rocks and hills of granite, oppose the labors
of the cultivator.   Industrious liberty teaches him the
art to extract comfort, competence and wealth from a
soil the most unwilling and ungrateful.

I knew that Boston was the great sea-port of New
England ; and thither I directed my steps, resolved
to leave a land however otherwise inviting, whose laws
would not acknowledge me a freeman.   As I approached the town, the country lost much of its picturesque
and hilly grandeur ; but this was made up for by the
greater beauty of its smoother and better cultivated

fields ; and by the pretty dwellings scattered so numer-
ously along the road, that the environs of the town
seemed a continued village. The city itself, seated on
hills, and seen for a considerable distance, gave a noble
termination to the prospect.

I crossed a broad river, by a long bridge, and soon
entered the town ; but I did not stop to examine it.
Liberty was too precious to be sacrificed to the gratification of an idle curiosity ; a New York mob had set
me free ; a Boston mob might perhaps delight in the
opportunity of restoring me to servitude. I found my
way, as soon as the crooked and irregular streets would
allow me, to the wharves. Many of the ships were
stripped and rotting in the docks ; but after some search
and inquiry, I found a vessel about to sail for Bordeaux.
I offered myself as a sailor. The captain questioned
me, and laughed heartily at my land-lubberly air, and
rustic ignorance ; but finally he agreed to take me at
half wages. He advanced me a month's pay ; and
the second mate who was a fine young fellow, and who
seemed to feel for my lonely and helpless ignorance,
assisted me in buying such clothes as would be necessary for the voyage.

In a few days, our cargo was completed, and the ship
was ready for sea. We dropped off from the wharf ;
threaded our course among the numerous islets and
headlands of Boston harbor ; passed the castle and the
light-house ; sent off our pilot ; and with all sail set,
and a smacking breeze, we left the town behind.

As I stood upon the forecastle, and looked towards
the land, which soon seemed but a little streak in the

horizon, and was fast sinking from our sight, I seemed to feel a heavy weight drop off me. The chains were gone. I felt myself a freeman ; and as I watched the fast receding shore my bosom heaved with a proud scorn,—a mingled feeling of safety and disdain.

" Farewell my country !"—such were the thoughts that rose upon my mind, and pressed to find an utterance from my lips ;—" and such a country ! A land boasting to be the chosen seat of liberty and equa rights, yet holding such a portion of her people in hopeless, helpless, miserable bondage !"

" Farewell my country ! Much is the gratitude and thanks I owe thee ! Land of the tyrant and the slave, Farewell !"

" And welcome, welcome, ye bounding billows and foaming surges of the ocean ! Ye are the emblems and the children of liberty—I hail ye as my brothers !—for, at last, I too am free !—free !—free !"

CHAPTER XV.

The favorable breezes, with which we had set out, did not last long. The weather soon became tempestuous, and we were involved in fogs, and driven about by contrary winds. Our labors and hardships were very great ; but still I found a sort of pleasure in them. It was for myself that I toiled and suffered ; and that thought gave me strength and vigor.

I applied myself with the greatest zeal and good-will to learn the business of my profession. At first, my companions laughed at my ignorance and awkwardness, and were full of their jokes and tricks upon me. But though rude and thoughtless, they were generous and good natured. In the very first week of our voyage, I had a fair fight with the bully of the ship. I whipped him soundly ; and the crew all agreed, that there was something in me.

I was strong and active ; and as I made it a point to imitate whatever I saw done by any of the crew, I was surprised to find, in how short a time, I was able to run over the rigging and venture upon the yards. The maze of ropes and sea-terms that at first perplexed me, soon grew clear. Before we were across the ocean I could hand, reef, and steer with any man on board ; and the crew swore with one consent, that I was born to be a sailor.

But I was not satisfied with setting sails and handling ropes. I wished to understand the art of navigation.

One of our crew was a young man of good education, who served before the mast, as is common with New Englanders, in expectation of presently commanding a ship himself. He had his books and his instruments; and as he had already been one or two voyages, he understood pretty well, how to apply them, and used to keep a reckoning of the ship's course. This same young sailor, Tom Turner by name, was a fine, free-hearted fellow as ever lived; but he was of a slight make, and his strength was not equal to his spirit. I had gained his good-will by standing by him in some of our fore-castle frolics; and seeing how anxious I was to learn, he undertook to be my instructor. He put his navigator into my hand, and whenever it was my watch below, I was constantly poreing over it. At first, the whole matter seemed mighty mysterious. It was some time before I could see into it. But Tom, who had a fluent tongue, lectured and explained; and I listened and studied; and pretty soon, I began to understand it.

All this time, we were beating about in the neighborhood of the banks of Newfoundland, and as we experienced a constant succession of storms and contrary winds, we made but little progress. We lost a couple of top-sails and several of our spars; and had been out some seventy days in very rough weather.

I took it all kindly though; I was in no hurry to get ashore. I had chosen the ocean for my country; and when the winds roared, the rigging rattled, and the timbers creaked, I only wrapped my monkey-jacket a little closer, braced myself against my sea-chest and studied my navigator;—that is to say, if it happened to be my watch below ; for when upon deck, I was always ready at the first call, and was the first to spring into the rigging.

At last, the weather moderated, and we made all sail for the coast of France. We had made the land, and were within a few leagues of our harbor, when an armed brig, with the British colors flying, bore down upon us, fired a shot a-head, and sent a boat's crew on board.

In those days, American vessels were quite accustomed to such sort of visitations ; and our captain did not seem to be much alarmed. But no sooner had the boat's officer reached our deck, than laying his hand upon his sword, he told the captain that he was a prisoner.

It seemed that while we were beating about on the Grand Bank, America, at last, had screwed up her courage, and had declared war against England. The armed brig was a British privateer, and we were her prize. At first we were all ordered below ; but presently we were called up again, and offered the choice of enlisting on board the privateer or being carried prisoners into England. Near half our crew were what the sailors call Dutchmen, that is, people from the North Sea, or the coasts of the Baltic. These adventurers readily enlisted. Tom Turner was spokesman for the Americans ; and when called upon to follow this example, he told the lieutenant, in a tone so gruff as to be little better than a growl, that " he would see him damned first."

For myself, I felt no patriotic scruples. I had renounced my country ; if indeed that place can be fitly called one's country, which while it gives him birth, cuts him off, by its wicked and unjust laws, from every thing that makes life worth having. Despite the murmurs and hisses of my companions, I stepped forward and put my name to the shipping paper. Had they known my history, they would not have blamed me.

After cruising for some time, without success, we returned to Liverpool to refit. Our crew was recruited ; and we soon put to sea again. Cruising off the coast of France we took several prizes, but none of very great value. We now made sail for the West Indies ; and, in the neighborhood of the Bermudas, while close hauled to the wind and under easy sail, we discovered a vessel a-head, and gave chase.

The chase slackened sail and waited for us to come up. This made us suppose that it might be a man-of-war ; and as we were more anxious for plunder than for fighting, we put up the helm, and bore away.

The chase now made sail in pursuit ; and as she proved to be much the better sailer, she gained rapidly upon us.

When we saw that there was no chance of escaping, we took in our light canvass, brought the vessel to, ran up the British flag, and cleared for action.

The enemy was an armed and fast sailing schooner— an American privateer, as it proved, about a fair match for the brig, in point of size and armament, but in much finer trim, and most beautifully worked. She ran down upon us ; her crew gave three cheers ; and shooting across our bows, she gave us a broad-side that did

much execution. She tacked and manœuvered till she
gained a favorable position, and then poured in her fire
with such steadiness, that she seemed all a-blaze. Her
guns were well shotted, and well aimed, and did serious
damage. Our captain and first lieutenant were soon
wounded and disabled. We paid back the enemy as
well as we could ; but our men dropped fast ; and our
fire began to slacken. The schooner's bow-sprit got
fast in our main rigging, and directly we heard the cry
for the boarders. We seized our pikes, and prepared
to receive them ; but a party of the enemy soon got a
footing on board the brig ; wounded the only officer on
deck ; and drove our men frightened and confused towards the fore-castle.

I saw our danger ; and the idea of falling again into
the hands of the tyrants from whom I had escaped,
summoned back my ebbing courage. I seemed to feel
a more than human energy springing up within me. I
put myself at the head of our yielding and dispirited
crew, and fought with all the frantic valor of a mad
hero of romance. I struck down two or three of the
foremost of the enemy ; and as they quailed and shrunk
before me, I cheered and encouraged my companions,
and called on them to charge. My example seemed to
inspire them. They rallied at once, and rushed forward with new courage. They drove the enemy before
them ; tumbled some into the sea ; and pressed the
others back into their own vessel.

Nor did our success stop here. We boarded in our
turn ; and the decks of the schooner saw as bloody a
battle as had been fought on those of the brig. The

fortune of the fight still ran in our favor, and we soon
drove the enemy to take refuge on their quarter-deck.
We called to them to surrender ;—but their captain
waving his bloody sword, sternly refused. He encouraged his men to charge once more ; and rushed furi-
ously upon us. His cutlass clashed against my pike,
and flew from his hand. He slipped, and fell upon the
deck ; and in a moment, my weapon was at his breast.

He cried for quarter. I thought I knew his face.

" Your name," I asked.

" Osborne !"

" Jonathan Osborne late commander of the Two
Sallys ?"

" The same !"

" Then die ;—a wretch like you deserves no mercy !"
and as I spoke I plunged the weapon to his heart, and
felt thrilling to the very elbow-joint, the pleasurable
sense of doing justice on a tyrant !

But justice ought never to be sullied by passion,—
and if possible, should be unstained with blood. If in
my feelings at that moment, there was something noble,
there was far too much of savage fury and passionate
revenge. Yet from what I then felt, I can well understand the fierce spirit and ferocious energy of the slave,
who vindicates his liberty at the sword's point, and who
looks upon the slaughter of his oppressors almost as a
debt due to humanity.

The crew no sooner saw their captain slain, than
they threw down their arms and cried for quarter. The
schooner was ours, and a finer vessel never sailed the
seas.

Every officer on board the brig was wounded. All confessed that the capture of the prize was, in a great measure, due to me ; and with the approbation of all the crew, I was put on board as prize-master.

CHAPTER XVI.

WE had a short passage to Liverpool. The schooner was condemned as a prize, and was bought in by the owners of the brig. They fitted her out as a privateer ; and as they had been informed how large a share I had in her capture, they offered me the command of her. I readily accepted it ; and having selected an experienced old sailor for my first lieutenant, I soon collected a crew and set sail.

The cruising ground which I preferred, was the coast of America. Off the harbor of Boston, we were so lucky as to fall in with, and make prize of a homeward bound East-Indiaman, with a very valuable cargo of teas and silks. We put a prize-crew on board and sent her off for Liverpool, where she arrived safely, and produced us a very handsome sum in prize-money. We now stood to the southward ; and for a month or two, we cruised off the capes of Virginia. As we kept well in to the coast, we often made the land ; and I never

saw it without feeling a strong inclination to send a
boat's crew ashore, and to kidnap from their beds,
such of the nearest planters as I could lay my hands
upon.   But I did not think it prudent to attempt the
carrying into execution, this piece of experimental instruction, of which the Virginians stand so much in
need.

My cruising adventures, chases and escapes would
fill a volume ;—but they are little to my present purpose.   Suffice it to say, that while the war lasted I
kept the seas ; and when it ended, most reluctantly I left
them.   My share in the prizes we had taken, rendered
me wealthy,—at least what the moderation of my
wishes made me esteem so.   But what was to supply
the ever varying stimulus and excitement, which till
now, had sustained me, and prevented my mind from
preying on itself, and poisoning my peace with bitter
recollections ?   The images of my wife, my child, and
of the friend to whom I owed so much, often, on my
voyages, flitted mournfully across my mind ; but the
cry of ' sail ahead' would call off my thoughts, and
dissipate my incipient melancholy in the bustle of action.   But now that I was on shore, homeless, alone,
a stranger, with nothing to occupy my mind,—the
thoughts of those dear sufferers haunted me continually.
The very first thing I did, was to find out a trusty
agent whom I might send in search of them.   Such an
one I found.   I gave him all the information which might
promote the object of his mission ; I allowed him an unlimited credit on my banker ; and stimulated his zeal by

a handsome advance, and the promise of a still larger reward, if he succeeded in the object of his mission.

He sailed for America by the first opportunity ; and I consoled myself with the hope that his search would be successful. In the mean time, to have some occupation that might keep off anxious doubts and troublesome anxieties, I applied myself to study. When a child, I had a fondness for reading, and an ardent love of knowledge. This love of knowledge, the accursed discipline of servitude had stifled and kept under, but had not totally extinguished. I was astonished to find it still so strong. Having once turned my attention that way, my mind drank in all sorts of information, as the thirsty earth imbibes the rain. I might rather be said to devour books, than to read them. I scarcely gave myself time to sleep. No sooner had I finished one, than I hurried to another with restless inquietude. I read on without selection or discrimination. It was a long time before I learned to compare, to weigh, and to judge. It happened to me as it has happened to mankind in general. In my anxiety to know, I was ready to take every thing on trust ; and I did not stop to distinguish between what was fact, and what was fiction. But while I allowed an abundance of folly and falsehood to be palmed upon me under the sober disguise of truth, I had but little taste for writers professedly imaginative. I could not understand why they wrote, or what they aimed at. I despised the poets ; but voyages, travels, histories and narratives of every sort, I devoured with undistinguishing voracity. Time and reflection have since enabled me to extract something of truth and philosophy from these chaotic acquisitions.

For a while, my studies had much the same stimulating and exciting effect with my former activity. They raised my spirits, and enabled me to bear up under the discouraging advices which I received from America. But they palled at last ;—and when my agent returned with the disastrous information, that all his searches had been unavailing, I found no support under the bitter grief that overwhelmed me.

From such information as my agent had been able to obtain, it appeared that Mrs Montgomery, Cassy's mistress, had become security to a large amount for that brother of hers, by whose advice and agency she managed her affairs. That brother was a planter ; and among the American planters, the passion for gambling is next to universal,—for it is one of the few excitements by which they are able to relieve the listless and wearisome indolence of their useless lives. Mrs Montgomery's brother was a gambler, and an unsuccessful one. Having ruined himself, he began to prey upon his sister. Besides embezzling all such money of hers as he could lay his hands upon,—and as he had the entire management of her affairs, her income was much at his disposal,—he induced her, under various pretences, to put her name to bonds and notes to a large amount. On these notes and bonds suits were commenced ; but this, her brother who strove to defer the disclosure of his villainies as long as possible, took care to conceal from her ; and the first thing she knew of the matter, her entire property was seized on execution.

Among her other chattels, my wife and child were sold,—for it is the law and the practice of America to sell women and children to pay the debts of a gambler !

Cassy and her infant had fallen into the hands of a gentleman,—such is the American phrase,—who followed the lucrative and respectable business of a slave-trader.   My agent no sooner learned his name, than he set out in pursuit of him.   But he found that the man had been dead for a year or two ; and that he had left no papers behind him, from which might be traced the history of his slave-trading expeditions.   Not yet discouraged, my agent traveled over the entire route, which he was told the deceased slave-trader had usually followed.   He even succeeded in getting some trace of the very gang of slaves which had been purchased at the sale of Mrs Montgomery's property.   He tracked them from village to village, till he brought them to Augusta in the state of Georgia,—but here he lost sight of them altogether.   This town is or was, one of the great marts of the American slave-trade ; and here in all probability, the slaves were sold ; but to whom, it was impossible to discover.

Thus baffled in his search, my agent had recourse to advertisements in the newspapers, in which the person of my wife was particularly described, mention was made of the name of her late owner, and a very generous reward was offered to any one who would give information where she or her child was to be found.

These advertisements brought him an abundance of communications, but none to the purpose ; and after having spent near two years in the search, he gave it up, at last, as unavailing.

Of Thomas he could learn nothing, except that general Carter had never retaken him. A man of his figure and appearance had been occasionally seen, traversing the woods of that neighborhood, and lurking about the plantations ; and it seemed not unlikely that he was still alive, and the leader of some band of runaways. Such was the information which my agent brought me.

While he remained in America, however little encouragement his letters gave, still I could hope. But now, the last staff of consolation was plucked from under me. Of what availed it, that I had myself shaken off the chains, which were still hanging, and perhaps with a weight so much the heavier, to the friend of my heart, to the wife of my bosom, to the dear, dear infant, the child of my love ? The curse of tyranny indeed is multifold ;—nay, infinite !—It blasted me across the broad Atlantic ; and when I thought of Cassy and my boy, I shrunk and trembled as if again the irons were upon me, and the bloody lash cracking about my head !—Almighty God ! why hast thou created beings capable of so much misery !

I recovered slowly from the shock, which at first had quite unmanned me. But though I regained some degree of composure, it was in vain that I courted any thing like enjoyment. A worm was knawing at my heart which would not be appeased. Never was there a bosom more inclined than mine to the gentle pleasures of domestic life. But I found only torture in the recollection that I was a husband and a father. Oh, had my wife and my dear boy been with me, in what a sweet retirement I could have spent my days, ever finding a new relish for present bliss in the recollection of ills endured and miseries escaped !

The sense of loneliness which oppressed me, and the bitter thoughts and hateful images that were ever crowding on my mind, made my life an irksome burden, and drove me to seek relief in the excitements of travel. I visited every country in Europe, and sought occupation and amusement in examining their scheme of society, and studying their laws and manners. I traversed Turkey and the regions of the East, once the seats of art and opulence, but long since ruined by the heavy hand of tyranny, and the ever renewed extortions of military pillage. I crossed the Persian deserts, and saw in India a new and better civilization slowly rising upon the ruins of the old.

The interest I felt in the oppressed and unfortunate race, with which, upon the mother's side I am connected, carried me again across the ocean. I have climbed the lofty crests of the Andes, and wandered among the flowery forests of Brazil.

Everywhere I have seen the hateful empire of aristocratic usurpation, lording it with a high hand, over the lives, the liberty and the happiness of men. But every where, or almost every where, I have seen the bondsmen beginning to forget the base lore of traditionary subserviency, and already feeling the impulses and lisping in the language of freedom.   I have seen it every where ;—every where, except in my native America.

There are slaves in many other countries ; but no where else is oppression so heartless and unrelenting. No where else, has tyranny ever assumed a shape so fiendish.   No where else is it of all the world beside, the open aim of the laws, and the professed purpose of the masters, to blot out the intellects of half the population, and to extinguish at once and forever, both the capacity and the hope of freedom.

In catholic Brazil,—in the Spanish islands, where one might expect to find tyranny aggravated by ignorance and superstition, the slave is still regarded as a man, and as entitled to something of human sympathies. He may kneel at the altar by his master's side ; and he may hear the catholic priest proclaiming boldly from his pulpit, the sacred truth that all men are equal.   He may find consolation and support in the hope of one day becoming a freeman.   He may purchase his liberty with money ; if barbarously and unreasonably punished he may demand it as his legal right ; he may expect it from the gratitude or the generosity of his master ; or from the conscience-stricken dictates of his priest-attended death-bed.   When he becomes a freeman, he has a freeman's rights, and enjoys a real and practical equality, at the mere mention of which, the prating and prejudiced Americans are filled with creeping horror, and passionate indignation.

Slavery, in those countries, by the force of causes now in operation, is fast approaching to its end ; and let the African slave-trade be once totally abolished, and before the end of half a century, there will not a slave be found in either Spanish or Portuguese America.

It is in the United States alone, that country so apt to claim a monopoly of freedom, that the spirit of tyranny still soars boldly triumphant, and disdains even the most distant thought of limitation. Here alone, of all the world beside, oppression riots unchecked by fear of God or sympathy for man.

To add the last security to despotism, the American slave-holders, while they fiercely refuse to relinquish the least tittle of their whip-wielding authority, have deprived themselves, by special statute, of the power of emancipation, and have thus most artfully and industriously closed up the last loop-hole, through which Hope might look in upon their victims !

And thou my child !—These are the mercies to which thy youth is delivered over ! Perhaps already the spirit of manhood is extinguished within thee ; already perhaps the frost of servitude has nipped thy budding soul, and left it blasted,—worthless. No !— oh no !—It ought not, must not, cannot, shall not be so ! Child ! thou hast yet a father ;—one who has not forgotten, and who will not forsake thee. Thy need is great—and great shall be his efforts ;—that love is little worth which disappointment tires or danger daunts.

Yes ;—I have resolved it. I will revisit America, and through the length and the breadth of the land, I will search out my child. I will snatch him from the oppressor's grasp, or perish in the attempt. Should I be recognized and seized ? It is not in vain that I have read the history of the Romans ;—I know a way to disappoint the tyrants ; the guilt be on their heads ! I cannot be a slave the second time.

FINIS.

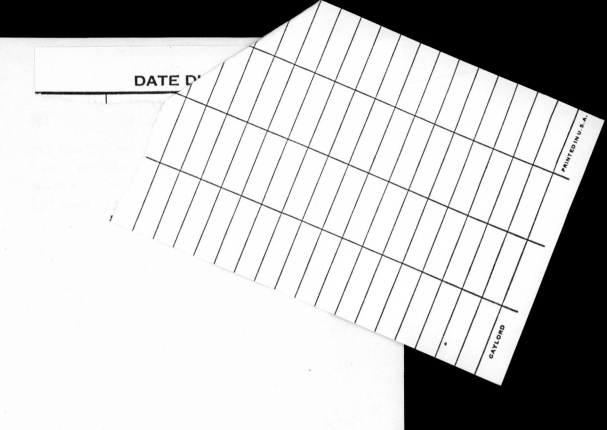